HUNTED

*For Jean, the mom I never thought I'd have,
and the most loving, encouraging, wise, beautiful-soul
person I know. I feel so loved by you and I treasure
our relationship.*

*For all survivors of abuse and those who've
experienced oppression, but especially for ritual abuse
survivors; I hope you find your voice, along with
healing, love, and safety,*

*And for all readers who like a good story,
I hope you find yourselves moved.*

HUNTED

Cheryl Rainfield

WestSide Books ®
Lodi, New Jersey

Published by WestSide Books
60 Industrial Road
Lodi, NJ 07644
USA

This is a work of fiction. All characters, places and events
described are imaginary. Any resemblance to real people,
places and events is entirely coincidental.

Library of Congress Cataloging-in-Publication Data

Rainfield, C. A. (Cheryl A.)
  Hunted / Cheryl Rainfield. -- 1st ed.
    p. cm.
  Summary: Cassie, a telepathic teenager, is on the run from government trackers be-
cause she is a paranormal in a world where being a "para" is illegal.
  ISBN 978-1-934813-62-1 (hardcover : alk. paper) [1. Telepathy--Fiction. 2. Govern-
ment, Resistance to--Fiction. 3. Science fiction.] I. Title.
PZ7.R1315Hu 2011
[Fic]--dc23

                                                                        2011028128

International Standard Book Number: 978-1-934813-62-1
Cover illustration by
Cover design by David Lemanowicz
Interior design by Chinedum Chukwu

Printed in the USA
10 9 8 7 6 5 4 3 2 1

First Edition

HUNTED

CHAPTER 1

Mom's gaze flicks to the rearview mirror for the thousandth time, like she's afraid someone's tailing us. I don't know how she thinks she can tell in the dark—or with her abilities shut off, leaving her as blind and dull as a Normal.

"There's no one there," I say, sharp like broken glass, as if I haven't been checking every few minutes myself. As if I haven't been reaching out around us for anything different. Anything off.

The truth is, I think she's right to be nervous. I can't feel anyone watching, can't even sense another Para close by—but they've been shadowing us too quickly lately, like they've found a way to zero in on my talent. But only another Para could do that, and I haven't sensed the metallic bitterness that comes from the Government Paras—the Para-slaves.

Just before we ran, I got the sense that I knew one of the trackers—or that they knew me. That's never happened before. It's too big to think about—one of our own, hunting us. Betraying us, without being forced to.

I glance at Mom. She's clenching the steering wheel so tightly it looks like she might wrench it off its hinges.

I wish she'd swallow her anxiety, act like the parent. The way she was before . . .

Mom loosens her grip on the steering wheel, turns to look at me, her eyes bloodshot. "You're sure no one's following us? Check again, will you, hon? We can't take any chances."

I grit my teeth, biting back words. I've never gotten used to her asking me to do what she used to on instinct. It's reversed our roles. Now I'm the parent and she's the child, needing protection.

I hunch against the car door, away from her, and open up more to the people around us. Their voices tumble and roll over each other chaotically.

. . . *shouldn't have had that third donut . . . can't do this . . . will he be waiting up for me? . . .*

I sift through them, feeling for power, for predatory instincts. For anyone focusing on us, when we should just be two anonymous blips in a car.

Nothing.

I reach out farther, toward the people off the highway.

. . . *who does he think he is, calling at three in the morning? . . . drank too much damned coffee . . .*

Then I reach past the stray thoughts, the people in their cars and beds. I reach for the strongest voices, the ones that vibrate at a higher frequency—the other Paranormals.

I sense a few hundred, maybe more, in the cluster of

buildings we're heading toward, but they're fast asleep, their energies focused on dreaming.

I do one more sweep, delving deeper—and that's when I feel it. The pinprick of attention, where there should be none. Someone watching us intently, hiding behind layers of others' thoughts.

I draw my breath in so sharply my chest hurts.

Mom glances at me. I force a smile, try not to let the fear show.

I've got to find out who the watcher is without them sensing me. I visualize a shield of energy around Mom and me. I blend it with the energy of our own bodies, building onto it.

Then I reach out gently for that hidden mind. The layers open up to me slowly—caution, a proprietary protectiveness, and intense concentration.

I laugh as I recognize the familiar mind pattern. My old Para-friend and contact, John. I've never met him in person, but he's helped us get to safety so many times over the years.

"*What are you doing, watching us?*" I ask, teasingly. "*I told you, we'll be okay.*"

I feel him startle—surprised, even annoyed, that I caught him keeping tabs on us. "*If you think I was going to let you face the wolves alone, you're wrong,*" John sends. "*I'll always watch out for you. Besides, you've had too many near misses lately. I want to make sure you're safe this time.*"

"Too many near misses" is putting it lightly. Normals

used to get suspicious of us—of *me*—once every six months or so. But lately, their target rate has increased—at least with me.

I rub my gritty eyes. *"You sense anyone with a lock on us?"* I ask John.

"No one. But something doesn't feel right. Have you sensed anyone?"

"No." But then I didn't last time, either—until it was almost too late.

"Keep your talent damped down, just in case."

"You mean try to pass as a Normal," I send, disgusted. I can't stop my gaze from sliding to Mom. She's worse than a Normal. She's deadened everything inside her so nothing gets out, nothing gets in. It's like her brain is a lump of cement, unreadable—instead of energy and thought.

"It's better to have a little discomfort and be safe," John sends.

"I know, I know." I jerk away from him grumpily, closing our connection. "Nobody's watching us, except John," I tell Mom. "Most of the Paras are asleep."

"Caitlyn Isobel Waters, you know I don't like you saying 'Para'; it's derogatory," Mom says, her voice as hard and brittle as an icicle.

"It's Caitlyn Ellis this time, remember?" I say.

"I remember." Her mouth tightens, then she glances at me, her face softening. "Thank you for making sure we're safe. I wish *I* could check myself."

I scowl and slouch down in my seat. *You could if you wanted to. If you tried.*

Mom takes a gulp of coffee. "You want to get some sleep?"

Like I could, knowing they're after us. And she'll need me. "That's all right. It's not that far now."

God. We're always so polite to each other. Like strangers.

I hate that I can't hear what she's thinking. I stare out into the murky night, my tinted glasses making it as dark as ink. Even at three in the morning, there are small yellow squares of light, testaments to the people still awake—dealing with crying babies, nightmares, heartache.

People's thoughts are coming at me faster now, little blips as we pass other cars, the buildings in the distance. We drive beneath a big anti-Para sign flashing its message:

BE A GOOD CITIZEN! REPORT PARA BEHAVIOR

I've seen that one so many times my eyes almost glaze over. The next sign is just as common:

DON'T LET THE PARAS TAKE OVER!

REPORT SUSPICIOUS BEHAVIOR

But the sign after that makes me sit up straight:

PARAS ARE UNNATURAL!

THEY DO WHAT NO HUMAN SHOULD

Shivers race down my spine. I've never seen that one before. I haven't seen so many anti-Para signs so close together in a while. I can almost feel the hate closing in around us. Why did John think we'd be safe here? But I know why—it's easier to hide in a city.

My eyes ache and my body's heavy with exhaustion. I try to focus on the rhythmic thrum of our tires on the road, the whisper of classical music from the speakers, the click-click of the turn signal as Mom changes lanes, but the Normals' mind-voices keep growing until they're a faceless roar.

We pass a ParaTrooper outpost, the building lit up in the dark, the barbed wire along the top of the fence gleaming like bloody teeth. I avert my gaze fast, as if they'll feel me looking. If they have a Government Para on staff, they might. Paras are forced to do the government's bidding against their will.

To protect us, I build the shield up around Mom and me again, gritting my teeth with the effort. I'm so tired that every little thing drains me.

Mom pats my knee. "We'll be okay, Cait. You'll see."

"Sure." She says the same thing every time—but we're still running.

Mom sighs. "It won't always be like this, honey. Someday, we won't have to run. Someday, we'll have rights, just like every other citizen. Every Normal."

I roll my eyes, quietly snorting. *That's right, Mom. Keep hoping.*

Mom sighs again, her sour-coffee breath filling the car. Her hair is greasy, her face lined, deep shadows beneath her eyes. She badly needs a shower; we both do. But there wasn't time. We haven't stopped driving except for gas and to pee.

We travel light—what we can each carry in one duffel bag and one backpack. It makes for a fast getaway, but I feel like a visitor in my own life.

Now it's my turn to sigh. I've lost so many people I care about—Dad, Daniel . . .

I squeeze my eyes shut. I don't want to get pulled into the undertow.

"Caitlin!" John sends.

Heavy, murderous thoughts seep into the car, filling my head, making it hard to think. I snap my eyes open, glance in the rearview mirror. A ParaTrooper patrol car is coming up behind us. They've got a Government Para with them; I can almost taste the bitter metal of the tracker embedded in his tongue. How could I not have noticed? I curse myself. I'm too drained to deal with this. But I have to. I reach for Mom's thigh, touch it gently, and build up the shield around us. "Patrol," I say softly. "Just keep driving."

Mom nods grimly, the knuckles of her hands bone white, her eyes as wide and as scared as I feel.

"Caitlyn! Do you feel them?" John sends.

"I don't just feel them, I see them," I send.

"Shit. Can you lose them?"

I put everything I have into shielding Mom and me, cloaking us in the night, in the thought-patterns of Normals as we pass them. Just nice, law-abiding citizens who hate Paras. I'd laugh if it weren't so sickening—people hating us just because they lack something we have.

The hatred is so intense my mind grows foggy. I shake my head to clear it. I breathe out the rotting decay and breathe in the sky, the night, pushing that energy out and around us—*Normals. We're just Normals.*

The patrol car draws nearer. Mom's gaze keeps darting to the windshield mirror. Sweat trickles down my back.

The patrol car coasts up on my side, level with us. I can see the beefy driver, his cheeks flushed with drink, his gut pushing at his black uniform, straining the buttons. His buddy beside him is playing with his gun, tossing it back and forth between his hands. Idiot. Stupid, mindless, bigoted idiot. And in the back seat—a Government Para, sitting iron-straight, body skeletal and emaciated, mouth hard.

The trooper playing with his gun puts it back in his holster, says something over his shoulder, and then draws his ParaController out of his breast pocket—the thin, black plastic device with a touch screen about the size of an ebook reader, that monitors a Government Para, and emits an electric shock to keep the Para in line. So he's the Para's handler. I'll bet he liked torturing animals when he was little.

The trooper looks at me sharply. I smile weakly and waggle my fingers at him, trying to look like I'm grateful that he patrols the city, keeping us safe from those big, bad Paras.

The driver winks at me, but his buddy frowns and jerks his chin at us, talking, his thoughts loud—why would a mother-and-daughter Normal be out traveling so late? Behind him, I can feel the Government Para probing, trying to penetrate my wall of energy, get past my surface thoughts into my heart.

I focus my energy, keeping it steady, filling my head with Normals' thoughts. And then I feel John's energy joining mine, adding to my façade of normalcy. It grows and becomes almost solid.

The Government Para backs off.

"Thank you," I send gratefully. I probably could have managed it myself. I have so many times. But I'm weary, and John gave me the boost I needed. And you never know with these Para-slaves. Some of them are so fueled by their own need for survival that they'll do anything.

I start to let down the façade—and then I feel the Government Para at me again, probing, still not sure.

I focus on making my mind seem as closed and as deaf to others' voices as a Normal, and I project that toward the Government Para. His interest in me wavers. But the patrol car keeps pace with us still.

Time for the big lie. I open the glove compartment, take out the folded anti-Para flag, and shake it open, flapping it in front of my window.

ParaTroopers think that we can't bear to spread anti-Para sentiments. And most of us can't. But I've had a lot of practice, at least with this flag. It's helped save us. And though it sickens me, I smile.

I can see them argue, but the flag has done the trick. The patrol car speeds ahead of us.

I let out my breath shakily and relax the shield just a bit, my hands trembling.

"Put that thing away," Mom says.

I cram the flag back into the glove compartment, out of sight.

"Well." Mom's voice is breathy, like she's just run a race. "They didn't stop us. Nice job, Cait. Your dad taught you well."

My chest aches, the pain spreading through me into my shoulder blades. I wish Dad was still here with us, with his rich laughter and his quick, creative mind. If he was still here, he'd be thinking up new and better ways to protect us from the Government Paras and patrols. Instead, I have only the shielding technique he taught me—and that was just for my comfort. That was before it was necessary to hide.

I rub my chest, trying to rub the ache away.

"Caitlyn—something's wrong!" John sends. *"Don't you feel it?"*

I jerk. He's right; something's been niggling at the edge of my shield, like a bird pecking against glass, since we shook off the patrol car. I was giving in to my exhaustion, instead of keeping alert. I grit my teeth and open up to it.

The scent of metal fills my mind with a tight, high energy. A different Government Para is searching for us—for *me*. She knows I'm arriving here tonight in a beat-up car with a deadened Para who reads like a Normal. She holds my photo to get a better fix on me but she can't quite get a focus.

. . . I've got the troopers shielded from the telepath. There's no way she should have detected them, not unless she's far more powerful than I was told . . . .

I pull out of her head, gasping.

"Caitlyn . . ." Mom says, a wobble in her voice.

I lean forward, peering through the darkness, shielding us both while reaching for the bitter metallic scent of the Para-slave.

There, up ahead—just around the curve of the road. Waiting for us hungrily, like we're prey.

I grab Mom's arm. "Turn off here!"

"It's not our exit!" Mom says.

"Trust me!" I say, reaching for the steering wheel, yanking it. The car jolts, and we edge into the next lane. Thank god there's hardly any traffic. Thank god there was no one behind us.

The curve looms toward us. The troopers, the Government Para, all waiting, intent.

"Caitlyn?" John sends, his mind-voice full of anxiety for me.

Mom dithers, keeping us on the road, past the exit, approaching the curve.

"Get off now!" I scream, yanking the wheel again.

Mom shoves me away, but she steers us over the cement meridian and onto the exit, metal scraping cement.

CHAPTER 2

"Caitlyn!" John sends. *"You've got to get away from there. Now!"*

"Oh my god, oh my god!" Mom says. We pull up to the crossroads.

"This way!" I say, pointing away from the troopers that I can sense now—away from the Para-slave. The Para-slave reaches for us, trying to get a lock. "Mom!"

Mom steps on the gas pedal and we jerk forward, driving into the outskirts of the city. "Were there troopers?"

"And a Government Para," I say. Waiting for us. For me.

Mom goes silent.

Pain tears through my head like lightning, momentarily blinding me. My whole body tenses up unbearably, muscles seizing, fingers stiffening against the pain, toes arching upward. I feel the Para-slave scream, her pain mine, and I know her handler is punishing her for losing us. The Para-slave's nausea shudders through me as the electric shock increases. All the sickos sign up to be ParaTroopers; they can torture us with full government approval. Even kill us if they go too far—and all they get is a lousy fine. I clench my teeth against the acid rising in my throat.

I feel Mom's warm hand on my forehead, hear her voice in the distance, and then feel the car jerk to a stop.

"No! Keep going!" I mumble.

The car jerks forward.

Pain rips through me again with jagged teeth, but it's lessening the farther away we get. Dad used to worry about how strong my talents are, even though he was proud—and I know he was right to worry. Someday I'm not going to be able to hide my connection well enough, or get away fast enough, and then I'll be like that poor Para-slave getting tortured.

I rub my face with my hands. I can't feel guilty for what happened to her. I have the right to stay free. Me and my mom both do. But guilt twists through my stomach.

I stare out the window. We drive past nightclubs, liquor stores, tattoo parlors. A storefront church crouches next to an exotic dance club, and more than one store advertises "free" payday loans. Some of the stores have anti-Para flags in their windows.

Mom flexes and unflexes her fingers against the steering wheel, a sheen of sweat on her forehead. She glances over at me. "You doing okay, hon?"

I nod.

She reaches past me and pops open the glove compartment, grabs a bottle of painkillers, and hands it to me without taking her gaze off the road. "Take two," she orders.

I swallow them dry.

Cheryl Rainfield

I don't hear sirens behind us. The Government Para is faint now. I think we've lost them.

"They knew you were coming!" John sends, his mind-voice rough with emotion. *"I don't know how they could, but— Are you safe?"*

"For now." I rake my fingers through my hair. I don't want to think about it. It has to mean that one of the Underground Normals betrayed us. It hurts to think that, though. They may be Normals, but they're part of our cause. Part of our safety net. *"Someone must have tipped them off."*

"I know," John sends. *"We've got a rat in the system. I'll hunt down whoever did this and fix them good—I promise."* His sadness rises up over his fear, washing through me like a wave. *"It's hard to believe anyone we know could do this. Even a Normal. Listen, don't go to the safe house; it might be watched."*

Du-uh. *"I know how to do this."*

"I know; you've eluded them for years. But be careful anyway. There's a lot of weirdness going on."

I grunt. *"You're right."*

"And don't reach out to any of your contacts until I find out who the rat is, okay?"

I want to snap at him that I've been managing just fine for years—but the fear in his mind-voice grips me tight. *"Okay."*

"Promise me. You know what those Para-hunters are like. Once they're on your trail, they'll never give up."

"I promise."

"Keep safe," John sends.

20

"Keep strong," I reply, the formal closing coming easily to me. We disconnect.

Mom's edging our car slowly down the road, craning her neck to peer out at the shabby buildings. "I take it our plans fell through."

I nod, lock my fingers together. "They were waiting for us."

"Waiting." Mom's voice is weary, an old woman's.

"Caitlyn—can you hear me? Let me know if you be okay. You should have checked in by now," Netta thinks at me worriedly, loud for a Normal. She's the contact John found me in this city, one that will lead us to a safe house.

I grip my hands between my knees and block her out, forcing myself not to respond. It could have been Netta, even though we only just connected. Or someone else she works with. I don't know who betrayed us, but it had to be a Normal. No Para could have done this without my knowing. The thoughts and emotions would have leaked through.

Mom turns the corner, our old car rattling. The houses and buildings on this street all look dingy, with peeling paint, shingles missing from the rooftops, fences leaning sideways. A motel hunches on the corner, half the lights are burned out on the sign.

Mom pulls up slowly to the curb. A window in the dreary motel blinks VACANCY.

"We have to go where they won't expect us to be," Mom says. "They know our pattern. Safe houses, underground hideouts . . . they've found them all."

I swallow the lump of guilt in my throat. They found *me*. "It's easier to hide in a big city."

21

"Exactly," Mom says, looking at me with her lips pressed softly together, like she knows how hard it'll be for me with all that mind-noise.

I swallow again. I don't think she can drive much farther, not tonight. And wherever we go, there will be Para-Troopers and Government Paras—unless we cross the border. But we can't cross it, not now. Not with Government Paras on every exit.

"Let's do it," I say.

We get out of the car together and stagger to the office, our legs cramped from the long ride.

◉

The motel room the owner ushers us into is dingy and small, the walls a dirty green, the TV so old it doesn't even have a remote. The double bed looks hard and lumpy, and the room smells moldy, like there's been a major water leak.

Mom wrinkles her nose, and I know she doesn't want to be here any more than I do. "Do you have another room? Perhaps a bigger one?"

The motel owner tightens her bathrobe around her scrawny body, glaring at Mom. "I told you, this is all we got. You want it, or not?"

. . . *Not going to give them nothin', wakin' me up like this* . . .

Her stringy hair falls in clumps around her face. She shoves it out of the way.

Mom turns to me.

I listen in on the woman.

. . . Shoulda asked for more. They can afford it. Look at them, too snooty for the likes of us. What are they doing out in the middle of the night, anyway? . . . Her eyes narrow as her gaze darts back and forth between us. . . . *I bet they're Paras. I could make a buck off them . . .*

I look past her, to Mom. "I can't believe the hotel double-booked us like that. Or that the manager was so rude."

"Yeah?" The woman squints at me.

. . . Shoulda worn my glasses. Knew it wasn't Henry; he never rings the bell. . .

"Well, what didja come here for?"

. . . Gotcha now. Nobody comes here for a good time. They come to repent, or to visit their loved ones in Para-jail, or to find others who wanna bring back the lynchings . . . but nobody ever comes here for a holiday—'cept for the Para Cleansing, but that's days away . . . "You here for Para Cleansing Day?"

I don't look at Mom. I can barely stop myself from shuddering. How can anyone let the day Paras were massacred just slip off their tongue so easily? But most Normals do, I know that. To them, it's a holiday, even though it was the beginning of all the riots. "That's a great day, no matter where we are," I manage to say. "But we came because we heard you have a good Para-capture record."

"The best in the country!" the woman says proudly. "This is one safe city. But why'd you come *here*? You look like you could afford something better, if you don't mind my saying."

"I'm afraid that was my fault," Mom says. "I made a wrong turn and got us hopelessly lost. We were relieved to see your place."

23

"Huh. So, do you want the room or not?"

. . . Shoulda never been so proud with Henry. Shoulda told him I wanted him to come by . . .

I wait, but she doesn't go back to suspecting we're Paraṣ. I nod at Mom.

"We'll take it," she says.

"Sixty bucks a night, two nights minimum," the woman says, holding out her roughened hand.

Mom pulls the bills reluctantly out of her wallet, her hands trembling slightly. We might look middle class, but we've been depending on the generosity of people in the Underground for a year or two now, since our savings ran out. Mom always finds a job, but it's never enough with the kind of work she can get, and paying first and last every few months hasn't helped. If she'd let me work, too—but schoolwork comes first, that's what she says. Schoolwork and keeping a low profile.

The motel owner turns to go.

Outside, something glistens. I take a step closer to the window and peer out into the gloom. "Mom, there's a pool!"

"The pool's an extra twenty-five a night," the woman says, holding out her hand again.

Mom bites her lip.

"It's okay," I say quickly. "I don't need it."

But Mom knows that I do.

She opens up her wallet and reluctantly takes out two more bills.

The outdoor pool is grungy. Leaves, twigs, and wrappers float along the surface. The tiles are cracked and stained, the diving board browned from years of dirty feet—but I don't care.

As soon as I dive into the water, the pain leaves. The voices that grate through my mind become whispers. I relax, muscles unclenching. I've never understood why water has that effect on me—it's not like thoughts are transmitted over sound waves—but I don't really care why. All I care about is the blessedness of almost quiet, the peace that fills me. It's like unfolding an extra pocket of time that no one else has, time that's woven from sunshine and cool breeze, soft grass and laughter. Time that spreads gently through me, massaging my thoughts into jelly-bliss.

The cool water enfolds me like an embrace. I duck under, so I'm immersed completely, and swim to the other end. I do lap after lap until my muscles protest, until I can't drag my arms forward anymore, and then I float on my back, water gently lapping against my face.

CHAPTER 3

"Do you know of any cheap places for rent?" Mom asks the motel owner standing behind the counter.

The woman doesn't look much better in the morning light—her hair is still stringy, her body still scrawny, underfed. "You could stay here," the woman says, and licks her lips.

Mom shakes her head wearily. "Too expensive."

"How much were you thinking to spend?"

"Five hundred—six at the most."

"You can stay here for that," the woman says, leaning forward.

"For a month?" Mom sounds surprised. She raises her eyebrow at me.

I haven't heard any suspiciousness coming from the woman this morning. Just a need for money—a desperate need.

"Yeah, for a month," the woman quickly agrees.

I decide to push her. "But we were going to get a two-bedroom. So I could, you know, have my own room."

The woman looks down at the faded countertop. "I was just being ornery last night. Didn't like being woken. I got a two-room available."

I poke beneath her surface thoughts, but there's no suspicion, no malice, just worry about money, the bills she owes, the creditors who are after her, a craving for cigarettes and beer, missing Henry. . . .

"But—but we'd need a kitchen," Mom says.

"All our units got bar fridges and microwaves—and I could lend you a hot plate," the woman says.

It's hard to feel her desperation. It presses against me, close and smothering. "Might as well," I tell Mom. "It's not like we've got another place lined up."

"Are you sure?" Mom asks.

"At least they have a pool," I say.

"I'll knock that off the price, too!" the woman says.

. . . *if Henry had come by—paid his share. All the money I owe—people aren't gonna wait much longer for it* . . . The anxiety fills her lungs like phlegm, thick and heavy, and I feel like I'm drowning from the inside.

I gasp for air. "Even better," I say, though I know she falsely charged us in the first place.

Mom exhales loudly. "Fine."

◉

Mom turns to me when we're alone in our new rooms—two rooms with an adjoining door. "You felt sorry for her, didn't you?"

I shrug. "I guess."

"And there was something else. You started to look . . . in pain."

"She was desperate," I say.

"You can't let other people's emotions decide what you're going to do. She's a Normal. She'd turn you in if she knew."

She's right. I don't know what came over me. Usually I can block Normals out better than this if I have to.

Someone from the Underground reaches for me— Netta. I keep myself disconnected, though I feel guilty. Netta sounded so warm the few times we connected. To ignore her without explaining, and allow her to worry . . . . But safety comes first.

It makes me anxious, being cut off from the Underground like this. I unzip my duffel bag, taking out my melamine dishes. They're light and unbreakable, easy to carry.

"What did the Underground say? When will they have another place for us?" Mom asks.

I set my plate, bowl, and cup next to the microwave. "I haven't asked."

"You haven't—?"

"Someone let us down. Someone in the Underground. All these months, I thought it was me. I thought I wasn't passing well enough, slipped up somehow." My voice trembles, and I struggle to get it back under control. "But that isn't it. Someone has it in for us. I don't think we can use them again. Not right now."

"But how will we get new ID?" Mom bites her lip. "You know I can't get a job without it. And we can't register you for school until. . . ."

She's right. We're even more of a target without ID. I close my eyes. There has to be a way. How do other people do it? Refugees, people on the run who don't have the Underground to help?

I pull out my cell, log on to my anonymizer, and search Google for "fake ID." A ton of sites come up. I start scrolling through them, checking the quality of the images they show, and then enter in Mom's and my new names. I order birth certificates, a driver's license and Social Security card for Mom, and school records for me. I pay with what's left in my PayPal account, checking off the fastest shipping method.

"All done," I say. "We should have them by tomorrow."

Mom tilts her head. "Do you want to tell me how?"

I turn my phone to show her the screen. She nods, slowly. "That should work, for now. As long as it's not a setup by the government or the ParaWatch to try to find stray Paranormals."

Shit. I hadn't even thought of that.

"But most likely it's not," Mom says, smiling bravely. "And of course we can manage without the Underground. It'll be just like before. Only better . . ." Her voice trails off.

I wince away from those long nights sleeping in the car, the smell wafting off our bodies, the way my stomach always cramped in hunger, the way I never spoke to anyone except Mom, and a few of the voices in my head—Paras I'd never met.

Mom looks away from my face, unzipping her duffel bag. She takes out her own dishes, setting them carefully beside mine. "It won't be the same; I promise. You're older. You can look out for yourself better. And things are different now. Normals aren't running around in mobs, lynching us."

But she doesn't sound so certain.

"If we can't trust the Underground, we can't trust the Underground." She opens the cooler bag, takes out the travel bread, almond butter, and soy milk, and puts them in the bar fridge. Her mouth has gone tight, the way it does when she's trying to hold in her feelings. I wonder if she's thinking of Dad. Of the way Normals murdered him.

"It won't be the same as before," she says again.

"Yeah—they didn't have all those anti-Para laws back then." I clap my hand over my mouth, regretting my words. It's the truth—but she knows it as well as I do. Maybe more.

Mom pulls out a bag of nuts, then a bag of dried fruit. "No, they didn't," she says quietly. "But people were taking things into their own hands, killing randomly. Beating people to death. We survived a long time without contacts; we can survive again."

I can't believe this is happening. The Underground has been our lifeline for years. It's the only place I know I can trust Normals—because they've been vetted by dozens of Paras and they're sympathetic to our cause. Whenever we were threatened, whenever Government Paras or Para-Troopers came too close, the Underground was there for us.

The Underground is more than just a network of Paras and Para-sympathizers. It's more than just a route to safety. It's an extended family. And it's the only sane voice in the torrent of hatred that surrounds us.

To have that security ripped away because one person—*one* Normal—infiltrated the Underground . . . . It makes me tremble with rage.

But even more than safety—the Underground is my one possibility of finding my brother. Of somehow connecting to Daniel again. If he's still alive, if his Para-abilities haven't been tortured out of him . . . .

I try to push away the waves of anger and despair that are pulling me under. I can't let one bigot keep me from something so essential. But I can't risk our safety, either.

"Caitlyn."

John. Reaching for me.

Has he found the rat? I'm almost afraid to find out.

CHAPTER 4

I chew on my lip. I don't know if I want to know who it is, or if I can bear the betrayal. But why should it matter, when they're just Normals? Normals who almost became friends.

"Caitlyn!" John sends, more insistent this time.

I sigh and open up to him. *"Did you find the rat?"*

"Not yet. But—"

"You'll tell me as soon as you know?"

"Of course," John sends, impatiently.

It's so familiar, the way he says that to me. We found each other in the Underground years ago. I helped him through some bad times, and he's helped me. We've never met face-to-face, but I consider him one of my closest friends. My family. We have a closeness that Normals can't even dream of. I know bits of his soul, and he knows mine. But as close as we are, it's not the same thing as seeing someone face-to-face. I long to be able to see him, to hug him, to smile and laugh with him, though I know we might never be able to—not in person. He's on the run almost as much as I am.

"Caitlyn," John sends again, pulling me back. *"I've found a temporary hideout for you—"*

"No."

"No? What do you mean, no?" John sounds surprised, worried.

"I mean no. We've been relying on the Underground too much."

"That's true, but I'm not just the Underground; I'm your friend. I didn't mean you should disconnect from me! Besides, I personally vetted the safe house workers, and I haven't let anyone know who will be staying there—"

"No," I send, more firmly this time. *"I trust you more than anyone else; you know that. But someone still managed to find out where we've been staying. I think you're right—I need to sever ties for a while. At least until I know it's safe."*

"And how will you know that?"

Mentally, I shrug. I can probe every contact I have, see who told who what, as far beneath the surface as I can reach. But it's hard to trust myself; I didn't sense the rat. And neither did John. It has to be someone we know.

"At least tell me where you are," John sends. *"Let me bring you money and supplies."*

"Thanks, but the fewer people who know where we are, the better. We're going to lay low for now. Blend in with the Normals."

"I don't like it. But I understand your wanting to fall off the radar." Fury builds in him, twisting and howling like a tornado. *"I can't believe Normals think they can treat us like this—hunting us down like animals just because*

Cheryl Rainfield

we're special. Different from them." Pain thrusts through him, sharp as a sword, the metallic smell of fear and blood rising up from his memories. He shoves them away, and I let him. Every Para has horror stories from their past, about Normals who hunted them or hurt their families. *"Maybe they* should *be afraid that we're the next evolutionary step,"* he sends passionately.

My dad didn't believe that. He thought we were all equals. But look where that got him—murdered by the ones he advocated for. Murdered by Normals.

"Then why do you keep blogging for them?" John sends. *"Why do you keep trying to change their minds?"*

I startle—but of course he heard me. I didn't disconnect. *"Maybe I haven't completely given up on Normals like you have. Maybe I believe they can change."* But I'm not so sure anymore.

"Hey—I work with the ones in the Underground, don't I?"

But I know that if he didn't have to, he wouldn't. None of us would.

I sigh. *"Listen—I don't want anyone zeroing in on us, so I'm going to go."*

I can feel his reluctance. But all he sends is *"Just . . . promise you'll connect if you need me?"*

"I will. And John . . . if anyone hears from a Daniel— a Daniel with talent . . ."

"I know." John pushes down his impatience, trying not to let me see. *"I'll tell you immediately."*

I disconnect.

I can't believe I just did that—rejected John's help. But

someone's been finding out somehow. Maybe there's a Para who's been listening in on us. But no. A Para would never betray one of their own. Though a Government Para would. They do every day.

"Anything I should know about?" Mom asks, setting a bag of granola on the counter.

I raise my eyebrows.

"You got that listening look you get," she says.

"Nothing important." How do I tell her that I refused money and a place to stay when we need it so bad?

It was better before Mom shut down her talent. We could never lie to each other before. Never hold anything important back. I wonder how Normals ever trust each other, when they can't hear each other's deep truths.

"You going to be okay, not connecting with anyone?" Mom asks.

"Sure." I shrug.

She looks at me sideways, then gives me a tight, fast hug, not saying anything. She knows me too well. If she had, I might have cried.

Mom clears her throat. "We should look into getting you enrolled in a school."

"I know, I know." I sigh. "Blend in with Normals as fast as you can. Never forget they're watching." Underground Survival 101.

Mom nods. "And I will look for a job."

CHAPTER 5

I take a long swim before heading off to the school, hoping the peace-bliss will linger with me, but people's thoughts still slither into my own:

. . . did Michael? . . . run in my stocking . . . damn coffee is cold . . .

I crank up the volume on my MP3 player, letting the white noise fill my brain. It doesn't help that I haven't slept, but I never can, not the first few nights in a new place.

The morning sun is hazy, veiled in gauzy clouds, though still warm on my skin. I pass a grimy tattoo parlor, a dollar store, a pawn shop with metal bars across its windows. I tune in and out of people's thoughts, getting fragments as I pass them, building a sense of the city.

There's a lot more fear here—more Para-haters than I'm used to—but there are also a lot more Para-supporters.

A blond boy runs past me, his sneakers shuck-shucking against the pavement, shoelaces untied. His glasses bob against his button nose, the way Daniel's always did when he ran. I grab his arm. "Daniel?"

. . . get off me! . . . The boy spins around. "Let go!"

It's not him. Of course it's not. Daniel wouldn't be eight anymore. He'd be seventeen, two years older than me.

I let the boy go and back away. "Sorry! So sorry. I thought you were someone else."

"Huh!" the boy says, screwing up his lips and arching his neck back like he wants to spit in my face—but his eyes hold pain. He knows, too, what it means to lose someone you love. I turn away, trying not to think of Daniel.

◉

I see it again—the mob with their torches and bats, their guns and knives, their faces twisted in hate. Mom pulls us both into the cellar—"Stay here, no matter what happens." The house shakes—Daniel and I huddle together, our minds locked on each other, trying to block it all out. I scream as Dad's unchecked cry of pain cuts through me. I run up the stairs and out the door, Daniel running after me, crying at me to come back. I can feel Mom sending calm into the mob, but it's not enough, just her alone by Dad's side.

The mob sweeps us up and pushes us along like a river, away from Dad, away from the horrible beating. Daniel clutches my hand. And then a woman with a deep thrum running through her, the prettiest woman I've ever seen, her eyes so large they make her look innocent, plucks me out of the crowd, and Daniel with me. She bends down to my level. "You have a gift, don't you, sweetheart? Something that makes you special." She holds out her hand. "This is no time to be out. Come with me, and I'll make sure you're safe."

I look up into her face, trusting the kindness she projects. I take her hand. Daniel glares at us. "We don't know her. And Mom told us not to!"

He clenches my hand, tries to draw me back.

"Your mom told me to come get you both," the woman says. Daniel looks up at her, and she touches his cheek gently. "I wouldn't forget you."

Something about the way she looks at him feels wrong, as if he's a donut she wants to eat up. I shake myself uneasily. *"Come on!"* I send. *"Let's go back."*

Daniel ignores me and takes her hand as the mob descends on us, hitting us like a giant wave, pulling me away from them. I lose sight of Daniel. And then suddenly our connection cuts off, like a moth snuffed out by an electric flare. *"Daniel!"* I shriek. No matter how hard I send to him, or how often, he never answers; there's just this empty void where he is, a void that widens to a chasm when I feel Dad's last cry.

I shake my head, trying to focus on the present. Daniel is gone.

But I can't help hoping that somehow, someday, I'll find him again — through the Underground. For now, it's just not safe. I push myself farther away from the others until it's like I've got cotton in my brain, or I've gone deaf.

I cross my arms protectively over my chest as I walk. I can't believe how alone I feel. How lonely, without that constant hum of conversation and connection. I feel so disconnected, like I could die and no one would know or care. Is this how Normals feel all the time? Is this how Mom feels now I shudder.

◉

The glossy red-and-black ParaWatch poster jeers at me from a pillar, the words as familiar as a playground chant. PARAS ARE A NATIONAL THREAT! REPORT SUSPICIOUS BEHAVIOR TO OUR HOTLINE.

I look around casually, feeling outward. No one's focused on me. I grab a silver marker from my backpack, scrawl two words, then drop the marker back in. The poster now reads, PARAS ARE NOT A NATIONAL THREAT! DON'T REPORT SUSPICIOUS BEHAVIOR TO OUR HOTLINE. I walk on, a bounce in my step. Let ParaWatch find *that*.

I shouldn't take such risks, but someone has to fight back. And it feels good. Man, does it ever feel good.

It's different from the fighting back I do on my blog. That feels more educational, more thought out—and safer, at least as long as my anonymizers and firewalls hold, and no one can trace it back to me. This—defacing a poster in daylight—could get me imprisoned, even killed. But still, I can't stop doing it.

I'm almost at the school; I can feel it in the bright, swirling energy, the chatter, the emotion emanating from the place. It's like teens amplify their thoughts, with all the feelings and hormones raging inside them. I have to fight extra hard to strain it out.

I'm thankful for the weight of my backpack on my shoulder, for my most precious things tucked inside—my tattered copy of *The Lorax* that Dad used to read me; my dog-eared copy of *Homecoming* that I read with my mom;

and a photo of Dad, Mom, Daniel, and me, just before everything went bad. Wherever I go, they're always with me—my turtle shell of a home, portable and heavy with memories.

"Books are your friends," Dad used to tell me. "They allow you to hope and to dream, but they also help to strengthen your talent. Never forget that." I read because I love to. Never thought I'd need to strengthen my talents. Never needed to. Now I wish I'd read more. Maybe it would have given me an edge.

I shift my backpack. I downloaded the local school's blueprints and studied them after my swim; I know exactly where all the exits are. I doubt they'll find us so soon, but it's better to be prepared. Especially if one of the Para-hunters has inside help. And from the blueprints, I know the school has a pool! I've got my suit on beneath my clothes, just waiting until I can use it.

The high school is a five-story building made of dark red brick, the color of dried blood. A group of kids cluster on the wide cement steps, laughing with one another, their strutting body language making it clear that they're the ruling power here. Others surge past them and are swallowed into the dark mouth of the school.

A man in a black suit stands at the top of the stairs, legs splayed in an army stance, hands held behind his stiff back. His balding head glistens in the sun as his marble-hard eyes scrutinize each student. Our gazes lock.

I shiver, goose pimples skittering along my arms. He's a Para-hater, for sure. I hope he's not one of my teachers.

Rich, deep laughter, easy and smooth, rises above the hubbub of noise. It reminds me of Dad—happy and secure. I turn and eagerly search out the laugher.

He's standing, head thrown back, full lips curved in a wide-open smile. His skin contrasts with his crisp white shirt. Narrow copper bracelets glint along one of his arms. He's so gorgeous, he must already be taken. But it's his laughter that's the best. It feels clean and pure, with no hidden malice or cruelty—just joy. I haven't heard laughter like that in such a long time. It makes me want to laugh with him, to find the world beautiful.

His head comes back up, his eyes snapping open, like he can sense me looking at him, and his brown eyes find mine, right through my dark glasses. Beneath his laughter is a kind of sadness, something wounded, even though it's held at bay by his cheerfulness. And there's a goodness in him that I can feel right to his core. He befriends outsiders, people who don't fit in anywhere else. That's who he's laughing with and I can tell they love him for it. He could be part of the in-crowd, but he's his own person.

His eyes draw me in. The mind-noise around me dampens, peace flooding through me. I've never felt so safe in a crowd before. I stare at him. I can't believe this is happening. I know it's because of this boy, but I don't understand it. Nothing like this has ever happened to me before.

He smiles at me, a warm smile, and it's like he's put his hand over my belly. I reach toward him, hoping he's one of us—but there's nothing. No vibration, not even a tingle.

But if he's not one of us . . .

I look away. The mind-noise comes crashing back like a thunderclap. I don't know how I could have been drawn to a Normal, or how I could let myself believe there was something special about him. It's not like we have anything in common.

A girl moves in front of me, blocking my view, her mouth moving, her hands gesturing as she talks.

. . . cute new girl . . . of course she likes Alex . . . everyone does . . . too bad she's straight . . .

I pull the buds out of my ears, the thoughts around me rising in volume. "Sorry, what?"

"I noticed you've got your eye on Alex."

"Alex?" My cheeks heat up like a sunburn.

"Yeah," the girl says, nodding toward the boy I was staring at. He's half turned now, to talk to his friends, but I can see from the way his shoulders are set that he's as aware of me as I am of him.

What is *wrong* with me? I force my attention back to the girl.

"You'd better be forewarned—he doesn't date. I mean *never*. You're better off not even thinking about him."

As if I would. I can't ever trust a Normal with my secret. So why do I want to? All because of some stupid laugh? I don't understand why I feel so connected to him, as if he can understand what it's like being hated. Being hunted for his life.

I look at the girl standing in front of me, watching me so closely. She's pretty in a tomboy way, with bright green eyes in a slim oval face, her long brown hair held back with an elastic band. Her thoughts are as loud as any Normal's.

My fingers itch to pop the buds back into my ears, but I know I can't get away with it much longer.

"What're you listening to?" the girl asks, and puts one of the buds to her ears before I can stop her.

She scrunches up her nose. "Static?"

I'm tempted to tell her that my MP3 player is broken, but I go for the truth. "It's white noise," I say. "Some people use it to relax." Others use it to drown out noise. Or at least I do. Without it, the city is a twenty-four-hour radio station inside my head.

The girl hands me back my earbud.

Be polite. Gain acceptance. Blend in. I mentally sigh, then pull the crumpled schedule out of my pocket. "You know where room 311 is? I've got English first period."

"Ohhh, Mr. Arnold. He's a real jerk." She purses her lips like she tastes something sour. "I've got him first period, too. I'm Rachel."

"Caitlyn."

"Come on," Rachel says, "I'll show you around."

I glance over my shoulder, but Alex is already gone. I'm surprised that I feel disappointed. *'Get a hold of yourself,'* I tell myself firmly. I follow Rachel up the wide cement steps.

The huddle of girls at the top watches us with disdain. We're clearly not good enough for them. One girl in particular—a girl with bleached-blond hair who the others keep glancing at, clearly the leader of their pack—radiates with ill will. I commit her face to memory; I need to stay away from her.

"Hey! Whatcha staring at?" the girl says, detaching herself from the group to block my way.

Up close, she smells of expensive perfume and bubble gum. Jealousy, anger, and fear all roil through her.

"I wasn't—"

"Leave her alone, Becca," Rachel says.

Becca doesn't even turn her head, like Rachel doesn't exist. She glares at me through mosquito-slit eyes. "In this school, there's us ParaWatch peeps, then there's the losers too scared to make a stand, and then there's Para-lovers. Where do you fit?"

I know what I should answer. I know what I have to do to fit in. But I just can't do it, not with this bigot. The rage in her is like a disease. "What you call losers, I call free thinkers."

Becca snorts. "Yeah, I figured you'd say that. You've got the look."

Well, she's got the look of a bully. I tighten my mouth to keep myself from telling her so.

"Listen, I saw you scoping out Alex," Becca says. "Lemme give you some friendly advice. You don't have a chance with him. You're just new trash, that's all. Worse than a Para.". . . *He's mine! Not yours, girlie . . . Just as soon as I make him notice me . . .*

I break eye contact and step aside to show I don't want a fight, though I actually want to shove her lips past her teeth. If anyone's trash, she is.

She blocks me again, sneering. There's a few like her in every school.

"Becca, come on. Leave her alone," Rachel says louder.

"Why do *you* care?" Becca snaps. "Unless you want to get into her pants?" The other girls cackle.

Rachel looks at her feet. . . . *oh god . . . not now . . .* The shame emanating from her is so strong it almost pushes me to the ground.

"Maybe someone would want to get into yours if you were a little nicer," I say.

Becca smiles, baring her teeth like a wolf about to attack. "You're new here, bitch, so I'll let you off this once. But nobody talks to me like that." . . . *gonna find some dirt on you and worse . . . major payback . . .*

What happened to my blend-in-with-the-Normals policy? I can't believe I'm messing it up already.

I look away from Becca again to let her think she's smarter, harder, than me.

Rachel's looking at me with hungry-dog eyes. . . . *god, she's not just cute, she's nice, too. Why does she have to be straight? . . .*

"Come on," I say to her, and shove through the heavy school doors.

CHAPTER 6

Thoughts rush at me, skewering my mind with jagged noise. Why do Normals have to be so loud? I focus on the sickly looking yellow-green lockers, the beat-up white-and-gray-speckled linoleum tiles, and the flickering fluorescent lights to ground myself, and the mind-noise retreats to a buzz.

Rachel turns to me, her face serious. "Look—uh—there's something I need to tell you." . . . *queer . . . lesbian . . . no, queer . . .*

We walk together, ignoring the slamming lockers, the students shouting, laughing, yelling. I try to look encouraging. I wish I could tell her that we actually have a lot in common. We both get judged or hated just for being who we are.

Rachel blows out her breath, her bangs fanning her forehead. "Okay. I'll just say it. I'm queer. I'm not going to hit on you or anything like that, but I thought you should know, in case you got a problem with it."

"Nope, no problem—as long as you're okay that I'm straight."

Rachel snorts. "I thought you would be. You still wanna hang out?"

"Of course." I can't believe she's asking me that. But then, she doesn't know that I'm a Para.

Rachel smiles at me, her cheeks flushed. . . . *why couldn't she be queer?* . . . "So—where're you from?"

"All over. My mom and I—we've moved a lot."

"Army position?"

"No. My mom—she just doesn't like to stay in one place too long. Not since my dad died."

"I'm sorry," Rachel says, touching my arm.

Jumbled thoughts and emotions burst through me. I catch a glimpse of her dad—red cheeked, broad shouldered, smiling, and then staring out a window, gray faced, eyes bleak and weary.

I move my arm away, then reach up to scratch my nose, trying to make it look like that's what I meant to do. I wish for relief, for anything to stop the noise in my head. "Is there a swim team here?"

Rachel blinks and the images fade. "Sure. They practice every day after school, but it's so late in the year, I'm not sure there'd be any positions open."

"No, but maybe I can swim a few laps."

"I can take you around after school, if you like. My brother's on the team."

"That'd be great!" I smile at her—a real smile. I'm starting to like her, though I don't want to. No attachments. It'll just make it harder when we move on.

A huge ParaWatch poster scowls at us from the wall.

It's double the size of the regulation poster, the text fresh-blood-red on nighttime black.

PARAS THREATEN US ALL. DO YOUR DUTY — REPORT A PARA. REWARDS GIVEN FOR ANY INFORMATION LEADING TO AN ARREST.

It's worse than the last town we stayed at. So many more posters. My breath shudders in my throat.

Rachel follows my gaze. "We're not all that dogmatic. Mr. Temple encourages the ParaWatch groupies."

"Mr. Temple?"

"The principal. He's a real bigot."

An image of the man with the balding head flits into my mind — the man who made my skin crawl.

Rachel looks at me out of the corners of her eyes. "He's racist, sexist, homophobic — and, of course, a Para-hater."

I blink. She's a Para-supporter! I knew I felt good about her.

. . . lookit that big lesbo and the new girl trash . . . going to take her down a notch . . .

The venom in the thoughts is so strong it almost snaps my head back.

I tug Rachel around so we're half facing Becca. "That's so cool that the school wants to start a gay-straight alliance," I say loudly.

"Uh — yeah?" Rachel says, her forehead scrunching up.

Becca stops an inch away from us, looking at me with disgust. I don't move, just look back, face neutral, waiting.

"Lesbo Para-lovers like you shouldn't be allowed to walk through these halls!"

"Becca, are you worried that you're a lesbian—or a Para?" I ask, keeping my eyes innocent-wide. "Because usually that's what people are afraid of when they talk like you."

Red crawls up Becca's neck and face, like tiny red ants. "Of course not, you—you—piece of Para-loving trash."

Becca stalks away from us, her back stiff with anger.

Rachel laughs loudly, her belly shaking. "Becca's the biggest homophobe and Para-hater in the school, in case you didn't figure that out. You just made my day. My year!"

"I'm glad." I grin. But fear rattles inside me. I've just drawn attention to myself—again.

The crowds are thinning out. Rachel looks at her sport watch. "We'd better hurry—Mr. Arnold hates it when you're late. He gives you a detention even if you've got a good reason."

She jogs up the stairs and I follow.

A tall man with a nose that looks too big for his face leans around a classroom door and glares at us, his glasses askew. "Hurry it up, Miss Levy," he says, in a nasal, almost whiny voice. "You don't want another tardy mark added to your record."

"Just forty-five minutes of purgatory to get through," Rachel whispers. "Remember it won't last all day—even if it seems to."

Rachel slips through the doorway.

Mr. Arnold stops me. "Take those sunglasses off. They look ridiculous."

49

I make a show of pulling out the "doctor's note" Mom scrawled out for me. "They're prescription glasses, sir. I need them to see."

"Oh, for—Very well." He impatiently gestures for me to walk in ahead of him, then snaps the door shut behind us. "There's an empty seat near the front."

I'll bet there is.

Students turn, curious. Dark brown eyes meet mine, the wide mouth curving into a happy-to-see-you smile. Alex.

I take a shaky breath, holding in my answering smile, but I can feel it flood into my eyes. I curse myself. He's a Normal. NORMAL. I must be losing it.

"Any day now, Miss Ellis."

I walk over to the empty desk and perch on the hard chair. I take my books out carefully, focus on my every movement to keep myself out of Alex's head.

Mr. Arnold stands in front of the smartboard. A few whispers start up, but when Mr. Arnold turns and frowns, his bushy eyebrows converging into one, they abruptly go silent. "If you've got nothing better to do, you can take out your scripts and read ahead while I put up these questions."

Everyone groans. I reluctantly open my battered copy of *Othello* while Mr. Arnold drones on and on, like a fly buzzing around the room. A whiny, irritating little mosquito.

"Miss Ellis? Miss Ellis, can you tell us the answer?"

I look up into his expectant face, seeing his I've-got-you-now expression. The answer is so loud in his head that it's hard to ignore. I know it's wrong, but I want to wipe the smirk off his face. "Brabantia accused Othello of using witchcraft." I think back to the scene—I read it at the last school—and add, my lips so dry they stick to my teeth, "He did it because he was a bigot." *Like most of you Normals.*

Mr. Arnold blinks. . . . *How did she—? . . . Swear I had her* . . . "That's correct. Although not everyone would agree with your assessment." He turns away.

People's attention swings to me like polar north. I slouch in my seat, pretending to be bored.

"Mr. Arnold, Mr. Arnold," a tall, confident boy calls, waving his arm like he's in grade three.

. . . Paul again . . . another student thinks.

Mr. Arnold sighs loudly. "Yes, Mr. Barrett? What is it this time?"

The boy doesn't glance in my direction, but I feel his awareness of me. "Isn't that like people today, accusing someone of being a Para when they're not?"

I stiffen.

The room erupts into voices. People's thoughts pulse with emotion so loudly I almost can't hear what people are actually saying.

I clench my hands in my lap, breathe slow and deep like Dad taught me to. I visualize people's thoughts being covered in layers of heavy air that dampens their volume, pushes them down like sand falling through water.

Everyone's focused on what the boy said. I'm sure he did it on purpose, but I don't think he meant to single me out.

I reach out toward him and feel it immediately, the way his thoughts seem to vibrate in and out of each other, like he can manipulate them. He's a telekinetic. He should know to be more careful! He put us all in danger, just by opening his mouth. And yet, I can't help admiring him for what he said.

I take another look at him. His curly brown hair frames his face like one of Michelangelo's cherubs and his green eyes are vivid and clear. His jeans and T-shirt fit him snugly in all the right places. And on top of that, he's brave, even if a little headstrong. Like I don't know anything about that. But how the heck did he get so confident, with him being a Para? I glance away, before he can catch me looking.

Mr. Arnold bangs his book against his desk and the room goes quiet. "We are not here to discuss current affairs; we are here to discuss English. The great masters of writing! Shakespeare! Perhaps you would save your question for a more appropriate class?"

Mr. Arnold reads aloud again, his nasal voice killing any dramatic effect the words might have.

I sneak another look at Paul. He catches my gaze and winks at me. I haven't been shielding as well as I thought. He knows, or at least he suspects, that I'm a Para. Unless he flirts with Normals, which I find hard to believe.

The intensity of people's thoughts lessens as Mr. Arnold drones on, and for once I'm grateful for a boring teacher.

When the bell rings, Alex is there beside me, smelling of soap, clean skin, and vanilla, and a faint whiff of chlorine. I think I could get drunk on his scent.

I shake my head, trying to toss the thought right out of me.

"I hear you like to swim, Caitlyn."

I wonder if I'm another of his outsiders that he's trying to make comfortable. But how did he find out so fast?

. . . asked her yet? . . .

I turn to see Rachel leaning forward, her gaze focused on us.

I look back into the heat of Alex's gaze. I feel myself being sucked into his eyes, wanting to smooth out the old pain I sense deep below.

Snap out of it! "I—yes. I love it. Swimming, pools . . ." It's like my body's taking over, leaving my brain far behind. I can't believe I'm going ga-ga over some Normal—or anyone for that matter. It's not safe; I know it's not.

I breathe out. I am not my body. I can control this. "I love the quiet of the water, the calmness—"

"Me, too!" Alex says, leaning forward. "The way it feels like the world disappears, and there's only you and the water. No noise, no clutter—just the water cradling you—" He stops, his face flushing. "There's a kind of peace," he adds, quickly.

"Yeah! I know what you mean." I stare at him. I've never met anyone who loves water the way I do, for the reasons I do. But I can't sense a fragment of Para in him. Why does he need peace so much? "It's like—all your problems go away for a while."

Alex nods his head animatedly. "Exactly!" He rubs his hair, and his curls stand up. "We've got a great pool here. I could show you around after school, if you like. I'm on the team."

He would be, with his broad back and narrow hips, and

his love of swimming. He shifts his feet, looking awkward when I don't say anything. "There's no pressure; I get it if you don't . . ."

I shake my head, force myself to focus. "Rachel's going to show me around," I manage to get out.

"She won't mind," he says, his eyes twinkling.

But she will. I can feel her misery, all the way from over here. And it brings me back to myself. "How about we all go together?" I say, then wish I could take it back. What am I *doing*?

Alex grins, his white teeth bright against the dark of his lips. "It's a date."

"If you're finished setting up your social life, perhaps you'd move on to your next class?" Mr. Arnold says, glaring.

Alex laughs. "You know you like us hanging around. It gives you something to talk about in the teacher's lounge."

Alex brushes my back with his fingers, then settles his hand on my shoulder, like that's where he meant it to be all along. A warm feeling fills my belly.

. . . *Why do I feel so good around her?* . . .

His thoughts are happy, bright as Christmas lights.

I quicken my pace to the door, just enough to break contact and stop the rush of his thoughts and emotions. I can barely control my own.

Rachel's waiting in the hall. Her lips turn upward uncertainly, like she's not sure whether she did the right thing or not.

"Rachel!" I gasp, yanking out my crumpled schedule. "Could you show me where my next class is?"

"Sure."

I turn to Alex, who's standing behind me, still as a mannequin. "See you after school." I rush Rachel down the hall, away from him.

CHAPTER 7

Rachel raises her eyebrows. "I thought you *liked* Alex."

"I do." God, I do. But I shouldn't. I can't. I'd always be worrying whether I could trust him, whether he'd turn me in if he got mad at me or if we broke up. A Normal and a Para could never make it.

Rachel pushes open the door, and we head down a flight of stairs, following the crowd. "So?"

"I don't even know if I like-like him." And I can't let myself want to. Besides, he's got a secret of his own, reasons he doesn't want to get involved.

"Oh, I think you're crushing on him. I saw your face."

It feels more than a crush. I'm drawn to his happiness, like sunshine warming my skin. I don't know how he can be so happy with all that's wrong in the world—people murdering each other, hating each other, raping, starting wars—but he is. Even with his own wound, whatever it is, he's happy. I wish I could be.

Rachel stops outside a classroom. "This is it." She hands me back my crumpled schedule.

Math. My least favorite subject. I find a seat, try to let the numbers, the equations, mean something to me. But over and over, my thoughts drift to Alex, to his wide smile and laughing eyes, and the calm in his heart.

◉

Rachel and I enter the pool area together. Only a few mind-voices pepper me; not many people are here yet. The smell of chlorine rises up all around me, and I breathe it in. The blue of the pool is unmarred, no one disturbing it yet, the thick navy lines on the bottom guiding the lanes. I ache to dive in.

Alex strides toward us in just his Speedo, a silver swimming cap, and goggles pushed up over his forehead. I try not to stare at his broad, muscular shoulders, his long, lean legs, and the bulge that makes up his suit. Oh my god. I can't wrench my gaze away. I have to get a grip!

I don't understand it. I've never fallen for anyone before. My safety's always come first.

Alex smiles. "I'm glad you came. Practice's in a few minutes if you want to stay and watch."

Rachel snorts.

Alex's smile freezes. "Your brother's already in the pool. You gonna go find him?"

They glare at each other, standing off like fighters.

I can't believe they're acting like this, like they're almost fighting over me. This kind of stuff only happens in movies, not in real life. At least not in my life. Part of me wants to bask in the moment, but maybe I'm reading it wrong. Besides, I can't let Alex get too close.

"I want to look around. Don't you?" I say to Rachel.

She nods. We take off our shoes and socks, then walk out onto the shiny gray tiles, Alex close beside me. My feet slap the floor, splashing through the shallow puddles of water, my soles automatically finding traction.

The pool is fifty meters long, just right for smooth, uninterrupted laps. I can almost feel the cool water caressing my skin, the peace-bliss of silence.

And then I sense another Para. A telepath.

Of course. She'd be drawn to the water, like I am.

I turn my head casually, and see a broad-shouldered girl in a dark blue swimsuit coming through the doorway opposite us. Our gazes lock.

"Stay strong," I send.

The girl stumbles. *"It's not safe here!"* She disconnects abruptly.

I rub the back of my neck. I'm used to Paras being cautious, but not so cautious that they won't even connect. . . .

She darts a glance at the wall behind me. I turn to look. A huge ParaWatch banner is draped over the entranceway, warning us all to be on the lookout for deviant Paras. This school has more anti-Para propaganda than I've ever seen.

"Coach opens the pool for a free swim at four-thirty, when practice is over," Alex says, looking at me. "You could stay and swim then, if you like."

I shake my head regretfully. "Not today."

"Tomorrow then." Alex flashes his smile at me, bright as sun glinting off glass.

I feel dizzy, short of breath.

I grit my teeth. This can't go anywhere. But I know that I want it to, even as I'm telling myself that it can't.

I turn to Rachel—but her gaze is on a slim boy with a white swimming cap, poised on the diving board. He springs, the board braying, and makes a near-perfect dive.

Rachel nods her chin at him. "My brother."

Across the pool, the coach blows a whistle, piercingly loud. I wince as it echoes through the pool area. "Swimmers in the pool!" the man yells. "Visitors on the bleachers—or out." He looks meaningfully at us.

Alex rubs his arm. "You staying to watch?" . . . *Say yes . . . no, don't . . .*

I shake my head. "Can't." Though I want to, just to be near him.

"Sorry you didn't get to see more of the pool," Alex says.

"Mr. Carter!" the coach bellows.

Alex waves. "I gotta go. See you tomorrow?"

"Yeah," I say, even as I shake my head no.

Rachel grabs my arm as we leave. "Somebody likes you!" she says in a singsong voice.

I laugh and swat at her, my breathing shallow. I do *not* care if some Normal likes me.

I catch the motel owner staring at me out of the grimy window as I approach the motel, but when I look at her, she moves away.

I reach after her. Nosiness, a wandering thought about whether my mom and I are Paras or are here to see a Para— but mostly I feel her desperation for money and to be loved.

She's thinking about fingering me and my mom, but she's not sure yet. She doesn't want another black mark on her record, but oh, she could use the money.

I walk into the lobby, smile at the owner like I can't hear her thoughts. "Nice day out."

She squints at me suspiciously; no one's ever that friendly with her. The kid must want something from her. But what? "Nice day if you like sweating," she says. She flicks her lighter, lights a cigarette, and inhales deeply.

"That's why I'm so glad you've got a pool," I say, trying to keep my voice light, the smile on my face. I wave at her as I walk to the elevators. I feel her gaze on my back. Will I end up like her one day—desperate and alone? Alex flashes through my mind and I push the thought away. Upstairs, I force myself to get through my homework. Then I log onto my anonymizer, and then my blog—*Teen Para*. Already there are 350 comments I haven't answered since my last post. A few of them are the usual Para-hater crap— "You don't deserve to breathe!" "Die Para-freak!"—but others are curious, thoughtful, even friendly. Mom would flip out if she knew what I was doing. But I think I'm helping some Normals, at least, realize that Paras are people. Real people who hurt and hope and dream.

"Sorry for my absence, peeps," I key in. "We had to move—AGAIN. Troopers were sniffing around our neighborhood. Someone must have snitched on us for the moola. Or maybe they think it's their duty. But how is it anyone's duty to enslave another human being? Did we learn nothing from the Holocaust? From slavery?"

I hover my finger over the "Publish" button. Some Normals will get all geared up over what I wrote. But what's the point of speaking out if you don't say the truth? I click the button.

"Caitlyn!"

John's upset. He must have had a Google alert on my blog, set to tell him as soon as I posted. I sigh. I already know what we'll both say. We've had this discussion so many times.

"Stop taking such crazy risks," John sends.

"It's not crazy if it makes a difference."

"You're wasting your time. Normals are never going to get it. They don't want to get it."

"Some don't. But some do. I've seen a few change, become more pro-Para. And isn't that worth it? We need all the support we can get."

"They're only like that when they have nothing to risk or to gain. Put their own families on the line or offer them a reward and they'll squeal on us like pigs."

I close my mind to John, ignoring him, though it hurts to shut him out. Hurts like slamming a door on my finger. But I wasn't going to connect with anyone from the Underground anyway, not until I find out who the snitch is. If someone's managed to overhear our conversations, then I'm not safe, not even being in contact with John. I've got to stay firm.

61

When I get to school the next morning, I can't stop looking for a friendly face—for Alex or Rachel—but I just see a lot of faces I don't know, all of them shutting me out. Loneliness washes over me—loneliness and that familiar dread that I'll never belong anywhere, that I'll be an outsider for the rest of my life, looking in on what other people have. I clench my teeth, pushing the tears back down. Tears make the new girl stand out.

Paul strolls toward me, smiling mischievously. Today his curls and rounded cheeks make him look like a Raphael angel. Cute, gifted—why can't my heart flutter for him? "Hey, pretty girl. What's there to be sad about? The sun's shining, we're alive, and—" His fingers brush my ear.

I feel his power surge, see his lips tighten in concentration. A chocolate bar rises out of his backpack and flies into his hand as he reaches for it.

"Here's something sweet for someone sweet." He draws his hand in front of me and offers me the chocolate bar.

I want to scream, "What are you doing? Don't you know how dangerous that is?"—but at the same time, there's a part of me that delights in his use of his power, and how he's getting away with it.

"Thank you," I say softly, taking the chocolate. I can't hold back a smile.

"You just moved here," he says, and it's not a question.

"Yep. How long have you lived here?"

"All my life," he says proudly.

Wow. It's hard to believe that someone who's as outspoken as Paul has lived here that long undetected.

Pain splinters through me. Why does Paul—who takes so many risks with being a Para—get to have a *home*, a community even, while I am forever on the run?

Paul winks at me and walks off.

I want to chase after him, ask why he took such a crazy risk to give me a bar of chocolate. But I think I know the answer. You don't feel much like living if you can't be yourself.

◉

Rachel finds me at lunch.

"The food here sucks," she says. "They try to pass it off as healthy, but most of it's full of fat or additives. And it tastes like crap—soggy French fries and cold nachos."

I shut my locker, clicking the lock closed. Hanging around with Normals is part of the blending in. But I actually feel myself wanting to spend time with her. Not that I'll be around long enough to really get to know her, so I can indulge myself. "You got somewhere else in mind?"

"The vegetarian grill across the street. It's got a lot of vegan food, but there's some meat-eater dishes, if that's what you're into. It's almost the same price as the so-called food here, but it actually tastes good—and feeds your body."

My mom would love her. I pick up my backpack. "I'm in."

The grill is bigger than I thought it would be, and a lot more crowded. People's mind-voices are louder than the din of conversation and clatter of plates. I dampen it down as much as I can, focusing on the warm, spicy scents, the colorful dishes of steaming and cold foods laid out along counters down the center of the restaurant. We get to help ourselves.

Rachel and I both have our trays piled with food when she stiffens. I follow her gaze.

Alex. The whole restaurant feels brighter, more vivid, the smells stronger. "What's *he* doing here?" Rachel mutters.

Alex looks around until his eyes meet mine. He gives me a wide, easy smile. Then he sees Rachel. His smile wobbles. . . . *always together . . . is she . . . ?*

How can I tell him I'm not gay? Wait—isn't it better if he thinks I am?

Alex walks over, taking long, relaxed strides. He smiles shyly at me. "Can I buy you two lunch?"

"No," Rachel says scornfully.

I've seen boys offer this to girls before. Seen the girls giggle and bat their eyelashes as they agree. I never understood their behavior. But suddenly I want to know what it's like. For once in my life, I want to feel what it's like to be normal. Not Normal, exactly, but . . . just a regular teen girl who doesn't have to hide or go on the run. Who can like any boy she pleases.

"Sure," I say.

Alex takes my tray and carries it to the cashier.

Rachel leans closer. "I've never seen him act this way before."

My heart flutters. "No?"

Rachel shakes her head. "He never acts interested in

anyone. Not until you. Becca's going to be in a jealous snit when this gets out."

Exactly what I don't need. Another reason I have to stop this before it goes anywhere.

"Caitlyn!" John sends. *"I know you need money. Let me send you some. Let me help."*

I grit my teeth and block him harder. It's getting easier to shut him out.

Alex comes back with my tray and a tray of his own. All thoughts slide out of my head.

"Guess I'd better go pay," Rachel says, and heads to the cashier.

"Where're you sitting?" Alex asks, standing a little closer than he needs to.

"We haven't picked a table yet."

I watch him scan the room. My knees are liquid, like I might fall over any minute. I bite the inside of my cheek, think about Rachel, the food, the obnoxious Mr. Arnold . . .

Alex touches my arm softly, like he's not sure he has the right to touch me. . . . *just being near her makes me happy . . . was it like that for my dad? . . . have to walk away . . .*

"Come on; someone's leaving," he says.

I follow him to the booth, where we wait for the smartly dressed woman to clear her stuff. She winks at us as she leaves. . . . *cute couple . . .*

Alex sets down our trays, then slides into the booth. I sit down across from him, a grin on my face. I feel almost high being around him.

No! It's crazy, stupid thinking. I'm not sure it's thinking at all.

I look around and wave to Rachel. She comes over and slides into the booth beside me, her plate loaded with lentils and rice, steaming vegetables, and salad. That same tension between Rachel and Alex is back—over me.

I take a bite of my falafel and rice and try to pretend I can't feel the undercurrent between them. Try to pretend I'm as blind and as deaf as they are.

"So, what'd you think of Mr. Arnold?" Alex asks fake-innocently, trying to hold back a smile.

"I think . . . he should've found another job," I say.

Alex laughs, raising his bottle of water like he's toasting me. "You said it. He sure kills any love of English. And that used to be my favorite class."

I can hear Alex trying to figure out whether I like him, whether I'd let him kiss me, even while he's telling himself to forget me. I see a gun in his mind, feel the explosion of sadness and guilt, but also relief.

I lean back, studying his animated face as he talks. I know if I reach for it, I can find out exactly what happened, what his locked-up sadness is about. But I don't want to find out that way. I want him to tell me, like he would in a normal relationship. I want him to trust me enough to tell me. So I focus hard on the meal, on what everyone's saying aloud, to keep myself from picking up anything else he may be thinking.

. . . *I'm really having fun* . . ., Alex says, leaning forward.

"I am, too," I say.

"Are, too, what?" His brow wrinkles.

Oh. My. God! I can't believe I slipped up like that! "Liking the food," I say quickly. "That's what I thought you were going to say." I shove more falafel into my mouth.

Sweat pricks my scalp. I can feel Rachel watching me like a cat as she eats, trying to put it together. Alex, too, is looking at me like he knows he missed something but can't figure out what. I curse myself for being so careless. *This is why it's important to never get involved. Because it's too easy to make stupid mistakes.*

"It's just that I've had so many rotten first few days of school, and you guys are making this one good," I say, grabbing my backpack from beneath the table. "So thanks."

"If today was good, why not have lunch with me again tomorrow? Make it *another* good day," Alex says, smiling at me winningly. . . . *love the way she looks at me, like she sees me . . . maybe likes me . . . but why does she keep running?* . . .

Tell him no. Tell him! "Sure," I say.

Alex turns, almost reluctantly, to Rachel, who balls up her napkin and tosses it onto her plate.

"Okay, I'm in," she says. "Same time, same place."

She gets up jerkily with her tray and walks to the cleanup area.

I follow her, scraping my leftovers into the compost bin. "I know you meant this to just be the two of us . . . ," I say.

Rachel looks at me, her eyes shiny with held-in anger. "It's not like I have any claim over you."

Cheryl Rainfield

All in a rush, I feel how much she wants me to fall for her the way I have for Alex. But I can't—and she knows that.

"We're friends," I say. "I know it's not the same, but it's what I can give."

Rachel flushes and looks away. "I wasn't—I hope—" Her voice wobbles.

"It's okay," I say, and it really is.

CHAPTER **8**

We've only just gotten back to school when the loud-speaker crackles.

"Attention, students—I want you to be careful on your way home today. There have just been reports that the Paras behind the terrorist blog, *Teen Para*—"

Terrorist? Now I'm a terrorist?

"—attacked a group of citizens. If you see anyone acting suspiciously, report them immediately."

The loudspeaker clicks off.

The hallway grows still, fear radiating from the other students. And then the noise starts up again, as people chatter and yell, their mind-voices as agitated as their regular ones. Some girls start screaming and a few boys punch their lockers. I stare at Rachel and Alex, not really seeing them.

"Holy shit," Alex whispers.

"I can't believe . . . ," Rachel says, then trails off.

They're blaming *my* blog for an attack on Normals? How could anyone even think I'd do something like that? No Para would. Attacking Normals will only bring increased Para-hatred, stricter punishments, harsher laws. Retribution and suffering.

My mind is so blank I feel dumb. I don't know why anyone would do this. And I don't know why they're blaming me.

No. I know why. Normals are devious. Especially the ones with the most power. They want to rile up the others any way they can. Keep the hatred bright.

It must mean that I'm making a difference. That some Normals are actually listening to me. Seeing us as people.

I clench my hands into fists. They're not going to shut me up that easily. "Gotta get to class," I say. I jog down the hall away from them without waiting for a response, yank out my cell, and log onto an anonymizer site.

Then I click onto Google. The news is all over. The photos of the beaten Normals, the note that was left, proclaiming "Para Freedom"—

I log onto my blog. Two thousand comments already.

"Teen Para did NOT take part in—or condone—this violence. We are looking for equality, for fair treatment through peaceful discussion—not to oppress others the way we've been oppressed. We are appalled at this violence."

I publish my post, log off, and run to class.

Everyone's talking loudly, right over Mr. Borris, the history teacher, who is as ineffective at his job as his bow tie is at dressing up his suit. Thoughts scream at me from all around, jagged and intense, blaming Paras, hating us. I lean into a conversation, focusing hard on the actual sound of the voices. I pretend to be interested, even though I feel sick.

"*Caitlyn!*" John. Again.

Of course he will have heard. I sigh and open myself up to him.

"*Caitlyn, we've got to get you out of there! They're out for blood.*"

"*No. We just got here.*"

"*Yeah—and that's what you said on your blog. That you'd relocated. You think they're not going to start looking at all the new students in every school? Come on; let the Underground help. I know you've had some close calls lately, but—*"

"*Too many.*" I know he can hear the firmness in my mind-voice.

"Sit down, people! Sit down!" Mr. Borris yells, slamming the classroom door shut, and finally, reluctantly, people return to their seats. I do, too, taking out my history book. Mr. Borris starts talking slowly, with almost no inflection in his voice, like he's trying to put us to sleep.

"*Promise me you won't post anything else on that blog of yours,*" John sends. "*At least not anything identifying. If they find you—*"

"*They won't.*" But I can't predict that; neither can he.

"*Caitlyn—*"

"*I promise.*"

"*The Normals—they don't see us as people; you know they don't. They see us as subhumans—puppets to control, or to kill if they can't. There's no reasoning with them. You've got to take down your blog. I couldn't stand it if anything happened to you.*"

"I think it's because of my blog that this happened. I think I am reaching them."

"Caitlyn, that's crazy. Normals don't listen to us. And why should they? They have all the power. Why would they want to share it with us?" Pain rips through him, rage tearing close behind like a sandstorm.

"Some are more human than others. Some actually listen."

"God, Caitlyn!" His worry unfolds until it surrounds me. *"I didn't want to have to tell you this, but—Caitlyn, there's a Para-killer out there."*

I laugh. *"I know that. All the ParaTroopers. And a bunch of Normals."*

"No. I mean someone who's really got it in for Paras. He tortures them before he kills them. Does something to them—no one knows what—that causes them to shrivel up before they die. And he only goes after Paras."

"What? Why haven't I heard of this?"

"The stories only started a few months ago. Around the time the troopers started targeting you more. I didn't want to scare you."

"You think"—I swallow, mouth dry—*"you think he's after me?"*

"I think he's after all Paras. But it makes sense he'd go after a powerful one."

"But nobody knows that I'm the Teen Para blogger. . . ."

"Some of the Underground Normals do. I know they've all been vetted, but—this guy is killing Paras in hiding. He's finding them faster than the ParaTroopers are.

Maybe that's why it hasn't been on the news—they don't want anyone to know that they're not in complete control."

I lean back against my seat. I knew there was anti-Para sentiment. You can't be a Para and not know that. And I knew some Normals hated us. But this? This is more than hate. This is sick. Sick and scary.

"They're starting to call him the Para-Reaper. So for god's sake, Caitlyn—be careful. These Normals—they're not worth your life."

But I'm not doing it for the Normals. I'm doing it for us *all*.

I disconnect, feeling shivery and cold. And that's when it hits me—John hid this from me.

Paras aren't supposed to be able to hide from each other. When we connect, we connect fully—mind-to-mind and soul-to-soul. We don't keep secrets, because we can't. I rub my chin. But John did. Somehow, he kept something from me that he was worrying about.

If John can hide things from me, what else is he hiding?

I shake my head, trying to halt the thoughts, but they won't stop. Maybe I don't know John so well as I thought I did.

I sit up straighter and focus on Mr. Borris droning on about some ancient war. It's hard to care about it when I'm afraid another war will happen right now, in my own lifetime. I just hope it won't turn into another Cleansing.

When the class ends, I gather up my books and backpack, then shuffle to the door with the rest of the crowd.

Becca's standing in the hall, arms crossed over her chest, looking at me through squinty eyes. Her blond hair looks as fake as her smile. Her posse stands around her, all of them with attitude.

I start down the hall away from them. I can't deal with this right now.

"Hey, new girl!" Becca yells in a voice that reverberates through the hall.

I stop and turn around slowly, my throat tight like it's been drawn together with string. I smile at her like I don't remember how rude she's been.

Becca sneers at me. Others crowd around us, sensing a fight.

"You come to town and all of a sudden Normals are being attacked?" Becca says. "I don't think that's a coincidence."

I force myself to breathe slowly. Becca can't prove I'm a Para. But suspicion and spite are enough to cause trouble. Just one call will bring an investigative team to check me out.

"What Para would be stupid enough to move here?" I ask, trying to sound like I think she's joking. "You guys have the best Para-catching rate in the country! Why do you think I *came* here?"

Okay, that's laying it on a bit thick, but it seems to satisfy some of the others. I can feel them backing off. Everyone but Becca.

…Snot-faced pie-hole! I want Alex; I've wanted him for years. He never looks at me, never even gives me the time of day, and now this—this trash comes and snares his

attention, just like that? She has to have some hold over him. I can cause trouble for her, keep her out of Alex's sight... "Yeah, well, anyone could say that," Becca sneers.

"But only people who haven't looked at their own crap try to take it out on someone else," I say.

Becca's anger flares to hatred and I take a step back, my mind slowing down, fear taking over as Becca's spite nips at me. I don't know how to diffuse this.

"Hey, what's going on?"

I feel his deep calmness, the mind-noise around me lessening, even before I see him. I want to smile at Alex, but I can't. His showing up now is just going to make everything worse.

"New girl," Becca says, jutting her chin at me, "transfers here just when Teen Para transfers to a new school? Take one guess what I think she is."

Alex laughs, his boisterous voice pushing hers back. "Come on, Becca, you say that about all the new transfers. Besides, what Para would want to come here?"

"That's what *I* said!" I say with relief.

Becca whirls on me. "You—you Para-trash! That's just what you'd say."

Shit. I shouldn't have said anything. I take a step back.

"Becca—I know you've got more reason than the rest of us to be sensitive about Paras," Alex says, shaking his head. "But making trouble for Caitlyn because you're jealous just isn't cool."

Becca bites her lip, her cheeks flushing. She stalks away, her posse following her.

The crowd thins out as people rush to class.

"I hope she didn't make you feel unwelcome," Alex says, his protectiveness pouring over me. "I, for one, am glad you're here."

I feel a rush of giddy happiness and slam it back down. "No, I'm good," I say. "Thanks."

"Where's your next class? I'll walk you." He takes my crumpled schedule out of my hands and flattens it out on his thigh. "Social studies with Ms. Edwards? You're lucky—she's one of the nice teachers."

We walk together—down the hall, up a flight of stairs, down another hall to the left. I am ultra-aware of Alex the whole time—his laughter, his sweet scent, and his desire to defend me. I hold my books tighter and keep myself from reaching out to touch him the way I want to.

I can feel his desire for me mixing with my own.

I stop. Am I really attracted to him—or am I just picking up on and feeding off of his attraction for me? Thinking about it makes my head ache.

"We're going to be late," Alex says, nudging me. I take the last few steps to the classroom and create distance between us. The mind-voices of everyone around us start to seep back in and the pain in my head grows sharper.

"See you after school? At the pool?" Alex says.

The pool will give me a break from all these voices, from people's desires and emotions and thoughts. It'll make the pain melt away.

And it'll be so much nicer to swim in a long, clean pool. How can I refuse?

◉

As soon as the last bell rings, I rush to the pool, shucking my clothes and shoes, my smooth turquoise suit feeling like a second skin. People's mind-voices are more muffled, already, the water calling to me. I stand at the edge, looking down at the blue of the water, breathing in the chlorine as deeply as I can. To me, this feels like home.

Two swimmers are doing laps. The swim team is practicing—again. I turn to go.

Alex enters, the calm he brings with him like a nap in the sun. "Caitlyn!" Alex calls. "Hold up."

I turn. His suit is so small and tight, I have to force myself to focus on his face. "I didn't realize you guys would be practicing."

"Coach isn't here yet. We're just warming up. You want to do a few laps with us?" He speaks coaxingly, like he can tell that I want to bolt. His brown eyes beg me to stay.

"Wouldn't your coach mind?"

"Nah. He's always late. Besides, I'm the swim captain."

Of course you are.

I dive in. The water envelops me, people's thoughts releasing their grip. Peace-bliss, that's all it is, I tell myself. Even though there's a pool in the motel, I didn't come here just to swim with Alex.

I slice through the water, fingers tightly together and slightly cupped. Alex dives in after me, the next lane over.

I see his sleek, muscular body pass me like a seal beneath the water. I swim steadily, the water smooth around me, my breath easy and sure.

As I near the edge, he passes me again in a sprint. He's an incredible swimmer; I can see it in the power and control of his strokes, in the way he glides through the water. But he's swimming too fast.

A few more laps like that and he'll have tired himself out. He's too good a swimmer not to know that. So why do it?

Because he likes me. Because he's trying to impress me.

I glide forward, the water making me as buoyant as I feel.

But whether or not Alex likes me doesn't change a thing. It can't.

I push myself a little harder, but still slow and easy, the water cradling me.

Alex passes me again, but I'm closer this time and I can feel him tiring. We do another lap almost in tandem.

Then a whistle screeches, shattering my quiet. I look toward the sound.

A large man in track pants and a gray T-shirt jabs his beefy finger at me, the whistle dangling around his neck. "You! What's your name?"

"Caitlyn, sir," I say, treading water.

"Caitlyn? Caitlyn, why the heck didn't you try out for the team at the beginning of the year, when we could have used you? What are you trying to do, make me cry?"

"I—"

Alex quickly swims up beside me. "She's new, coach. Just transferred in."

I look at him gratefully.

The coach puts his hands on his hips. "Fine. Look, Caitlyn—I can't have you in my pool with the team, not when they're training. But you can come by for the free swim afterward."

I nod, then swim to the side and haul myself out, Alex close behind me.

The coach walks over, his flip-flops slapping against the wet tile. "You better try out for the team next year, young lady. Your school needs you."

"Yes, sir." Water drips off me onto the tiles and I shiver.

"Get yourself to the showers!" he says, and then turns to the others. "The rest of you—let's see some laps!" He walks down the side of the pool, watching the swimmers, yelling instructions.

"He's a great coach," Alex says. "He really cares."

"I can tell."

"You want to stay? We could go somewhere afterward."

"I can't." I grab my clothes and bag and head for the girls' locker room.

His hurt and bewilderment punch into me but I keep going. It *has* to be this way.

The motel owner is at the window again when I get back. She needs to get a life. Before I even put my hand on the door handle, she's swinging the door open.

"Terrorists! I just knew they'd turn on us one day." Fear emanates from her, making it hard for me to breathe.

"I don't think anyone's going to come after you," I say, trying to calm her down.

The motel owner crosses her arms over her chest, scowling. "What—you don't think I'm important enough for some Para-trash to notice me?"

"No, no—I just meant—the media blows things up bigger than they are all the time. Maybe they're not really terrorists."

There's a silence. The woman looks at me sideways out of narrowed eyes. "You takin' their side? You one of them, girl?"

Sweat pricks my back. "Would I take their side if I were one of them? That would be pretty stupid, wouldn't it?"

"It sure would!" The woman laughs a hard, short laugh. Then she narrows her eyes again. "Unless you're one clever Para. I'm gonna be keeping my eye on you." She reaches for the cigarette pack in her pocket, then puts it back. "You want a beer?" she asks and I feel her loneliness like a pit in my abdomen.

"A beer? My mom would freak."

"Or a soda? You can have one for free."

I just can't deal with anything more. Not today. All I want to do is to crash—not watch every word I say. "Can I take you up on that another day? I've got so much home-work I'm not sure I'll even finish before bed."

"Sure," the woman says abruptly. She takes a deep drag on her cigarette. "I'm gonna find out what you're up to."

I hope I didn't make her more of an enemy than she already was.

◉

Mom's pacing back and forth, waiting for me, when I reach our motel room. "Did you see the news? That Teen Para—I can't believe one of us would be that stupid! Attacking Normals, bringing the sky down on us all."

"Exactly!" I say. "Mom—no Para would do that."

"Not willingly, anyway," she mutters.

"You think a Government Para beat up those Normals?" I ask.

"They must go a little crazy, being forced to turn on their own kind. Or it could be a government setup—you know they try to discredit us any way they can." Mom's face is tight, lines stemming from her lips. "I'd feel better if we left right now. But I'm not sure that that's the smart thing to do. Leaving so soon after such news might make someone suspect us. They might even be watching for people on the move after that news report."

"So we're not going to leave?"

"No," Mom says. "Not yet. Not unless things get a lot worse."

Happiness fills me like helium, making me light enough to float.

CHAPTER **9**

In the morning, Alex and Rachel are both waiting at my locker, glaring at each other.

I slow down, not sure what to do.

"Caitlyn!" Alex looks pointedly at Rachel. "I want to talk to you. Alone."

"So do I," Rachel says. "What makes you think that what you have to say to her is more important?"

Alex pats the air. "Be easy." He turns to me. "There's a swim meet at the rec center tonight. You wanna go with me?" His face is hopeful, vulnerable.

I'd love to! "I can't."

His cheeks flush.

"My mom's really strict about stuff like that," I say quickly—which is true. "But we're still on for lunch, right?"

"Right," Alex says, smiling crookedly. "See you then." *. . . better anyway . . . shouldn't have asked . . . what am I doing wrong? . . .* He walks away, his tan backpack slung over his broad shoulder.

I want to tell him I'm not interested. But I don't know if I could say the words and mean them, even though I know I'm putting myself in danger just letting myself think like that.

"Why'd you turn him down?" Rachel asks.

"My mom is strict—no joke."

"But she wouldn't have to know. You could always tell her you were at a friend's house. At my house."

A friend. I haven't had a friend—a real friend—since before the riots. Before Dad died. Before Daniel disappeared. I smile at her. "Rachel—you have a devious mind," I say, trying to keep it light.

Rachel strikes a pose. "I do, and I'm proud of it."

I open my locker, shove my math and history books in, and take out *Othello*.

Rachel leans against the lockers. "Listen—I wanted to make sure you're doing okay. I know Becca's had it in for you since you got here."

I shrug. "She's no worse than any of the other bullies I've had to face. Being the new kid tends to draw them out."

"That blows." Rachel rubs the back of her neck. "I was hoping you weren't going to give Becca too strong a payback."

I look at her, surprised.

Rachel grimaces. "I know, you'd think I'd be the last person to stick up for her, after the way she treats me. But Becca—well, she's been through a lot."

"And that makes it okay to treat people like shit?" I say.

Rachel chews on her lip. "Everybody else here knows, so you might as well, too. Becca's mother is one of the three who set off the riots. She's the one who teleported all the kids out of that bus before it crashed."

"Oh," I say slowly. "And—people gave Becca a hard time because of it?"

"Oh, yeah. She and her dad are on the government watch list. I think that's why Becca accuses so many people—she's trying to take the heat off herself and put it on someone else. You know, suck up to the ParaWatch. She was a bit of a pariah around here for a few years."

I feel sorry for Becca. She must have felt so alone. Hated, even. But that doesn't excuse *her* from becoming a Para-hater. I shut my locker and click the lock closed. "Thanks for telling me. That helps me understand."

I rub my eyes beneath my glasses. Becca's not just a regular Para-hater. Her hate is so loaded. I almost wish I hadn't stopped her from bullying Rachel the other day—but no, I can't wish that. Rachel is worth a hundred Beccas.

"English class?" I say.

"English it is."

Mr. Arnold frowns at us when we come in. "Hurry it up, girls. Less talk, more walk."

He's the one who should talk less. I don't think he realizes how boring he is. Why'd he ever become a teacher, anyway? It's not like he cares about teaching . . .

. . . though once he did. But that was before his daughter died of cancer—a long, slow death over six agonizing years, when he read to her every night and kept praying for a miracle.

I pull out of his head, fast. I didn't mean to do that. I wish I hadn't. Now I feel sympathy for him—and I don't want to.

I think longingly about the school pool. It's so close, it's hard to just sit here when I know water would give me an instant buffer from people's thoughts. I wish I could go dive into it right now. And Alex . . . No. I can swim at the motel.

Mr. Arnold drones on, his voice a monotone, but I keep getting glimpses of his daughter's pale, wan face, the bruises beneath her eyes, the way she cried when he'd leave her, but god he had to, though it tore him up inside, he had to work to pay the medical bills—

I stare at my book, forcing the words to come back into focus.

What's happening to me? People's secrets don't usually bombard me like this, not unless they're really upset. It feels like someone's stripped away my defenses. I reach out but no one's focused on me except for Alex, who's admiring the curve of my neck, the way my hair falls. He's thinking about the way I swam last night, and about how I stood up to Becca, gutsy and strong—

I shiver, goose pimples rising on my skin.

I slam the feeling away. Could the government have found a way to make Paras intensely attracted to Normals?

Maybe to get us to reveal ourselves? But no—if they had, I'd know. And this thing with Alex doesn't feel orchestrated. It just feels . . . natural. But it can't be.

Still, I can't stop thinking about him—about how I want to kiss him and wrap my arms around him. How I want to feel his arms around me. How I want to unlock his sadness, help it flow away. I bite my lip. I want to tell him about me and have him see me for who I am. I don't want to hide the truth from him anymore. And I don't want him to keep things from me.

Sentences blur in front of my eyes. I definitely can't meet Alex for lunch, not even with Rachel there.

When the lunch bell rings, I head straight to the library, not looking at anyone, not making eye contact. I'm being a coward and I know I'm hurting them both. But this is the way it has to be. Paras can't be friends with Normals. And a Para can't love a Normal. I'll tell them I felt sick, got my period. Tell them I forgot. And then I have to create distance between us.

Or maybe if I don't say anything at all, that'll be enough. Maybe they'll be so hurt, they'll never talk to me again. That's what I should be hoping for. Instead, sadness sits like a tight, hard fist inside my chest. I breathe out, trying to soften it.

The calm of the library enfolds me like soothing water. There's hardly anyone here, and the mind-voices are more subdued with people lost in books. Green plants grow on every bookshelf, and thin carpet covers the floors, muffling sound.

A large woman with graying hair and a peace-symbol

necklace looks up from the front desk as I enter, her face welcoming. "I haven't seen you here before. I'm Mrs. Vespa."

"Caitlyn."

"Looking for anything in particular, Caitlyn?"

I think about the last book that gripped me so much I didn't want to put it down, the book that I had to leave behind when we ran.

"*The Hunger Games,* by Suzanne—"

"Collins." The librarian smiles warmly, the skin around her eyes crinkling. "I knew you were a reader. I could just tell."

She takes off her glasses, letting them hang from the chain around her neck. As she moves, they bump against her large chest. "I like her work. Strong characters. Fast pace. Lots of richness."

"Yeah. I can't wait to get my hands on it," I tell her.

Mrs. Vespa stands, her chair groaning. "I'll show you where it is."

The windows that line the hall-side of the library don't make for good cover. I try not to look over my shoulder. I'll know if Alex or Rachel spot me—I'll feel it. But I'd rather not deal with the anger and pain. I need to get to the shelves where no one can see me.

I follow the librarian, feeling safer once we're behind a row of shelves. The air smells different here—like yellowing paper and ink, musty and full of promise. I breathe it in.

The librarian pulls the thick book down and hands it to me. "Have you read her work before?"

"I was halfway through this one before . . . we had to move."

The library door swings open and I jerk around, leaning past the edge of the bookshelf to look. Just a pimply boy with bad hair, no one I know.

When I turn back the librarian is watching me, her smile slipping into concern. "You need anything else, dear, please let me know."

Great. Now she thinks I'm being bullied. So much for not drawing attention to myself.

I sit in a corner with my book and find the place where I left off. As good as the book is, I keep reading the same paragraph over and over, not taking in the words. Alex and Rachel keep pushing into my mind. They'll probably end up hating me. I shouldn't care—they're just Normals—but it hurts already. Still, a little hurt is nothing compared to becoming a Para-slave.

I sigh and turn the page.

Mrs. Vespa appears in front of me, holding out a plate with half a sandwich—looks like cheese, tomato, and lettuce, and half an apple beside it. "Noticed you didn't have any lunch. Want to share?"

"I—" Tears prick the inside of my nose. I'm not used to Normals being nice to me. Not used to anyone outside the Underground being so kind. We move too often to develop real relationships. First I start to bond with Alex and Rachel when I shouldn't, and now I'm falling apart when a librarian is nice to me? I'm going soft.

"Go on. It's just a bit of food," Mrs. Vespa says gruffly.

"Thank you." I reach up and take the plate from her, careful not to let our fingers touch.

I eat slowly, letting the book pull me back in.

My scalp prickles like someone's watching me with their talent. I look around casually. No one seems to be looking at me, but the feeling gets stronger.

"Look behind you, Caitlyn," John sends.

I almost whirl around, but I'm too careful to do that. *"John? What are you doing here?"* I feel him all around me now. I drop my pen on the floor.

"You wouldn't tell me where you were, so I found you."

I lean down to pick up my pen, looking over my shoulder as I do. The boy's sandy-blond hair is swept back from his forehead, his face gaunt and vulnerable, his blue-gray eyes laughing with some secret joke.

My breath lodges in my chest like a brick. He's older, thinner, more hardened, with deep pain and sadness crouching behind the laughter in his eyes—but it's Daniel. I'm sure of it, even as fear blooms through me like blood in water. So many near misses—so many trails that ran cold—and now Daniel is here? I almost can't believe it, and I don't know if I can trust it.

"Daniel?" I cry, half standing. After all these years of searching, of looking for him—but how can it be? And what's Daniel doing here, instead of John?

But his mind-voice—Daniel *is* John?

I feel dizzy and sick with hope.

The boy stands, too, and takes two big steps toward me. *"It's me."*

I reach out and hug him.

He flinches, his arms stiff around me.

CHAPTER 10

"Daniel—is it really you?" I can't believe it. But I know it is. It's him! I've got to tell Mom—

I pull away from Daniel and look up into his face. He's taller than me now, and so thin, like he hasn't been fed well.

I want to hug him and shake him at the same time. *"Why did you let us worry—let us think you were dead? And why did you call yourself John? How did you hide from me?"* How did I not know it was him? I feel so betrayed. And relieved. I float outside of my body, watching us both. Daniel. Here. Really here with me.

"Use your voice," Daniel sends. *"We're in public."*

"Why didn't you tell me who you were? How did you keep it from me?" The words tumble out of my mouth, jostling into each other. "When did you find me? And how? We've been looking for you ever since you disappeared."

Tears are streaming down my cheeks, hot and fast. I don't bother to hide them.

Daniel looks around the library. It's almost deserted—just fifteen minutes until class. Mrs. Vespa's watching us curiously.

Daniel pulls me over behind a bookshelf. "You can never be too careful," he says quietly. "You know that. People betraying each other. The Normals after us. And my talent—it was dampened for a while."

That's no answer. Not enough of one. "Don't you know how hard we've looked for you?" I hiss, gripping his arm. "How long we hoped, and then lost hope? How could you not—"

Daniel jerks his arm away. "Because I'm not free." He sticks out his tongue, and I see, with horror, the metal tracker punched right through it.

"You're a Para-slave!" A tool. Of all the things I worried about, all the things I imagined, I never really thought that would happen to Daniel. It was a possibility, of course. But it was too awful to think about. I imagined him with an adoptive family. Imagined him on the streets, imagined him dead. But I never imagined him being a Government Para. I kept my thoughts far away from that, as if somehow that would prevent it from happening.

Now I feel the metallic scent laced through all his thoughts. The scent I dismissed as fear. I swallow hard and reach out to touch him. He jerks away.

"Are you . . . okay?" I ask.

"What do you think?" he spits, venom in his voice.

His grief and rage at being abandoned slap into me.

"Daniel—we didn't leave you. We never stopped looking for you." I grasp his roughened hands tightly, send waves of comfort to him—the years and years of searching, of worrying, of putting the word out to the Underground, of praying and hoping and yearning to find him . . . .

Daniel shakes loose, but I feel his pain and fury dissipate, smoothing over.

I look at him uncertainly. *"Can you—come home?"*

Daniel shakes his head. *"They track wherever I am; you should know that. The government owns me."*

I do know that. I curse myself for letting my need for him take over. Tears fill my chest, my throat, so thick I choke on them. *"Daniel—I am so sorry for that day. So sorry that woman took you. It was all my fault."*

"No. It wasn't." Daniel looks away. *"I chose to go with her. I was . . . flattered."* The pain inside him cracks open, spilling over me so strong I have to struggle not to cry out. And beneath it runs that thread of anger and blame.

Fear blossoms in me. *"Daniel—if you can't come home—"*

"What did I come back for?" Daniel asks bitterly.

"No! I'm glad you found me. Just . . ." I can't send it, can't think it, but it comes unbidden. *"Are you going to turn me in?"*

"What do you think I am?" Daniel's fists clench and he turns away—but I can feel that he's thought about it, and that he's wanted to, sometimes.

Government Paras are given easier lives, more privileges, when they turn other Paras in. But if their trooper discovers that they've been hiding another Para, they'll be tortured. I can hardly bear to think about it—to think about what Daniel must have gone through—

"It's all right. They treat me all right now," Daniel sends.

But I feel the twisted pain in his soul, the way his joints

ache at night, the way he sometimes wakes screaming as dark memories claw at him.

I want to hold him, to hug his pain away, but I know he doesn't want me to touch him.

Is it because he's hiding something?

"They monitor us," Daniel says quietly. "Not just our bodies—our brain waves, our heart rates, our sweat—but also our emotions. Too much fear, or anger, or happiness, and my trooper comes trotting over, all eager to zap me. Even when I'm working undercover, like now. They're willing to mess up an entire operation to get one Para. They've got me on a long leash—but it's a deadly one. I don't want my brain to get fried. I need to be careful."

I feel his emotions smooth over again, like a putty knife smoothing over plaster. *"Is that why—,"* I start to send, then block the rest. But he knows what I was going to say.

"I'm not used to hugs anymore. To touch that doesn't hurt."

He shudders, pain radiating through him, into me.

I send him more comfort, as much as I can.

"Caitlyn—you know things are getting worse. The ParaWatch is getting stronger. Troopers are getting more aggressive. The government's punishing the Normals who help us even harder—and is rewarding Para-haters more. And there's that crazy Para-killer out there."

I nod with the truth of what he's saying.

"I came here to make sure you're safe—but I also came because I need your help. There's a group of us— we're fighting the government from the inside."

I stare at Daniel, fear sucking away my breath. *"They'll kill you if they find out."*

"You think they're not going to kill you—after they torture you—for your blog? Caitlyn, you're taking crazy risks with that blog of yours. And you're all alone. But this group I'm in, we have power together. The power of hundreds of Paras all secretly working together."

"How is that different from the Underground?" I ask.

"The Underground!" Daniel sends scornfully. *"They're just a bunch of frightened Paras and Normals scurrying from one rabbit hole to the next. We're working for real change, Caitlyn. We're working to make a difference."*

There's something he's not saying. Something just below the surface. . . .

Daniel laughs. *"I never could get one past you. The fact is—the government's captured some high-powered Paras lately—Paras so new they're too scared to fight back. We need more talented Paras on our side, and you are one of the strongest. You always have been,"* he sends proudly. *"With you beside me, I think we'll have a real chance."*

"A chance to—?"

"To stop this madness! To regain our equality. Will you help?"

It sounds right, but something makes me hesitate. *"What would I have to—"*

The bell rings shrilly, interrupting us.

Daniel shakes his head. "We'll talk more later." *"Right now, it's better to blend in. I don't want anyone fingering you."*

I grit my teeth, but he's right. "Promise me you won't disappear on me again."

"I promise." Daniel smiles, but there is pain in his smile, and something else twisted up in the pain, something I can't decipher.

"But what about Mom?" I ask. *"What do I tell her?"*

"Don't tell her anything; not yet. I want to be the one to. Now go on. You need to work on blending in."

Don't I know it.

But after seeing Daniel, I can hardly concentrate. In science class we're dissecting frogs, and the formaldehyde smell is overpowering. I keep reaching for Daniel, for reassurance that I didn't imagine him, that he really is here. I feel him, but muffled, like a sponge is absorbing his presence. No—like *he* is—so the trooper monitoring him doesn't come to check up on him.

The sadness splits open inside me, and tears burst out. Thank god for the frogs.

Mr. Kinley comes over, wearily pushes my frog away, pats my shoulder clumsily, and tells me I can go see the nurse or the counselor if I want to. His embarrassment at my outburst almost overwhelms me.

I shake my head and swallow back sobs, trying to get myself under control. Mr. Kinley leaves me to it.

In my next class, history, Alex is there. My heart lifts but his shoulders go stiff with anger at the sight of me, his eyes shuttering over. It takes me a moment to remember why—my skipping out on them.

All through class, I am so aware of Alex, of the pain

coursing through him. But I can't tell him why. Can't even say I'm sorry without it sounding trite.

I turn away from him miserably and hunch my shoulders. I listen to Mr. Borris go on and on about World War II, ignoring the war that happened right here, and that's sparking again between Normals and Paras.

For once I actually want to leave before Mom thinks we should. I want to start all over.

But I could never leave Daniel. Not now that we've found each other.

Alex avoids me and I'm grateful. I get through the rest of my classes by reaching for Daniel and finding him over and over again, until he gently pushes me away. *"I'm here. I'm not going anywhere. Stop worrying; you're worse than Mom ever was."*

"But when will I see you again?"

He doesn't answer. I feel like I'm losing him all over again.

I reach for him as hard as I can, but I can't find him.

I need to scream, but instead I arrange my face in a bland mask. Nothing feels real. Not the other students, the classrooms, or the teachers' voices droning on and on. Only finding Daniel, then losing him again.

I float through the classes until the last bell rings, and then I wander unsteadily to my locker, not caring when people bump into me, their thoughts exploding through me like grenades.

Alex and Rachel are standing at my locker.

Alex grips my arm, fingers pressing too tight. "Where

were you? Why'd you blow us off like that?". . . *thought she liked me . . . stupid to care so much. . .*

I look from him to Rachel, then back again, my cheeks warm as a slap. "I'm sorry. I just—" I look into his dark, narrowed eyes. I can't stand him being so mad at me, being so hurt. But I can't let myself care.

"You just what?" His fingers dig into me. "Didn't want to be around the black boy and the lesbian?"

"What? No!" I recoil from their pain, yank my arm away. I can't believe they could think that. "I got scared," I say, looking away. I stare at the worn linoleum tiles, color faded from years of shoes walking over them.

"Scared of what?" Alex says, his voice distant, like he doesn't care what I say.

"Scared of how much I already like you," I say, and press my fingers against my lips. I can't believe I said that. Am I trying to make sure we'll have to move?

"Why?" Alex asks softly.

I look over at Rachel, at her arms crossed tightly over her chest to hold in the hurt, and I know I'm about to make another mistake. "My mom—she doesn't like to stay in one place too long. We've moved so often that I try not to get attached to people. It hurts too much when we leave. And we *always* leave. But I like you both—a lot. I'm sorry I was such a jerk, ducking out on you."

"Hey, it's okay," Rachel says, uncrossing her arms. "I know how parents can mess you up, especially when they don't have their own shit together."

"Yeah," Alex says, rolling his eyes. "Parents do all

sorts of crap. Mine sure did. But that doesn't mean you have to, too."

His natural happiness pushes back up like a sunrise, warming me. I grin at him. "Just don't do that to me again, girl," he says. . . . *I don't think I can take it . . .*

The loudspeaker crackles. "Attention, students." Mr. Temple's tinny voice echoes through the hall, bouncing off the walls. "You'll be happy to know that we've just made our school a safer, better place. State ParaTroopers arrested a dangerous Para who was hiding in our school!"

My stomach churns.

"Paul Barrett has been found guilty of unregistered telekinesis and is being transported by guard to a holding cell, thanks to a tip given by our very own Becca Johnson during a basketball game. We'll have a half-day tomorrow to celebrate. Let's all be as civic-minded as Becca and keep our school safe for everyone."

Paul. Oh my god, *Paul.* I slap my hand over my mouth to keep the sound in.

The loudspeaker shuts off. There's a poignant silence, and then the hallway erupts into students cheering and whistling and stomping. Even the teachers are clapping.

Acid rushes up my throat. They're *happy.* They're actually happy about another person being unjustly taken prisoner, and stripped of their family and friends, their home and possessions, and all their rights. Their happiness is not a clean happiness, though—it feels like blood-lust, the kind of euphoria that hunters get just after the kill, when the animal lies there bleeding its life away. I swallow and concentrate on not vomiting. That'd be a real giveaway. Sometimes humans are so inhumane.

But not everyone is cheering. Rachel has gone still and quiet beside me, and there are a few others who are looking at the jubilant crowd with dismay. I dart my gaze around, barely touching on the others. Maybe ten out of the forty or fifty aren't hooting like crazed animals. That's a lot more than I expected.

Alex claps my shoulder. "My god, that's going to be a real hit for the basketball team," he yells. "I'll bet his teammates are freaking out right now. They were playing with a Para! A freakin' Para. He could've killed them."

I wrench away, afraid I really will vomit now.

"Becca's a real bitch," Alex yells over the noise of the cheering, shouting students. "But she sure knows how to sniff 'em out."

I shudder. How could I have thought he was special? How could I have even thought about trusting him? He's just like all the rest.

"What's wrong?" Alex asks, leaning closer and shouting so I can hear him.

"You're talking about Paul like he isn't a person," I shout back. "Sure, he's a Para—but he's human, too. And how do you know he's actually dangerous? Using telekinesis in basketball doesn't sound dangerous to me. Unethical, maybe, but not dangerous."

Alex squints at me like my words are too bright. "I can't believe you'd say that! Another Para off the streets makes for a safer world."

"Oh, use your head!" Rachel shouts, her cheeks dark with emotion. "How would you like it if the government started rounding up all the blacks? Or the queers? Or the Jews?"

"It's not the same!" Alex says, stepping back. "We didn't go around hurting anyone."

"You don't know that Paul was, either."

Alex looks back and forth between us, his forehead crinkling. He looks around, and lowers his voice. "What are you, Para-lovers? You can't trust a Para!"

I can't believe I was ever drawn to Alex. Can't believe I let down my guard as much as I did with him. "How do you know? Have *you* ever even talked with a Para?"

"I don't have to."

"You're so stupid!" Rachel yells, spit flying from her mouth. "Haven't you read *Teen Para*?"

My blog—she's read my blog!

"Why are you coming on so strong about this?" Alex says.

"Because I don't like persecuting people!" Rachel snaps.

The others are still cheering, a teacher smiling benignly over them. My chest aches. I can't stand it in here anymore.

"Come on, Rachel," I say. "Let's go."

Alex reaches out toward me. "Caitlyn—"

I ignore him, my heart closed tight as a rusted-shut window.

Rachel tucks her arm into mine and I see her father again, gray-faced, going out to meet the men in black uniforms with red stripes down their sides.

Rachel pushes open the door and I turn back. Alex is standing there, arms dangling.

I walk away.

CHAPTER 11

We head to the grill. Rachel's hands are shaking so badly, she can't pick up her glass without sloshing her carrot juice. She lowers her head, her hair falling like a veil in front of her face.

"Rachel—what you said back there—"

"It was nothing! Just forget it. It was stupid," Rachel says, throwing the words at me.

"No—it was *wonderful*."

Rachel lifts her head and stares at me through her hair. "I shouldn't have said anything," she whispers. She clenches her hands together, her knuckles white, her thumbs deep red.

"Rachel," I say slowly, though I already know the answer. "Rachel, do you know someone who's a Para?"

Rachel looks down at the table like it's the one talking to her, not me.

"Rachel," I say softly. *"Look at me."*

She jerks her head up, hair whipping back.

I casually tent my hands together so that I make the letter P.

Rachel looks at me blankly.

My mouth goes dry as sand. She doesn't know the sign.

I suck my lip inward, ripping at the skin with my teeth. I haven't given anything away yet. Not really. She wasn't looking at me when I sent to her. But if she's not in the Underground . . .

I lean forward. "Rachel—I know you don't know me, not yet, but I believe in what you said back there. If you know someone who's a Para, they're lucky to have you."

Rachel swipes at her eyes. "Some people in our neighborhood still remember. It's not like it's a secret. He's registered." She blows out her breath shakily, then looks at me, her eyes bright and intense. "My dad . . . he's a very low-level clairvoyant. You know, he can tell you who's going to phone a minute before they do, that sort of thing. Nothing big. But when it became law, he registered."

Pain tightens her face. "The government took him away, even though he's so low level he's practically useless to them. Most of the time they just treat him like a lab rat, studying his brain, trying to see how his talent works. We've hardly seen him the last ten years—not even on holidays. When they do let him visit, he's monitored like a criminal. That's how they treat him—my dad, who still believes in the government, even after all they've done to him."

She sniffs. "They take me and my brother in for testing every year—but neither of us have shown any signs of our dad's talent, thank god."

"They shouldn't be able to take him away from you like that," I say. I can feel my secret sitting inside my throat, bursting to get out. *She* trusted me. True, her father's registered; it's public record, anyone can look it up. But she didn't have to tell me. And she doesn't exactly seem pro-government.

No. I can't risk it.

I sit on my hands. I can't put Mom and me in danger like that. "You must miss him so much."

Rachel half sobs. "It's like he abandoned us. Only I know he never meant to. And Ben—" She twists her hands. "Ben's so afraid they'll take him, too, even if he never develops a gift, that he's afraid to even dream, to plan a life for himself, only to have them take it away from him, too. I know they're trying to protect us, but sometimes I think they hurt us more." She claps her hand over her mouth, looking around furtively.

"It's okay," I say, knowing how useless that sounds, how little words can mean without the emotional truth, the sureness of mind-to-mind connection. "I won't tell anyone what you said, I promise. I'll swear it on any oath you want."

Rachel wipes her cheek and gives me a small smile. "I knew you were one of us."

The hair rises on the back of my neck. "One of us?"

"A Para-sympathizer," Rachel whispers, leaning forward. "There's a lot more of us than the government wants to admit."

A Normal who supports us—and isn't even part of the Underground. She's someone who doesn't have that added support.

"You are brave," I say.

"I have to be. He's my dad." Rachel presses her trembling fingers against her lips, smiling as tears drip from her chin. She's made herself vulnerable to me—incredibly so. I want to offer her something back. Something to show she was right to trust me.

"My dad was killed in the riots, trying to make peace," I say, pain splintering through my chest like a cracked bone. The words are out of my mouth before I've thought them through. I tense, waiting for her to see the obvious.

"God, I'm so sorry. He must've really cared about people's rights."

I swallow. "He did."

I see him, shouting at Mom and me to get back inside as the people swarm around him with torches, bats, and guns, forcing the unprepared government agents back. Hear him send to us, one last time, *"I love you. Always remember that."* Watch him lead the mob from our house, getting farther and farther away, until we can't see him anymore. I feel Daniel and I shuddering in each other's arms, shuddering with the violence all around us, terrified, and later feel the shriek of pain as Dad's mind and heart are extinguished, like they never existed. And then Mom leaving, too; though her body is still alive, she's as far from me as any Normal. It's like I've lost them both.

"All this hatred is gonna make us one screwed-up generation," Rachel says.

"Or a stronger one that wants to stop the craziness— but not with violence because we've seen too much of it."

"Yeah," Rachel says and reaches for my hand.

I squeeze her hand before I let go. It feels so good,

talking with her; it's almost like I have the Underground back. But I can't trust her like that. No matter what she believes, she's not the Underground. And even in the Underground, there are traitors.

I keep thinking about Paul as I walk back to the motel. I can't stop wondering what's happening to him, thinking how it could have been me.

Why do Normals hate us so much? Why are they so afraid of us, when they're the ones using violence? Why are they so threatened by anyone who's different from them?

I think of Paul's angelic face, his kindness, his bravery in standing up for Paras in class, and I want to weep. It shouldn't have been him. It shouldn't have been anyone—but he stood up for us. He tried to make a difference, while all I do is hide behind my blog. I force back the tears. I *will* join Daniel's cause. Even if I get tortured for it. I have to take a real stand, not hide in the shadows.

Paul must feel so alone and scared, riding in a van with guards beside him, his wrists cuffed, his ankles shackled. I pray that he wasn't beaten or raped, that the guards didn't take their pent-up anger out on him—but I know that they often do. I've seen it happen. Felt it. And his family . . . I don't know what my mom would do if the troopers captured me. Or what I'd do if they took her.

I draw breath deep into my lungs. I've got to do something, not just think about him and feel sorry for him. I focus on Paul, reach for that mixture of sauciness and sincerity, for that vibrating energy that his telekinesis gives off.

He's there, but growing fainter, even as I listen—yet still in my reach.

I chew on my lip. I'm taking a crazy risk. If he slips and says my name, even by accident, it could lead the Para-Troopers right to me. But it could have been me. And I'd want someone to do the same for my mom.

"Paul," I send. *"Keep safe."*

"What? Er . . . keep strong. . . . Who are you?"

"It's Caitlyn. From English class."

"Caitlyn." His terror, his grief, are barely controlled. *"I thought you might be one of us. But I wasn't sure."*

"I know. I'm sorry." I send him calm. *"Paul, listen. Do you want me to pass on a message to your family?"*

"I—" Cold fear slices through him. *"You'll warn them I've been taken?"*

"I will."

"All right. They live in a bakery on Lennox Ave. It's about four blocks from school—"

"I think I know where that is. Just hang on."

I've already memorized the streets around the school—a typical safety measure. I turn back, away from the exotic dancers' club, the billiards and pawn shop, and head north, watching the street signs as I go.

The houses and stores get a little tidier, not so seamy looking. I pass a used bookstore, a craft store, and then a bakery.

The bakery windows are dark, the door half open. I hope I'm not too late.

I swallow, my throat as dry as parchment, and edge into the doorway.

A woman in a flour-blotched apron sits weeping at a table, an older woman beside her talking intently. A white-haired man fastens a box with trembling hands. The younger woman shakes her head, weeping harder, and the older woman leans forward, her voice louder. I recognize her voice. I'd recognize it anywhere. It's Netta, my Normal contact from the Underground.

I hesitate in the doorway. What if she's the one who set me up?

"I tell you, we have to get you out of here now. You may not think you care, but a year or three in prison will change that," Netta says.

"What does my life matter without my son?"

"Margaret, you have to go. You know you do. We talked about this day."

I grip the door frame, the metal cold beneath my fingers. Netta's voice is caring, intense—just like her mind-voice. They don't differ.

"Caitlyn?" Paul says. *"Are my mom and grandpa still there? Are they okay?"*

"Yes."

The old man looks up, narrowing his eyes. "We're closed. Family emergency."

Netta's gaze locks on mine. "Shoo, now, child; there's been a—a death in the family."

At that, the woman beside her cries harder.

Netta doesn't recognize me. But of course she doesn't. She's a Normal, and we've never "met."

I grip the door frame so hard my fingers ache. Netta's worry for Paul and his family are genuine. She doesn't feel like someone who would turn in a Para. But whoever it is, I haven't sussed them out yet. And I should have, by now.

"I'm Caitlyn," I send. *"You were my contact."*

"Caitlyn!" Netta's mouth drops open, and she stands. *"I'm right glad to see you, lass! But you shouldn't be here. There's too much danger."*

"Paul wants to give a message to his family."

Netta's eyes fill with tears. *"You shouldn't take that risk. Though god knows we could use it."* She sits back down. "Margaret, I tell thee, it's time to leave. You must go now. You can't help your boy from prison."

"I can't help him free, either!" the woman cries.

I clear my throat. "I know Paul."

The old man stands up, his gnarled hands clenching and unclenching. "Get out of here! Get out!" he yells, his neck and face reddening like he's been burned.

"Keep safe," I say, and make a small P with my thumb and index finger.

The old man sags back into his chair. "Sorry," he mutters.

I shake my head. "No, I'm sorry. I should have started with that."

"What's happening?" Paul interrupts. *"Caitlyn?"*

"Your mom and grandpa are still here. But they won't leave."

109

"Tell them I love them. Tell them I'm sorry. Tell them—"

Paul's thoughts grow fainter. He must be getting farther away. Farther than I'm used to reaching. I clench my fists, panting with the effort. *"Tell them yourself."*

"Mrs. Barrett—Paul wants to tell you something."

"Paul!" Mrs. Barrett staggers up, looking around wildly. "Is he here?"

"No, I—I'm a telepath."

Paul's mom covers her face with her hands. Paul's grandfather looks at me with strained hope.

"Paul—your mother won't leave, and if she doesn't, the troopers will take her to jail, her and your grandpa both. You know they will."

"Okay," Paul sends. *"Tell them—"*

"Wait. I'm going to try something." I focus on the thread that connects me to Paul, then connect up to Mrs. Barrett, then her father. My legs feel rubbery.

"Go ahead, Paul," I send.

"Mom? Grandpa?" Paul sends.

"Paul?" Mrs. Barrett gasps.

"It's me, Mom. You have to get out of there. Get you and grandpa safe. I couldn't stand it if they took you, too."

"Oh, my love, my son."

"Promise me, Mom." Paul's mind-voice is firm, even though it's faint. *"I can get through this easier if I know you're safe."*

"I promise," Paul's mom says. *"But Paul . . ."*

My legs feel like they're going to give out. I'm not sure how much longer I can keep this up. Paul must be miles and miles away. And connecting two Normals with a Para at once—it's more than I've ever done. A fluttering sound fills my ears.

"Paul, son"—his grandfather's voice is choked— *"We love you so much. We'll do everything we can to find you. I don't know how, but—just hang on. I couldn't be more proud of you."*

"I can't hold the connection open much longer," I send. *"Paul—you know the Underground?"*

"Yeah."

"Use the password. Maybe you can reach word to them—"

"I will. And I swear on my life, I won't let anyone know about you. Mom, Grandpa—I love you—"

Blackness fills my mind. Blood gushes from my nose, some of it down my throat, and I swallow it, choking on the saltiness.

Netta is there, her lilting voice soothing me, her warm hand on my back. She tilts my head forward, pinching my nose. "It's all right, lass. Breathe through your mouth, now. Margaret, do you have ice and a cold washcloth for her?"

I feel cold against the back of my neck. I'm gagging on my own blood, struggling for air. I spit blood out, then draw in a breath. The flow of blood slows, then stops.

The room comes back into focus. Netta is there beside me, her one brown eye and one blue eye worried and kind.

"Is she all right?" Paul's mom asks in a hushed voice.

"I'm fine," I say, and stand to prove it.

The bakery tilts around me, lights piercingly bright.

Netta steadies me quickly. "Sit down, lass, take it easy."

"Really, I'm okay." But it scares me. I've always known I get drained if I use my gift too much. Known my eyes become extra sensitive to the light. But nosebleeds? That's new.

Paul's grandfather grabs a bottle of orange juice from the glass-doored fridge and hands it to me. "Drink that. It will help."

"I'm fine, really."

"Drink it," he says firmly. "A little sugar always helps Paul when he's overextended himself."

I take a gulp of the sweet juice, then another. I feel less shaky now. The lights are still too bright, my eyes burning fiercely, but I talk past the pain, grateful for my dark glasses. "Listen, you heard what Paul said. You need to leave. Get yourselves safe. Who knows, maybe you'll find another telepath who can connect you."

Paul's mom rushes over and hugs me tight. "Thank you," she whispers hoarsely. "God bless you."

She turns to Netta. "I have a duffel bag packed just for this. I'll go get it."

Netta squeezes my shoulder. "Thank you, lass—you did a good thing here."

"Where are you settled? Do you still need help? John said—"

"Don't tell anyone you saw me today," I send, impulsively. *"Don't even tell John. Okay? It's important."*

Netta looks at me uncertainly, but I know she senses my urgency. *"All right, lass, you have my word."*

I don't know why I said that. I just know there's been too many near misses lately, and I need to keep my whereabouts as secret as possible. And I don't want Daniel to get mad at me for putting myself at risk.

Paul's grandfather stands before me, looking at me gravely. He clasps my hand in his warm, dry ones. "Thank you for what you did for Paul and his mother. I pray you stay safe." He turns to Netta. "I'm ready."

They carry his box out to the car together, then Mrs. Barrett's duffel bag.

I watch them drive away, my body heavy with sadness.

CHAPTER **12**

The motel owner is at the window again, watching everyone pass by. Her gaze narrows when she sees me. Maybe we shouldn't have come here. I take a deep breath and open the door.

"What's wrong with your nose?" the woman asks sharply.

I wipe at my nose. The blood is dry and crusted. "Nosebleed."

"Someone hit you or something?"

"No." I shake my head. "I just get nosebleeds sometimes. It's no big deal."

. . . she's hiding something, I just know she is . . .

"My brother used to get them all the time, too," I say. And I realize, with a jolt, that he did.

"Your brother?" The woman leans forward, her nostrils flaring like she's caught the scent of a secret. "Why isn't he with you?" *. . . bet anything they're visiting him in Para-jail. And Paras run in the family . . .*

I lick my dry lips. "I don't know where he is. He ran

away years ago." Half truths are always more believable than lies—and they're easier to remember.

"Huh," the woman says.

I heft my backpack. "I've got a lot of homework to catch up on." I turn toward the elevator, and she lets me go.

Mom knows there's something wrong as soon as she gets in the door. Her mind may be closed off from mine, but her intuition is still strong.

"Caitlyn—what happened?" she asks, dropping her grocery bags and coming to sit with me in the dim light of the motel room.

I struggle to keep my face still, to not show her how much I hurt—over Paul and his mom and his grandfather. Over Alex. Over Rachel's dad, and all those kids cheering in the hallways. I don't want her to talk about leaving again.

Mom smooths my hair back from my head, then tucks her hand into mine. I am startled, as always, by the lack of anything there—no thoughts, no emotions, not even what I'd sense from a Normal, just the warmth and soft strength of her hand. Usually it makes me feel more alone, but tonight I find it soothing.

She'll find out about the arrest soon enough. It will be on TV, and all the newsfeeds, websites, and radio shows. I lick my dry lips. "A Paranormal was arrested at my school today. Another student."

Mom's hand tightens on mine. "Did you see it happen?"

"No—but the principal announced it to the whole school. He's giving us a half day off Monday—to celebrate."

"That sicko!" Mom mutters. She shakes her head, her lips tightening in on themselves the way they do when she needs to cry. "Oh, that poor boy. His poor family. I wish there was some way we could help."

"If it'd been me . . . ," I say, my voice breaking on the words.

"Caitlyn, honey," Mom murmurs, pulling me to her. "It would devastate me. But it wasn't you. You're safe."

I nod, my throat too tight to speak.

Mom squeezes me, then lets me go. "How did the others react?"

"Most of the kids started cheering."

Mom frowns. "Of course. That's typical."

"But there's more, Mom. I wasn't expecting it, but there were a bunch of kids who didn't cheer. And one actually yelled at the others for not seeing that we have rights. There're more Para-haters here, but there're also more Para-supporters who speak out, more than anywhere else we've been."

"But you're still worried about something."

At times like this, I wonder if her talent has come back. I reach for her mind, half hoping—but I meet a steel wall.

I can't tell her about helping Paul. If he slips my name . . .

Mom waits. I flash back to Alex's satisfaction, only a few hours ago, that they'd caught a Para. To his insistence that we're all murderers.

"There's this boy I liked. . . ."

"Oh, Caitlyn," Mom says, a catch in her voice.

"I liked him. I liked him a lot. He was sweet. And then . . ." Tears fill my throat.

Mom smooths my hair. "And then he cheered with all the others?"

I nod.

Mom rests her hand on my head. "I know it hurts. But it's better to face it now, instead of after you've fallen for him so hard your heart breaks. You know you could never be with a Normal anyway."

It didn't used to be like this. Back before the riots, Mom used to tell me I could be with anyone—whether they were like us or not. I shrug away from her. "You used to say that all that mattered is that we love and accept each other."

Mom sighs heavily. "I used to believe that. Used to believe that our differences didn't matter. But that was before the riots. Before your dad was killed," Mom says, her voice deepening. "You know he started the peace talks. I'm sure that's why he was murdered." Mom rubs her cheek. "He was a hero, Cait. And he loved you very much."

I clench my hands together like a prayer. "I know."

Mom gently unpries my fingers. "All I'm saying is— your heart is important, but so is your head. If you see there's danger, don't walk into it."

What would she do if she knew about my blog? If she knew that Daniel was back—but enslaved to the government?

I've got to tell her. But I can't.

◉

Alex phones my cell five times on Saturday, and ten on Sunday, but I ignore his calls. I can't stop hearing him say that Paul might have killed someone. Fun loving, brave, kind Paul. And I can't stop thinking that it could have been me.

Monday afternoon, Alex is waiting for me on the side-walk outside school. I straighten my shoulders, lift my head higher, and march past him.

"Caitlyn, wait!"

"What is it?" I ask without turning around. I can't stand to look at him.

"Why didn't you answer my calls?"

I shrug, turning to face him.

"I don't know if it's the Para thing that got to you . . . ," he says.

I stare at him stonily.

"Or if I did something, but whatever it is, talk to me! We can work it out."

No, we can't. Not ever.

Alex takes a step toward me. "It's the Para thing, isn't it? Listen, I've been thinking about it—you were right. If they were doing this to blacks or to Jews, it'd be a crime. It's just—we weren't a threat to the human race."

"Who says Paras are?"

He's trying, I know he is, but it's not enough. I turn away.

"Caitlyn!" Alex grabs my arm. "Look—I never thought about it much before. Of course Paras shouldn't be dragged off like criminals, or like slaves, the way my people once were. No one should. My dad—he used to say Paras caused all his problems—made him lose his job, drink, and hit my mom—but I can see now that's just an excuse. I was wrong to believe it." . . . *I'm not like Dad. Am I? . . . blaming everyone else, hating them . . . god, is that what she sees in me? . . .*

"You're not your dad, Alex. It sounds like hate drove him—hate and lies and excuses. But thinking all Paras are dangerous or evil when you've never even met one, never even talked to one—that's bigotry."

Alex flushes. He looks down at his shoes, swallowing, then back up at me, his eyes bright. . . . *try so hard to be a good person . . . is she right? . . .*

"I think . . . you might be right," Alex says slowly. Shame fills him, spreading out hotly toward me.

"It's not your fault," I say softly. "The schools, the ads, the government—they all say the same thing, that Paras are dangerous. That Paras are a threat. It's hard to think past the garbage that's spewed at us all the time, especially when no one around us challenges it."

"God," Alex says and rubs his face with both hands. "This is huge, you know? This is really messing with my mind, that I might have been bigoted, exactly the way people are with me. . . ."

His pain rips into my chest. I pull him to me and hug him hard. "It's okay," I say. "It's okay. Just try and change how you think about it."

Alex shakes his head, tears streaming down his cheeks. I see the gun—Alex cowering with his momma, so scared he's peed his pants, his toy truck forgotten on the floor, and his momma's arms wrapped around him tight. "It's okay, baby," she tells him.

His daddy stands there, swaying, the gun pointed at his mom.

"I'm gonna kill you, you bitch! You and that brat of yours. Looking at me like that, judging me, all because some Para shit cost me my job. . . ."

Alex can smell the booze on his daddy's breath, can feel his momma's hitched breathing.

"Don't do this, Tom," she cries, but his daddy pulls the trigger and his momma jerks back away from him, blood spattering Alex. Then his daddy turns the gun toward Alex, his hand wobbling. Alex looks up at him mutely, waiting, frozen in fear. And then his dad turns the gun on himself. The gun goes off again and his dad falls hard to the floor, part of his head gone, pulpy blood spattering everywhere. But Alex doesn't look at him, won't look at him; instead, he scrabbles toward his groaning momma, the blood spreading across her shirt.

"Call 911, baby."

And he does.

Now, in my arms, Alex shudders. "Everything I've done—I've tried to be the opposite of my dad." . . . *never getting serious about anyone, not getting involved, not until you, never drinking, holding myself in tight . . . but god, I'm just like him, hating others . . .*

"You *are* the opposite," I say. I send him love, all the love I feel for him, and for the little scared boy that he was. I wipe the tears from his cheeks. "You're gentle and sweet, and you stand up for other people. I don't see you hating anyone. Maybe you were just . . . not thinking about what you were parroting, or that it could hurt someone. But I didn't feel you hating—not like most Para-haters. You're not your dad, Alex. You're *you*."

Alex laughs self-consciously, then pulls away. "Thank you." He touches my cheek softly, a sweet caress.

"Caitlyn!" Rachel calls, running toward us. "Have you seen it yet?"

"Seen what?" I ask, turning to her.

Rachel comes panting up. She raises her eyebrow, looking back and forth between Alex and me. . . . *should I wait?* . . .

"It's okay, Rachel—whatever it is, you can tell us both."

Rachel looks at me doubtfully, but she presses a button on her cell phone and hands it over. I watch the video clip, my body growing cold. Alex leans over my shoulder to watch.

"Yes, Stacey, that's right. A group of Paras held up the First National Bank today, getting away with more than twenty million in cash," the announcer says, her voice so bright it's as if she isn't connecting to what she's saying. She stands in front of the bank, yellow police tape flapping in the wind. "One robber threatened to squeeze everyone's heart shut with telekinesis if anyone made a move. The robbers left behind this note—'In support of Teen Para. Change is coming!' Apparently it's an exposé blog written by an anonymous teen Para, chronicling her life on the run—"

I can't breathe. Someone's trying to bring my blog down and destroy everything I've worked for—all the goodwill and understanding I've tried to create between Normals and Paras. It feels pointed, like someone's got it in for *me*, not just for any Para. But why would someone target me?

"It's crazy," Rachel says. "Why would a Para do this?"

"A Para wouldn't," I say slowly.

"Because that would make everyone think they're as bad as everyone says they are?" Alex asks tentatively.

"Oooh—loverboy's been boning up on Para-rights!" Rachel says.

Alex and I both flush.

I grip the phone. The ParaTroopers found us too quickly the last few months. Somehow this robbery feels connected. Uneasiness shifts in my stomach as I think about how I let Netta know I'm here. But her concern for Paul's family, and for me, was real.

I hand Rachel her phone and pull out my own.

I have to get on my blog, deny any involvement— again—in a crime. But how long are people going to keep giving me the benefit of the doubt? I have to find out who's doing this and stop them.

I do a YouTube search on the heist. Two thousand hits come back—and it can't have been very long since this happened. "It's gone viral," I say.

"Yeah," Rachel says quietly. I know she's worried about her dad. Her brother. Herself.

I click on one of the links and watch a different reporter tell the same story, blaming my blog with fervor and reminding Normals to turn us in.

"This is a setup," I say grimly. "It has to be. It's capitalizing on people's fears—and it's so close to Para Cleansing Day. That can't be a coincidence."

Rachel looks at me, startled, and I know I sounded too definite.

Alex watches us both silently.

"I mean, you said it yourself," I say. "It doesn't make sense for a Para to have done this, and so publicly. It's only going to make Normals hate them more." And I still have no clue who's behind this. Who's setting me—and every Para—up.

I want to ditch school, go to the bank that was robbed, and try to figure this out. That's what someone would do in a movie. But this isn't a movie and I know it'd be too dangerous.

"This really bothers you, doesn't it?" Alex says quietly. "People spreading hate."

"Yeah, it does," I say.

"You're amazing," Alex says, admiration in his voice.

Rachel harrumphs.

"You both are!" Alex says quickly.

Rachel rolls her eyes and I have to stifle a laugh.

I itch to research this more, but I have to keep to my routine, blend in. I check my watch. "Got to get back inside. Don't want to miss class."

I trudge up the school steps, Alex and Rachel beside me. Rachel glares at Alex like he's got an offensive smell.

"Oh, crap," Alex says, his face tight. "I forgot to study for my test next period—" He touches my hand. "We okay?"

"Yes."

"Good." He grabs my hand and squeezes it. "See you later." He runs off down the hall, his knapsack bouncing against his back.

Rachel and I walk more slowly. "You sure care a lot about this," Rachel says, sneaking sideways glances at me. I realize, suddenly, that she suspects—maybe even knows—that I'm a Para.

I stare at her, dry-mouthed. "Well, if we don't stand up for people who can't speak out, who will?"

"True." Rachel hesitates. "Caitlyn—do you know who Teen Para is?" . . . *is she Teen Para?* . . .

I make my face look as blank as I can. "How would I know?"

"You're right," Rachel says hurriedly, like she's rushing to reassure me. "It was a silly question. But if there's ever anything you want to talk about, I can listen. I'm good at keeping secrets."

God, she figured it out. She's so perceptive. "Rachel—you know how your dad registered . . . ?"

Pain closes her throat and I can feel her struggling to breathe.

"I wish he never had," she says, her voice low and hoarse.

"Even though it's the law?"

"Laws aren't always right. Weren't you just suggesting that?" she says.

I take a shallow breath, my head so light I can hardly focus. "I think you've figured out my secret."

Rachel's mouth opens. "You mean—you're—"

"I'm a telepath," I send. *"I can sense people's thoughts and emotions, and send mine to others. That's why you can hear me."* My heart pounds in my ears. *Shut up!* I tell myself. But I can't. It's such a relief to be able to talk about it. *"That's why I listen to white noise. It helps me block it out. And yes—I'm Teen Para. And I did not rob any bank or kidnap anyone."*

. . . oh my god . . . no wonder she understands . . . and she's telling me . . . wait, can she hear me? . . .

"Yes. But not all the time. I try not to eavesdrop on people."

There's quiet all around us. The halls are empty.

"We're going to be late," I say.

"Who cares?"

"I do," I say. *"I need to not draw attention to myself."*

"Oh—of course." "What class do you have?"

We both peer at my schedule.

"Free period! You're lucky. You know where the library is?"

I nod, trying to look calm, like it's every day I trust a Normal with my secret. I'm letting my guard down too much with Rachel and with Alex. I'm taking too many risks.

"Okay. Well, talk to you later." Rachel turns to leave.

"Wait!" *"I need you to promise you won't tell anyone."*

'I promise!' Rachel thinks fervently.

"It can mean my life if you slip up," I add.

"You can trust me," Rachel says quietly. "I've done this before."

Of course. Her dad. But still . . . it's hard to be calm when it's my life, and my freedom. I watch her walk away. I hope my instincts are right.

I turn—and almost bump into Daniel standing just a few inches from me. I frown. Why didn't I sense him?

Daniel's lips pucker with worry, the way they used to when he was little. *"You're trusting her—a Normal—with your secret? With your life?"*

"She's a Para-sympathizer. Her dad's a Para. She won't turn me in."

"Everyone has their price; you know that. You saw how they rushed to hand that poor guy in—Paul, was it?"

My eyes sting with held-in tears. I reach for Paul but can't feel him. He must be too far away. Either that or they figured out how to cut off his contact with other Paras. I shiver. Let him be safe.

"He'll be okay," Daniel says gruffly. "He'll survive. I did. And the tracker is just a nuisance—unless you mess up bad and your trooper fries you."

That makes me want to cry even harder.

"You know we have to stop them, Caitlyn. We can't let them get away with this. They're destroying so many lives."

"But what can we do? They even twisted my blog around—made it a reason for Normals to hate us." I press my hand against my stomach.

"That's what I wanted to talk to you about," Daniel sends, looking deep into my eyes. *"I want you to join the fight."*

"The Underground? But I'm already—"

"No; we're much more organized than that. We make a real difference, instead of just hiding people or bellyaching about it all." He looks at me. "Will you come?"

"Okay. But where—?"

"You'll see."

High-heeled shoes sound down the empty hall. We shouldn't be out here, not without a hall pass. I push myself back against the cold brick wall.

Daniel looks at me sideways. *"Don't worry; I got it covered."*

I feel his power surge, the air around me crackling. *"You don't see us,"* he commands. *"The hall is empty."*

The teacher strides by without even glancing in our direction.

My eyes widen. "How did you—?"

"Aw, come on—don't tell me you never put a 'suggestion' into a Normal's head?" Daniel laughs, his voice echoing through the hall. "You haven't? You don't still believe that crap Dad spouted about never using our powers on Normals, do you? If I'd done that, I'd have been dead years ago, just like Dad. This is a kill-or-be-killed world, Caitlyn—haven't you figured that out yet?"

My heart clenches so hard, pain pierces my chest. *"But Daniel, you shouldn't—"*

"Don't tell me I shouldn't; you weren't there! Dad could have protected himself if he'd wanted to. But no, he let himself be killed by the Normals he was trying to protect. Well, I did what I had to. I survived. And so would you."

My throat is raw with grief. I don't know this Daniel.

He's different. Harder. But he's right—I don't know what it was like. I'm not a Para-slave.

I owe him this. I owe it to him to at least hear him out. And if it *can* really help make a difference, then maybe . . .

"All right," I say. "Show me."

Daniel smiles, then heads down the hall. I follow him down one flight of stairs, then another. We pass the gym, the pool, the scent of chlorine calling out to me. I take deep breaths, wondering if Alex is there, practicing. I shake my head and follow my brother.

Daniel leads me to a red metal door and we cut through the furnace room, the air hot and loud with banging, and then we head down a tiny flight of stairs into a basement I didn't know existed.

The room is deep and shadowy, unfinished, and with a cold, unpainted concrete floor. But on the ceiling, something casts little shards of light. I look up. The ceiling is coated with sheets of aluminum foil.

Before I can wonder about that, two people step forward out of the gloom: a boy about my age, maybe a year or two older, with dark messy hair; and a short, thin, auburn-haired woman wearing a trooper uniform, her huge doe eyes focused on me. I look wildly at Daniel. Has he betrayed me, turned me in?

"I apologize for the stark meeting place," the woman says, "but it's the best we could come up with."

My heart tightens. I recognize that voice. Those eyes. It's the woman who took Daniel. Who tried to take *me*. I back away. "You're—you're—"

"Sorry, Caitlyn, I should have told you," Daniel says. "This is Ilene, my mentor. And my friend Zack."

"But she—she—," I splutter, pointing at the woman I can hardly look at.

"Took me. I know." Daniel nods. "But she also taught me a lot."

I back up another step. "I don't understand." Is this a trap?

"It's not a trap," the woman says, holding out her hands beseechingly.

I see now that her uniform is not quite the same as a trooper's. There are three thin red lines running down the sides, rather than one, and there are gold stars on her lapels. She's higher up than a trooper! Cold sweat breaks out on my skin.

"Don't you trust me?" Daniel sends, hurt threading through his mind-voice.

I do. I have to. But—

"It's okay." The woman sends calming waves at me.

I block them, hard. "Don't do that to me," I say. "Let me make up my own mind."

Ilene laughs. "You're right, Daniel. She is powerful. Most Paras don't sense my touch—unless I want them to." The woman turns to me. "You can trust us, Caitlyn. We want the same things."

"Yeah? Like what?" I cross my arms over my chest. I can't help being prickly, suspicious of this woman who stole my brother and caused us so much heartache. This woman who's wearing the uniform of our enemies.

"We want equality. Freedom. The same basic rights that everyone should have."

Of course. I nod.

"We want the war with the Normals to end," Daniel says.

I look back and forth between them. I can feel how much they mean what they say. How passionate they are. "I want that, too. But how?"

"With action," Daniel says quietly. "Your blog—it was a great effort, Cait—but it was *talk*. To make effective change, we have to actually change the laws. Change people's minds. And to do that, we have to change the ruling power."

"I still don't understand."

"We're talking about replacing the government with something more . . . equitable."

"Replacing? But—?"

"I knew it would be too much for her," Zack interjects, speaking for the first time. "She's just a cosseted Para. She's never been a Para-slave."

I bristle, wanting to smack him. It's not like things have been easy for me.

"Hey!" Daniel says sharply. "Caitlyn's not like that. She's different."

"We'll see," Zack says, his voice a snarl.

"I just don't understand how you'll do this," I say. "Three Paras—"

"Oh, there are a *lot* more of us than you see here," Ilene says, laughter in her voice. Her huge, doelike eyes draw me in. "We have Paras placed in positions of power all over the country, just waiting for our signal. Paras on the inside—in the government, like your brother and me—and Paras on the outside. I myself oversee all the Para-Troopers in the state—and, of course, all the Paras under their control. Between us, your brother and I, and our contacts, we have a lot of clout."

"Yes, but how—?"

"You know how Normals are big on appearances," Daniel says patiently, "because they don't know how to listen inside?"

I nod.

"Well, we're going to capitalize on that. They'll look at the Paras in positions of power—Paras passing as Normals like Ilene here—and trust them." Daniel giggles suddenly. "Ilene's the one that got me positioned here, undercover—to find you. You'll find I'll be in some of your classes. And for Government Paras who've aligned with the oppressors or been outed, we'll use our . . . influence, the way I did earlier. Normals are very susceptible to the strongest of us. And that's where you come in."

I shift uneasily. "I'm not sure how comfortable I am with that. It doesn't seem quite . . . ethical."

Zack spits on the floor. "I *knew* she wouldn't get it."

"Give her a chance," Ilene says.

"Caitlyn," Daniel says, pain deep in his eyes, "we're not doing anything like what they do to us. We're not hunting them down and taking away their families and homes. We're not torturing them and we're not killing them. We're talking about influencing them to do what's right." Daniel cocks his eyebrow. "Do you think it's okay, the way the government treats us? The way they treated me?"

"Of course not!"

"And don't you think that if we can change things—if we can gain equality and freedom—we should?"

"Of course!" But I feel all muddled up inside. It doesn't help that the woman who stole Daniel keeps smiling at me and that Zack keeps scowling. It makes it hard to think.

"Daniel—do you really believe this is the best way?" I ask.

"Yes," Daniel sends passionately. *"With all my heart."*

I can feel how much he cares about this. How much he believes it's right. "Then I'm in," I say aloud.

Ilene approaches me and clasps my hand in hers. "Welcome!" she says.

CHAPTER 13

"What will you need me to do?" I ask.

"Influence Normals."

"Who?"

"We'll tell you when the time is right. Right now, we need you to practice."

They don't trust me, not completely—which I get. They're in a vulnerable position, making themselves known to me. But I'm vulnerable, too. And I'm irritated. I thought the point of all these tests was to trust me. But if we weren't self-protective, most of us wouldn't survive.

"Okay," I say. "Show me how."

Zack steps forward, holding out his hand. His scowl is replaced by a contrite look. "I misjudged you. I'm sorry. Some Paras bury their heads in the sand—but I can see you're aware of what's what."

"Thank you," I say, shaking his hand, feeling oddly pleased.

"Come on," Daniel says, jerking his thumb at the door. He grins. "Let's go practice on some Normals."

For a moment I feel like we're kids again, standing on the corner near our house, listening in on all the people as they pass and trying not to burst into giggles. And then I remember where we are and the joy fades. I check my watch. "I have social studies in ten minutes."

"That's perfect!" Daniel crows. "Let's see if you can convince the teacher that you're really there."

◉

"Focus!" Daniel sends crossly. *"This should be easy for you. Your talent is so strong."*

"*I* am *focusing!*" I snap back. But I'm an uneasy jumble of thoughts and emotions. I can't help feeling that I'm invading someone else's mind. More than invading—that I'm doing something almost abusive by trying to put a thought into her head, even if she is a Normal. Even if it's something as harmless as convincing Ms. Edwards that I'm in class when I'm not.

"Do you think Normals think about ethics when they strip us of our rights? Or when they torture us? Caitlyn, you have to know how to protect yourself against them. And how to protect the rest of us."

I sigh and turn back to the open doorway. From where we're standing, I can just see Ms. Edwards sitting on the edge of her desk. I like her. She's one of the few teachers here that makes her subject come alive. She actually cares about the things she talks about, and I know she cares about us, too. It makes me all the more uncomfortable doing this to her. But I do it anyway.

"Caitlyn Ellis is present. Caitlyn Ellis is present," I send like a mantra, putting all my focus into it.

Ms. Edwards rubs her forehead, looks up at the class. "Caitlyn—will you come up here and pass these papers out? Caitlyn!"

Ms. Edwards looks around the classroom, her forehead wrinkling. "Where did she go? I swear I'm losing my mind. Bobby, will you come up instead?"

Daniel high-fives me. *"You did it!"* he sends, ecstatic.

But I feel slimy. Ugly inside.

It's both incredible and terrifying that I can control another person that way. It's a talent no human should have. It is too tempting, and in the wrong hands it could be disastrous. And how do I know that I won't *become* the wrong hands if I use it too much?

Maybe the ParaWatch is right. Maybe we all *should* be under guard.

I smile weakly at Daniel, trying to shield my thoughts. I don't want another lecture.

"Now just do that a hundred more times and you might catch up. Remember—you hold the lives of other Paras in your hands. You have to be ready to use whatever abilities you have to protect them—and yourself." He stands. *"I have a lot to do today. But now you know where to find me."*

"Daniel—" I reach for his arm. He flinches and I pull back, cursing myself for forgetting. *"Please think about seeing Mom. Or at least letting me tell her that you're alive."*

Daniel scowls at me, but his scowl doesn't hide the sudden sheen of tears in his eyes. *"I'm too different now,*

Cait. I've been hardened by the torture. I know you've felt it."

I nod, reluctantly.

"*Give me time. Let me get back to knowing how to be a family with you. And then we'll tell her—together.*"

There's a hesitation in his thoughts, like he wants to say something more, but I don't probe it. I let him have his privacy.

I hoist my backpack over my shoulder and start down the hall. I've got to find another Normal to practice on.

"*Caitlyn,*" Daniel sends.

I turn.

"*I really am glad I found you.*" He smiles uncertainly, his vulnerability showing.

"*I'm glad you did, too,*" I send with a rush of affection.

◉

Alex looks awkward when he sees me in English and I know he's embarrassed to have broken down in front of me. But I love him for it; I love his vulnerability and his willingness to open up.

I smile at him, hoping he can see the caring and respect in my eyes. I worry, too, though. What if he makes the same connection Rachel did? He's only just opened up to being pro-Para. Could I really trust him with my life?

I'm sure Daniel would think this the perfect opportunity to practice persuasion—that I should convince Alex to forget me, or maybe to be loyal to me forever. But I look at

Alex's broad back, feel his gentle soul, and I can't do it. Instead, I persuade Mr. Arnold not to look my way as I pull out my cell. I feel ashamed using my talent that way, but he's a weasel and would hurt me if he had the chance.

I plug my earbuds in and watch another video of the robbery, scanning the background—but nothing I see tells me who could have done this, or why.

Rachel looks back and forth between me and Alex, worry emanating from her. Maybe she's right to worry.

All around me, people are whispering about the robbery, speculating on how much money the Paras got away with and what they'll do with it. No one doubts that it was a Para who did it. No one but Rachel, and now Alex, though not so fiercely. I want to shout at them all to think it through—why would a Para bring trooper attention to themselves? I can't stand it that people are so full of hate that they assume it was a Para even when it doesn't make sense.

And then a thought comes to me—a sneaky, appealing, horrifying thought. I could use this new skill Daniel's teaching me to convince the entire class of the truth. To make them see it.

I could make Alex a 100 percent bona-fide Para-supporter, and then we could hide out together, just the two of us, and never be separated.

No. I recoil from the thought, my skin rippling. I can't believe I even thought that. This Para-talent is powerful—maybe too powerful for *anyone* to have. How do the other Paras Daniel's taught keep themselves in check?

I feel cold inside. What the Normals can do to us—it's horrible and wrong. But this—this is almost worse, because it's so insidious.

I shake myself. No. Torture is worse. Kidnapping people, stripping them of their rights, taking their lives—all are far worse than any control I could exert. And I haven't seen anyone misuse this skill yet. But the potential is there. Or maybe it's only there in me. I'll have to keep a close watch on myself.

When class ends, Alex strides toward me. "I didn't hear anyone do anything but blame Paras," he says quietly. "'Dirty, thieving, conniving, dangerous Paras.' I never noticed how common the hatred is." He looks at me hesitantly. "But are you *sure* Paras didn't do it?"

"It just doesn't make sense," I say, a vein thrumming in my throat.

"No, it doesn't, does it?"

"Stop loitering and get to your next class," Mr. Arnold says snottily behind us.

"We're going!" Alex says, rolling his eyes at me. Then he nudges me toward the door and out into the busy hall.

The loudspeaker crackles. "Students—please be advised that because of recent unsettling events, all schools will now be staffed with a resident ParaTrooper who you can turn to if you need assistance, or if you notice any suspicious behavior. Government Paras will rotate through our area schools, and our ParaTrooper will arrive tomorrow morning. I expect you to treat him with the utmost respect and show him what patriotic citizens we are."

I swallow, my throat tight. It feels like the world is

closing down around me—around all of us Paras—and that someone's behind this, orchestrating it all. Daniel was right.

I walk fast away from everyone, my cell open, and log on to my blog. "Peeps," I text. "Teen Para does NOT support the recent robbery that took place. Nor does she believe it really was Paras who committed the robbery. Every Para knows that we have to keep a low profile so the sea of hatred doesn't drown us. No Para would take such a crazy risk. Don't be fooled—it wasn't us."

Just in the time it took me to write that, dozens more raging comments appear on my blog. I don't know what else to do but what I'm already doing.

Even on the way back to the motel, I can see the effects of the news story. There are dozens more ParaWatch posters and flags up—on poles, on mailboxes, in the windows of houses and stores. People dart suspicious glances at one another as they pass by, their steps short and quick, like they want to get out of a storm.

◉

For once, the motel owner isn't at the window when I get back. I think that's a good thing, but when I open the door, I'm hit with a burst of grief so strong it's hard to keep standing. I step inside.

She's not standing behind the counter. Not staring at the little TV in the cubby. Not chain-smoking as she watches me. But the grief comes in waves, pouring through me, making my heart hurt.

I hesitate. I hear sobs through the door behind the counter. I don't know if I can take any more emotion today; I'm already so wrung out. But I don't think I can ignore this, either.

I step behind the counter. The door is open a crack. I stand there, not sure what to do—and then I hear a deep, wrenching sob. I tap lightly on the door. The sobbing continues. I push open the door to see the motel owner—I don't even know her name—curled up in a ball on the ground, her face red from crying, her cheeks wet. The grief is overwhelming.

I walk in, crouch down beside her, sending her comfort. Her boozy breath fills the air. "Can I help?" I ask.

"He left me!" the woman sobs brokenly. "He left me for another woman—and she wasn't even younger! He said I wasn't good enough!"

And in her head, I hear the echo, "You're not good enough! You're a worthless piece of shit!" I see an older man looking at her through alcohol-blurred eyes, his face hard—her father. "I don't care if you die!" he says.

The grief cracks through her.

"He was wrong," I say. "You are good enough. You're better than anyone who could say that to you."

The woman starts brokenly sobbing again.

"It was cruel," I say. "And you don't need to be around anyone cruel. You don't deserve to be treated like that."

The woman swipes at her eyes. "No, I don't." Her grief lessens a little, the old wound closing up. She props herself up on her elbow and stares at me. "What are you doing here? Who asked you to come in?"

"I heard you crying," I say awkwardly.

"I'm fine, I didn't ask you to come in," the woman says, sitting up abruptly. She swipes at her eyes again, as if that could stop the tears streaming down her cheeks. "Now leave me alone! Go!"

I feel her shame at having someone see her so vulnerable. I want to tell her that I don't judge her, that I'd never use it against her, but instead I just leave.

CHAPTER 14

Dinner is quiet. Mom frowns as she drinks her coffee, listening to the news on low. She glances at our empty duffel bags and I know she's thinking of running.

A piece of broccoli lodges in my throat. I swallow convulsively, forcing it down, then try to distract her with tidbits from school.

"Shhh! This is important!" she says, and turns the volume up on her radio.

"What greater measures can we take to catch Paras before they act?" the radio host asks. "More severe penalties, increased rewards, or Government Paras in every community? Or should we grant ParaWatch members temporary arresting power? What do you think, callers?"

The food starts to come back up my throat. I can't sit there and listen, even though I know Mom thinks I should; she says we need to know what the enemy is up to. I dump my food in the trash, wash my plate and fork, and go to bed.

Nothing's different in the morning. If anything, things are worse. ParaWatch members patrol the streets in twos and threes, heady with their new sense of power. Nothing's been decided, but they're already flexing their muscles. Anti-Para posters and pamphlets litter the street, and people aren't so talkative or so friendly as they usually are.

I walk quickly, keeping my gaze averted from other people's, not wanting to draw attention.

TV crews mill around the school yard, where reporters are interviewing students with a predatory intensity.

Heavy dark clouds hang in the sky. I keep walking around the school until I get to the back entrance, but it's locked.

I tug the door harder, rattling it so hard that my teeth jar. And then I notice the sign on the door: FRONT ENTRANCE ONLY, AT THE PARATROOPER STATION.

A ball of fear sits hard and hot in my stomach.

Another student appears around the corner, making for the back door, her head down like there's a weight attached to her eyes. I reach toward her with my mind. Not a Para, just shy, with old emotional wounds scarring her, making her not want to face the crowds. She stops abruptly when she sees me and then the sign.

"Isn't that a fire hazard?" I say, thumbing at the locked door.

The girl looks around, as if I might be talking to someone else, then back at me. "It's probably only locked from the outside," she says, her voice hoarse, like she's not used to using it. "Crowd control, I guess."

"Yeah. That makes sense." I send her waves of confidence and watch as she stands a bit taller.

"Guess we're stuck with the front door," she says and starts toward it.

I follow her, my shoes dragging against the asphalt.

The mind-noise from the reporters and the crowd of students waiting to get in is so strong, it almost makes me sink to my knees. I steel myself and join the crowd.

They seem to be letting in only one student at a time. At this rate, we're all going to be late for our first class of the day.

I feel a surge of hope that maybe the ParaTrooper will slow things down so much, the teachers will protest and the trooper will be removed. But then two more students are let in, then two more in quick succession, and the crowd moves forward again.

Reporters surge around us, talking into cameras, accosting students. I keep my head down, trying to look unapproachable.

The front door opens, swallowing two more students. The rest of us inch forward and I practice looking calm and bored.

Finally the door opens to admit me. It doesn't look like the same school I left yesterday. I'm herded into what looks like an airport metal detector, with a waist-high bar keeping me from moving forward. A muscular ParaTrooper in a crisp black uniform with the familiar red stripe blocks my way. Some miserable, shivering students are already locked in a small, penned-in area of the hallway. Their fear shakes through my bones like bass drums. Two of them are Normals being abused; one is carrying weed, and one hates authority. But three are Paras. Their terror makes me nauseous.

The ParaTrooper steps closer to me, hand on the gun in his holster, his body alert, even after so many students.

"Name!" he barks.

"Caitlyn Ellis."

"Caitlyn, do you like Paras?"

"No, of course not," I say, trying to look offended.

"Why not?"

I know the answer he wants, the answer he's expecting. I can hear it reverberate through my mind, even past the other students' terror. It's the standard government answer.

I swallow. "Paras are dangerous," I say haltingly.

The trooper studies me with narrowed eyes, his nostrils flaring like he's trying to sniff out my talents—like he can. Only another Para could do that. But if he's been around Paras enough . . . if the training was good enough . . . he might be able to tell. Sweat breaks out above my lip.

"Are you a Para?" he asks.

"No, I am not," I say stiffly, my pulse beating in my throat.

The trooper moves in closer to study me, so close I can see the dark hairs sticking out of his nostrils, can smell the stink of his sweat.

. . . Most of these losers are nervous, like they've got something to hide. The guilty ones I can smell a mile away. This one, though—I'm not sure about this one. There's something about her that seems off, like she's laughing at me . . .

I focus on the trooper the way Daniel taught me. *"I should let her go."* I send firmly, but not too hard.

The ParaTrooper rubs his forehead, frowning. He slowly opens the gate. "You can go," he says.

I step through and into the school, my legs shaky. What I did isn't unethical if it keeps me safe, right? I don't know, and right now I don't care; I just want to get as far away from the trooper as I can.

But I can't leave all the other Paras here. The ones he's singled out.

I look back. The trooper has opened the doors again and admitted two more students.

The students waiting to be transported fidget and shiver in the pen. I stare at the trooper, focusing on only him. I send *"None of these students are Paras. I got overzealous. I should let them go. I don't want any trouble from higher up."*

The trooper frowns and pauses in his questions of the student before him.

I pull up all my energy inside me, along with the feeling of how right it is, how much I *need* to free the others. *"I should let the students go. I don't want any trouble,"* I send over and over, imagining the thought drilling into the trooper's skull. I feel him resisting; it goes against all his training.

Then another energy joins mine, pushing with me.

"Aw, what the hell," the trooper mutters, and presses a button. The small corral opens and the students look up, their faces pale, their bodies tense and still. "You can go," the trooper barks. "Go on, get out of here."

The students race out of the corral and disappear into the school, the trooper watching them with a confused look on his face. He turns back to the student he was questioning and waves her through, too.

I feel drained of energy, like I need to sink to the floor and sleep. I stagger a few steps forward, not sure where to go.

Then someone grips my arm. *"Caitlyn. This way."*

It's Daniel. I stumble with him down the hall.

"You did a brave thing back there. Brave—but foolish. What would you have done if I hadn't been here to help? These ParaTroopers—they've had training to resist us."

I shake my head wearily. *"That was you?"* I can feel it now, the familiar echo. *"Thank you."*

"Don't thank me. It was stupid! What if he'd realized what you were doing? He would have taken you, too."

I want to snap at him that he's the one who taught me the technique. And what did he expect me to do—leave the others there?

We enter the basement room. "Caitlyn just saved some of us," Daniel says.

"Well done!" Ilene says, stepping out of the gloom. "It's a good idea, though, to use stealth. We don't want them getting wind of us too early."

Her, too? "So I should have, what? Left them to be taken?"

"It would have been safer," Zack says, coming to stand beside Ilene.

"Maybe for you, but not for those Paras."

Ilene frowns at Zack. "Of course you couldn't leave them there. But now that ParaTrooper will report what happened to his superiors, which means increased danger for all of us here, not just the three the trooper found."

She knew. They *all* knew that the trooper had caught some Paras and they were just going to let them be taken. But I can almost understand the logic, from afar, of saving many instead of only a few. But it seems cold and calculating, and more about saving their own skins.

"Caitlyn—becoming a Government Para is horrible," Daniel says. "But you survive it and you keep going. If a few of us have to endure that to save us all, isn't it worth it?"

I don't know. "How does it save the rest of us?"

"We're looking at the big picture. When we take the government down, Paras aren't going to be people they can dump on anymore. We'll have equality."

His fervor reverberates through my mind, and beneath it, rage. I reach for it but it's gone. I look at Daniel uncertainly.

"Caitlyn—you know things are getting worse. Having those crimes blamed on Teen Para is making everyone jumpier. The Normals who were on the fence are ready to come after us now."

I get a fragmented thought who Daniel knows something about my blog getting the blame for the robbery. Maybe he even knows who's behind the setup. I reach for it but the flash is gone like it never existed. And did it, really? I rub my jaw, unsure.

"Things are only going to get worse. We need to stop this craziness by forcing change. They're not going to start treating us as equals just because we make some noise," Daniel says.

"I'm already on your side," I say.

"One hundred percent?"

"One hundred percent."

Daniel looks at Ilene significantly and she shakes her head.

Something is passing between them, but I can't quite pick up on it. I strain and catch their mind-voices whispering—and then I'm thrown out like a bird hitting glass.

Daniel turns to me. "You've got to keep practicing, then. You've got to get better at this so you're ready when the change comes. We need every Para we can get on our side—especially powerful ones like you."

"I'll be ready." I glance at my watch. "Class has already started. I don't think today's a good day to be late."

"It's the perfect opportunity for you to practice some more," Daniel says. "Come on, I'll walk you back."

"Practice every moment you can," Ilene says. "We're going to need you."

Her words, heavy with responsibility, weigh on me.

Daniel and I walk back in silence.

"Daniel . . ." I hesitate.

Daniel stops and looks at me. "What is it?"

"Earlier—I got this sense that you knew who blamed my blog."

Thoughts rip through Daniel. . . . *need to end the persecution, to show everyone just how far Normals are willing to go to keep their power, need to convince Paras on the fence to join our side. Caitlyn's blog is the perfect catalyst . . .*

I stare at Daniel. "You set me up? You made people think I did those crimes? Why?"

I can't believe it. I feel like I've been punched in the solar plexus, all my air gone in a rush. I almost fall to my knees with the betrayal.

"Caitlyn." Daniel grips my arm, his fingers pinching my skin. *"Don't you see I had to? To get you on our side? To show everyone how bad the government really is? I had to snap people out of their complacency. It's only when things get really bad that people finally act."*

I can almost follow his convoluted thinking, but it doesn't make the betrayal any smaller.

"Caitlyn—millions of us will be imprisoned or killed, and nobody will do anything unless we make them. We have to wake people up. Especially other Paras."

I pull away, my eyes stinging.

"But you made it worse!" And you messed up everything I've worked for.

"No—I made people see how bad it is."

Did he really come here for my help? Or just to destroy my blog?

"Caitlyn, I'm sorry I used your blog. But sometimes you have to make sacrifices for the greater good."

I feel how fiercely he believes that, and how sorry he is that he's hurt me. But that doesn't change what he did. A heaviness settles in my chest. *"I have to get to class."*

"Caitlyn—"

"No. I can't right now."

Daniel nods miserably. *"I'm here if you want to talk."*

Getting into class is easy—too easy. I use my mind to

convince the teacher that I was already there, but had left to use the bathroom. It makes me feel powerful and invincible, like I can do anything, and I don't like that in me.

I can't believe Daniel betrayed me like that. I don't know how I'll be able to trust him so easily again. I know that being a Government Para has changed him. How could it not? But I'm afraid he's lost his moral compass, along with his innocence. Even if he's trying to do what's right.

I flash to that whispered, hidden exchange between him and Ilene. I don't know how they managed to shut me out so completely, so that I almost wasn't aware of their conversation. It was more by intuition than anything else that I caught on.

I shift uneasily. Daniel can do things I didn't even know were possible. And now I have to wonder why. What are he and Ilene up to?

I can understand his hatred of Normals after what they did to him. I know the glimpses I got were just that—glimpses. But to condemn an entire group of people because of something a few did—that's too close to what the Normals do to us.

Someone's trying to get my attention. I open myself up.

"Caitlyn, can you hear me? Are you okay?" Rachel thinks at me.

"Yeah."

"I was worried when you didn't show up in class—with the ParaTrooper here today."

"I got through. Some others before me almost didn't. Do you know if the trooper took anyone?"

"Just one, I think."

One who I didn't protect. Whoever it was must have come after I did. But at least I saved three of us. I can't help wondering, though, who the trooper took. Was it the telepath I felt in the pool? Or another telekinetic like Paul?

I pull my thoughts away, trying not to focus on the pain. It must be on the news, with all those hungry reporters crawling outside the school. Mom will have heard about it by now.

Mom! I text her, let her know I'm okay. I wonder sometimes if I forget to text her because I'm angry that she doesn't connect with me mind-to-mind anymore. It was so hard to train myself to communicate with her the way Normals do. I sigh and turn off my phone. I feel guilty not telling her about Daniel. But something doesn't feel right. And I don't want her getting hurt more than she already is. It *is* Daniel, I'm sure of it. But he's changed so much.

For years I've had to pretend to be as restricted as a Normal. Pretend to *be* a Normal. But with this new technique Daniel taught me, I don't know if that's necessary anymore. If I can convince Normals that I was in class all along, what's to stop me from using a little persuasion anytime I need to?

I wonder if it works on other Paras. Can I use it to force Daniel to tell me what's really going on? He shouldn't be able to keep anything from me now.

The bell rings and I walk out into the hall with the other students to find Rachel waiting for me. "It feels weird having a ParaTrooper in our school. Like we're a military state. I don't think anybody likes it—except the die-hard Para-haters."

We turn the corner and almost bump into Becca. "Speaking of which," I say in an undertone.

Rachel smothers a laugh.

Becca narrows her eyes at me. "So the trooper didn't take you, new girl? I'm surprised."

"You never know, there's always tomorrow," I say and keep walking.

Rachel scurries after me, laughing with wide eyes. "Why did you say that?"

I shrug. But I know why. Sometimes, if you don't laugh, you'll burst into tears. And that attracts attention.

We reach the stairwell and I say, "See you later!"

Rachel scrunches up her nose. "Isn't your class the other way?"

"I've got something to do. I'll explain later." *If I can.*

I head down the stairs into the basement. I can feel Daniel's presence the closer I get.

Daniel meets me in the boiler room. "Caitlyn. You want to ask me something."

"You're keeping secrets from me—you and Ilene."

Daniel looks at me, his face smooth, his emotion hidden. "We were waiting until we thought you were ready to hear everything."

Because he thought I wouldn't like it. My chest is tight. "Tell me now or I walk."

Daniel stands there, his eyes sad. He blows out his breath loudly. "Okay. You have the right to know. Ilene was the one who thought we should wait. . . . You saw what the

153

crowd did to Dad. Normals are never going to *give* us equality; we have to take it."

He gives me a sidelong look and I know something big is coming.

"If any of them tries to stop us—well, this time we're not letting them."

Suddenly, flashes of Normals being killed, screaming under torture, and enslaved to Paras, tear through my mind.

I stare at Daniel, my eyes so wide they hurt. "But Daniel—if we do the same thing to Normals that they've done to us, it makes us no better than they are."

"Do you really think we can keep living like this?"

"But you're talking about murder. Slavery. Torturing them if they don't comply."

"Yes." Daniel looks at me steadily. "They've had their chance to rule fairly and all they did was oppress us. They've brought this on themselves."

I want to shake him; I don't get why he can't see that what he's planning on doing to the Normals is the exact same thing Normals have done to us—and it's why he hates them.

Daniel shakes his head. "We're not oppressing them; we're righting a wrong. Surely you can see that?" A muscle clenches in his jaw. He's as frustrated as I am. But that doesn't make him right.

I reach out to him. There's a hardness in his core, like stone, that didn't used to be there. All the torture, the training—it's changed him. He is my big brother, but I don't know him anymore.

"Dad would never approve," I say desperately.

"They *murdered* Dad. How do you know what he'd think if he came back? I doubt he'd be so quick to forgive. How can you even *be* on their side, after what they did to him? After what they did to *me*?" Daniel turns away, his voice short and clipped, and I know he's trying to hide his pain.

"I'm not on their side!" I cry.

"You're either with them, or you're with us," Daniel says hoarsely, his back stiff. He turns around, his face carved in pain. "You've got a lot of talent, Caitlyn. We can accomplish great things if we work together. We can bring real freedom to Paras throughout the country, even the world. We can end all the misery and unfairness. But you have to want it."

"I do want it. But not this way!"

Daniel looks like he's going to cry. It makes my chest ache, but beneath the tears, I see a coldness that doesn't go away.

"Ilene said you'd be like this, but I didn't believe her. You're too smart. And you *felt* Dad be killed by the Normals. I know you did."

I look at him, startled. He could feel me after we got separated—and he didn't connect?

Daniel pushes out his breath. "You've got a few days to change your mind, Caitlyn. Maybe a week, tops. But when the revolution starts—if you're not clearly on our side, then you're against us. And we'll treat you that way."

"Daniel!"

He shakes his head and walks away.

CHAPTER **15**

Alex is leaning against my locker, looking casual and beautiful. My heart pounds so hard I can't quite catch my breath.

Alex pushes off my locker when I get close. "It's freaky having a ParaTrooper right in our school, isn't it?" he says.

"It sure is," I say.

"I keep thinking about that guy—Paul—who got arrested. If there's any other Paras here, they must be shitting their pants."

I nod, not knowing where he's going with this.

"I wish we could do something to help them, you know?" he says. "I mean—it's like we've got the Gestapo with us. 'Heil Hitler' and all that."

"I know," I say quietly. "Just . . . don't say that too loudly. They're probably going to come down even harder on Para-supporters."

"I'm not sure if I *want* to keep quiet," Alex says stubbornly. "Doesn't that just condone it?"

I smile at him. New Para-supporters have zeal. "But if we all get put away, who will support the Paras?"

Alex rubs his chin. "Good point. You're smart, girl."

I grin. "I know."

"We on for lunch?"

I nod. "You, me, and Rachel."

Alex looks disappointed when I mention her, but he recovers quickly and says, "Good."

Rachel, Alex, and I all fit into a booth again, like we belong there. It's a good feeling, but the ParaTrooper in the school has my stomach tied tight and I don't feel like eating.

Rachel looks at my almost untouched meal, then pushes her plate toward me. "You want to try these sweet potato fries? They're delish."

I shake my head.

Rachel leans forward, lowering her voice. "You think this is a permanent thing, the ParaTrooper at school? Everyone's so jumpy, like they're all waiting to accuse someone or to be accused."

"I hope not." I turn my fork over and over in my hand. "I don't see why they'd pull back now, though. They take power; they don't give it up."

"Yeah," Alex says, shaking his head. "I gotta agree with you. Most slave owners had to be forced to give up their slaves, and that took a long, bloody fight."

Rachel hunches her shoulders. "You're right. But for Paras to have to go through this every day—waiting to see if the trooper will single them out"—she glances at Alex, then away—"it must be so hard for them. I don't know if I could take it." She pushes her plate farther away, then looks at me. *"It's gotta be so much worse for you. But I keep worrying that my dad's genes will set off something in me."*

I lean forward. "It must be like waiting for someone to turn on you, and not knowing if they will. Not knowing if they know your secret or not."

"It's gotta be hell," Alex says.

"Hell," Rachel says, nodding.

What little food I've eaten sits heavily in my stomach. I have a feeling the Para-hatred is going to keep getting stronger. And my own brother is making it worse.

◉

After my last class, I start walking away from school, my feet heavy. It feels like my world is falling in on me. Para-hatred is getting stronger. Freedom is getting more and more restricted. And Daniel . . . My throat closes. I can't believe he really thinks that what he's doing is the best way to solve things.

I rub my forehead. It's another few steps before I realize that something is wrong. I feel weak and dizzy, like something's draining my energy. But it's not me that's being drained. It's another Para, somewhere close by—her talent getting sucked from her like the blood from her veins. *"Help!"*

I run toward the fading energy, my breath harsh in my throat. *"Hang on!"*

But the Para is weakening fast, her mind almost completely shut down.

I round the corner, back toward the school, but then I've run right past it. I turn back. There's a narrow alleyway between two storefronts. I swallow my fear and start forward—and then I lose the connection.

She's gone.

I know it before I even see the girl's shoe, her leg awkwardly splayed, her body emaciated, like she died from suddenly aging at least a hundred years. But even so, I recognize her face—a girl I've passed in the halls and seen at the cafe.

Fear holds me rigid. This has to be the work of the Para-Reaper. I should get out of here—now.

I peer into the alley, past the girl. I don't see anyone, but I get a flash of an emotional high—utter glee—vibrating through the air toward me and then it's gone.

I turn and vomit, my lunch coming up in a sour rush. I heave until nothing else comes up, then shakily wipe my mouth with the back of my hand.

"Daniel!" I send, like a cry. The way I used to when we were little and something bad happened.

"Caitlyn, what is it? What's wrong?"

I send him jumbled images, mixed with my terror.

"My god. Get out of there, Caitlyn!"

"But what about the girl? Her family?"

"I'll tell Ilene and the others. We'll get a group down there to claim her body before the ParaTroopers find it, and

someone to notify her parents. But Cait—you need to get out of there right now. *It's not safe."*

I know he's right. There's nothing I can do for the girl, not any more.

My feet feel like lead weights. I shake myself and head back toward the motel in a daze. This isn't the work of a trooper. It can't be. I shudder, wishing I could get the sight of the girl's shriveled body out of my mind. Someone runs up behind me and I whirl around—but it's just Daniel.

"Cait, are you okay?" he says, touching my arm. It's the first time he's voluntarily touched me. His fear and pain is as jagged as mine.

I notice the gesture, but all I can think about is the girl my age—the girl who went to my school—who was killed because she was a Para.

"Ilene sent someone out to take care of it," Daniel sends. *"At least her family will know what happened to her."*

But that's cold comfort. It's not like it can make her alive again or stop the Para-Reaper.

"Did you see anyone? Sense anyone?" Daniel asks.

"No. And I should have. But I think the killer—the Para-Reaper—isn't just doing it because he hates us. I think he's doing it to pull in energy. That's what it felt like—that her abilities and life energy were being drained right out of her."

Daniel's face pales. *"Is that even possible?"*

"That's what it felt like to me."

"That's sick," Daniel sends.

"Yeah."

"You want me to walk you back?"

"No, I'm okay," I say.

"All right," Daniel says. But I feel him watch me walk all the way down the street.

●

The motel owner doesn't look at me when I walk into the lobby. Her shame spreads thickly into me. . . . *I can't believe I let her see me like that . . .*

"Hi," I say, forcing brightness into my voice.

She looks up briefly, her eyes not quite meeting mine. . . . *How did she know where I was anyway?. . .*

I stand there awkwardly. "I hope you didn't mind my coming by yesterday. I could hear you crying—"

The woman looks up at me then. . . . *Did she read my mind?* . . . "Naw, it's okay," she says, shaking her head.

"Okay. Well, if you need to talk . . ." I can't believe I'm offering that.

"Naw, get on with you!" the woman says, and laughs painfully. "I'm better off without that jackass anyway."

Mom's sitting tensely listening to the radio when I get back to our room. "They've blocked off all the exits," she says, her voice wobbling. "Everyone going in or out gets scanned by a Government Paranormal. They're looking for Teen Para, damn her."

"You don't still believe she committed those crimes, do you?"

"It doesn't matter whether she did or not. We're the ones paying for it." Mom puts her head between her hands.

"I don't know what to do. Maybe we should take you out of school. Hole up until this passes over."

"We'd look more suspicious."

Mom lets her hands fall. "I know. And they're talking about starting up patrols, setting up a curfew." She looks up at me, her eyes haunted. "I don't know how to protect you anymore."

I pull a chair over and sit down beside her. "It's okay, Mom. I can protect myself."

Mom squeezes my hand. "Sure you can," she says, her voice high.

I don't need to read her mind to know that she doesn't really think I can.

⊙

In the morning, tension and fear ripple off people as they rush through the streets, heads down, not looking at one another. I've only gone a block before I see a Para-Trooper patrolling the streets, his black boots thumping along the sidewalk, one hand on the gun in his holster.

I walk faster, keeping my gaze averted, hoping he doesn't look my way.

It's almost a relief to get to school and be admitted by the ParaTrooper I've already dealt with. He glares at me like he remembers me. I can feel him waiting for me to look at him the wrong way or to answer with hesitation so he can send me to lockup.

"Let her go," I send, pushing at his mind. *"She's boring. Normal."*

The trooper frowns at me. His fingers twitch on his gun.

I push harder, the effort making my head ache. Warm liquid trickles down my nostril. I wipe at it. Blood.

Not now! I sniff it up, trying to hold it in.

"Let her go," I nudge him harder. The ParaTrooper waves me through.

Rachel's waiting for me at my locker. "So you got through okay."

"Yep." I glance at her sideways.

"Caitlyn—you're bleeding!"

"It's nothing," I say quickly, but she's already pushing a tissue into my hand.

I hold it there until the bleeding stops.

"Someone punch you?" Becca asks sweetly, stopping in front of me. "I would have loved to have seen that."

Thank god we don't all have the same symptoms and that Normals haven't clued in.

"I think you're more of a target than I am, with your attitude problem," I say.

"That's what you think," she says. Then I hear her think, " ...*Just you wait, Para-trash!*..." Becca laughs snidely. The warning bell rings, and she whirls around and stalks away.

Rachel grabs her bag. "We're going to be late."

I don't know if I care. *I should*. Blend in, stay unnoticed. But something feels wrong. Something bigger. I'm breathing shallowly, like I'm waiting for something bad to happen. Waiting for Daniel to do something—because he will; I know he will. Daniel never gives up.

I keep pace with Rachel and try to ignore the bad feeling.

Lockers slam shut, girls check their makeup, boys shove each other, sneakers squeaking in the hall. Zippers unzip, flesh slaps against flesh, laughter rings out. And threading throughout it all is the mind-noise of people's thoughts, constant and unrelenting.

. . . help me . . .

The mind-voice is tight and high with panic. But underneath it is a goodness I know.

Alex? I stop in my tracks.

Someone bumps into me, their thoughts like a slap. I reach for the panicked voice.

. . . somebody help me . . .

Alex. God, it's Alex!

. . . can't breathe . . . too tight . . .

I get a flash of darkness, cold metal pressing against cheek, stuffy air, dirty-feet smell, trouble breathing.

If I help him he'll know. There's no way he can't.

I tremble so hard my teeth chatter. He could turn me in. But I can't let him suffer.

Rachel's saying something to me, but I can't hear her words. I focus all my energy, send as loud as I can. *"Alex— where are you?"*

"Caitlyn?" Alex sounds startled, hopeful. *"How—? . . ."*

"Just tell me where you are."

"I don't know. Somebody's locker. The cowards jumped me from behind. It's hard to breathe."

"Okay. Hold on, I'm coming. Just keep thinking at me."

Fear and hope crash into me like a body slam.

I shove aside my own fear and stride down the hall toward his thoughts.

Rachel grips my arm. "What is it?"

"It's Alex. Someone's shut him in a locker." And I think I know who that someone is. I walk faster.

There aren't many people left in the halls.

. . . choking . . . chest aching . . .

I run.

Rachel runs beside me. "Can I do anything?"

I shake my head, tears streaming as I run.

The hall's almost empty and our footsteps echo loudly. Classroom doors close; the PA system screeches as it turns on, the national anthem blaring out.

I reach out, pushing past all the jumbled voices until I feel Alex's weakening voice again.

. . . can't believe I didn't see . . . this is why she's so aware . . . don't let this be our last . . .

I run down the hall toward his voice. His fear gets heavier, pressing down on my chest like a slab of marble.

"Just hold on." I turn the corner, my sneakers squeaking against the polished floor, Rachel right behind me.

Cold anger whips into me. Daniel is leaning against a pus-yellow locker, his arms crossed over his chest. *"You're going to risk your freedom for a Normal? But you're not willing to risk anything to help your own kind?"* Disgust and loathing billows off him, stronger than his incredulity, his pain at my betrayal.

"Of course I'll help other Paras. But not through

killing, or slavery, or abuse. Now step aside, Daniel. Let me get Alex out before he suffocates."

Daniel's eyes narrow. Hot jealousy rushes through him. *"You think it's that easy? You think you can just save your boy and walk away?"*

"I think we should be on the same side."

Daniel smiles thinly. *"That's up to you."*

"Caitlyn—you still there?" Alex's voice is louder, reverberating inside my head, making it hard to think.

Another flash. Breath rasping in throat, dirty sock stuffed in mouth, head dizzy, sweating.

"How sweet. You've let a Normal into your secret. Now he holds your life in his hands."

I ignore Daniel. *"Still here, Alex. Try to breathe slowly."*

Daniel pushes up off the locker and turns to face me, his eyes hard as iron, his teeth bared in a half smile. "Get out of here, Cait, before something happens to you." *"Before I make it happen."*

He's not bluffing.

I take a step forward, then another. Will his own technique work on him?

I reach for Daniel's thoughts. *"I don't want to hurt them,"* I send, trying to match his thought patterns, to make them vibrate with rage and pain the way his own mind-voice does. Trying to weave the thought into his own. *"I'm going to walk away."*

I'm doing something I never thought I'd do. But I can't let Alex die.

Daniel half turns away, then swings back to face me.

A door snaps open in the hall, and Mr. Arnold frowns at us. "What are you doing out here? Get to your classes."

I take a shuddering breath. "I can't, sir. Someone's in trouble."

Mr. Arnold frowns deeper, then steps out into the hall and closes the door behind him. Faces appear at the small window in the door, pressing up against the glass like captive fish staring out of their tank.

"Later," Daniel mouths at me, then saunters away.

"Where do you think you're going, young man?"

"To class," Daniel says, not bothering to stop.

Mr. Arnold points his finger at Daniel, then lets it drop. He turns to me, the lines deepening around his thin mouth. "Now then, Miss Ellis, what's all this about? I hope you're not playing some kind of prank."

"No, sir." I've slowly been inching my way down the hall, pulled toward the dizzy, suffocating feeling, toward Alex's voice. I'm close to where Daniel was standing. The dizziness is so strong it's hard to stand, but it's not right, not yet. I take another step, then another, light bouncing off the floors, harsh and bright. "There's someone stuffed inside one of these lockers."

I don't know why it helps me to reach out with my hand when what I hear and sense are in my head, but it does.

"If you're trying to be funny . . ."

Two more steps, another locker, Alex's voice filling me now, pressing at me from all sides, the dizzy, suffocating feeling a constant. My hand shakes as I press it against the cold yellow metal. "Right here. Please, can't you help him?"

I tug on the lock, but I know it won't open before I try. I pound on the metal door, feel it shudder. "Can you hear me?"

Another classroom door opens, and a cross-looking woman sticks her head out. "What's going on?"

"This girl seems to think that someone's stuffed inside one of our lockers," Mr. Arnold says, like he's humoring me.

There's a muffled thump, then a banging sound. We all jump.

"What was that?" Mr. Arnold tugs on his nose.

"I told you, someone's trapped in there," I say, trying to keep the impatience out of my voice. "It sounds like he's having trouble breathing. Can you get him out?"

Mr. Arnold turns toward his classroom, and the student faces vanish from the window. "I'll call the janitor."

CHAPTER **16**

The janitor rams the blades of his metal cutter into the lock and pushes down hard, grunting.

The lock clatters to the floor.

Mr. Arnold yanks open the locker—and Alex drops out, hitting the floor hard, a sock stuffed in his mouth, his hands tied behind his back. He rolls over on his side. His eyes flutter, lashes like tiny dark wings.

"Alex!" I cry.

"You all right, son?" Mr. Arnold kneels down and yanks the sock out of Alex's mouth. "Who did this to you?"

Alex gasps for air. "Didn't see . . ."

His eyes find mine. *"Caitlyn, thank you . . . and god, I'm sorry."*

"I'm glad you're okay."

I feel him in my mind, sweet and warm, our connection deeper than ever. It's going to be all right. He won't turn me in. Will he?

Alex's eyes flicker, roll back in their sockets, and his head falls back, his skin bleaching lighter.

"Alex!" I reach for him, but his thoughts are wrapped in cotton, pillow thick.

"He's fainted." Mr. Arnold pulls out a cell phone from his vest pocket, flipping it open. "Is the nurse in today?" he barks. "Good, send her up immediately. We have a situation." Students are pushing out the classroom door like soda from a can, eager and horrified.

Mr. Arnold turns back to me, his shoulders rigid. "And you—get yourself down to the principal's office!"

"What for? I didn't do anything."

The class stands behind me, their thoughts rushing at me like hail. . . . *How did she…?* . . . *gotta text this* . . .

Mr. Arnold glares over his glasses at them. "Get back to class. *Now*. Lisa, you're in charge." He waits until they straggle away. "How did you know Alex was in there?" he asks me grimly.

I raise my head. "I heard him."

"You heard him—with a sock stuffed in his mouth? Come on, you'll have to do better than that." . . . *She must have seen who did this* . . .

"I heard him, too," Rachel says.

Mr. Arnold harrumphs.

"Alex is unconscious," I say. "Shouldn't we be doing something—sir?"

Mr. Arnold stiffens. "The nurse will examine him. And you will take this matter up with the principal—both of you. Now get going."

I start down the hall, my legs heavy like I'm pushing through sludge, Rachel walking silently beside me. I want to stay with Alex, make sure he's all right—but that would draw too much attention. What is it about Alex that makes me lose my caution? That makes me forget how to protect myself?

I push open the door and start down the stairs.

Rachel hasn't said a word, though fear shivers through her. I look at her pale face. "Thank you."

"Why would anyone do that to him? Alex is harmless. Everyone likes him."

I bite down on my lip so hard I taste salty blood. It sounds too narcissistic to say that it happened because of me, so I don't say anything.

But maybe no one's safe around me—not so long as Daniel's here.

Mr. Temple looks at me unblinkingly, his eyes stony. His office chair is at least five inches higher than the visitor's chair I'm sitting in, making him look more imposing, which I'm sure is exactly what he wants.

I force myself to relax. There's something about Mr. Temple that isn't right. I can't read anything off him, anything at all—but he's not a Para. I'd know if he was, especially one strong enough to block me, the way Daniel has. I don't know how he's doing it. I don't know what it means.

"Can you describe what you heard, Ms. Ellis?"

I clear my throat. "A thump, and a muffled, strangled noise." Close enough to the truth to sound right.

Mr. Temple leans back in his chair, lacing his hands behind his head. His scab-colored tie leans off to one side. "Mr. Arnold said you knew there was a boy jammed in the locker. Not just a student, but a boy in particular. Care to explain how you knew that?"

He knows.

"I just assumed it was a boy. It's the kind of thing boys do to boys. The things girls do to each other are different."

Mr. Temple nods, as if he's considering what I said. "And how did you know that Alex was having trouble breathing?" He leans forward. "There's no way you could have known he had a sock stuffed in his mouth." He jabs his finger at me. "Not unless you saw it happen — in person, or in your mind."

Cold sweat rolls down my sides. "Mr. Temple, are you accusing me of being a Para?" I put all the disgust I can into my voice. "If you are, let's get the ParaTrooper in here. I've got nothing to hide. If not, I'd like to go back to class."

I can't believe I just said that. I run my tongue over my dry lips. But if he's as Para-hating as people say he is, then he's probably already accused two Normals in his quest to rid his school of Paras. Maybe he doesn't want to risk the huge fine and mark on his record that comes from accusing three "innocent" Normals.

I stare at Mr. Temple. His face is expressionless, but his Adam's apple is bobbing up and down. I think I must be right.

Mr. Temple clears his throat. "Sure you don't want to tell me who did this?"

"How could I know? I didn't see it happen."

Mr. Temple leans back so far it looks like he's going to tip right over. I wish he would. "All right, then." I get a flash of sadness and rage, tinged with a metallic scent.

Daniel's been here. He's talked with the principal, influenced him somehow.

Mr. Temple presses his hands against his desk and stands, his chair squeaking. "We're done here. But Caitlyn—I'm watching you."

I swallow noisily. "You're *watching* me?"

"I know you have a . . . talent, and I'm going to get proof."

My heart feels like it's going to pound right out through my rib cage. I can't let Mr. Temple turn me in. I stare at him, focusing all my energy. *"Forget."*

He blinks and scratches his head, like he can't remember what he was saying.

My god. What did I do?

We stare at each other.

Mr. Temple rubs his forehead. "What was I—? Never mind. You can tell Rachel Levy to come in now."

I sprint out of his office.

CHAPTER 17

Rachel's sitting needle-straight in one of the plastic chairs lined up against the wall, her thin fingers picking at the skin on her elbow, her foot jerking up and down. I walk over, try to look calm. "He'll see you now."

"I'll just stick to the story—we heard him banging, right?" Rachel thinks at me as she stands.

"Yes. Thanks."

There's a ParaWatch pamphlet pinned to the bulletin board behind her. I look past it, as if it means nothing.

The secretary watches us over her glasses, her thin lips pressed tightly together. *. . . teenagers these days . . . what I have to put up with . . . no appreciation . . .*

Rachel touches my arm. "Don't worry; it'll be all right."

I'm cold and shaky, but I manage to smile. Then she's in the office with Mr. Temple, the door shutting behind her.

The secretary's still watching me.

I smile prettily at her. "Thank you for your help."

She gawks at me like I just told her what color bra I'm wearing. I suppress a smile, but it's gone just as fast.

I clench my backpack as I stride down the empty hall. I don't want it to happen all over again. The running. The accusations. The beatings and murders. But the fear and ha-tred — and the accusations — are gaining strength. There might just be another riot, another Cleansing. God, I hope I'm wrong.

I close my eyes. I can already see Mom sucking the worry up inside her so strong that it devours her from the inside, making the lines in her face deeper, her smile more brittle. I don't know if she can survive another series of riots and Para-murders.

Anger pricks like hot needles at my scalp. "You blow me away," a voice says.

I snap my eyes open. Daniel's standing there, sneering. "What?"

"You just go running to protect your little Normal friends, though they'd never protect you."

My throat closes inward.

Daniel steps closer. "You're a Normal-lover, Cait." He says the word like it's a stinking pile of feces. "You want to be accepted by them, be like them. But you'll never be one of them. And they'll hate you for it."

I clear my throat, a sandpapery stutter. "They're not all bad." And we're not all good.

Daniel laughs harshly. "It only takes one Normal hat-ing us to make things worse."

I step around him, as if I can't feel his anger. *"Don't do this, Daniel. Don't turn people against each other more than they already are."*

"Too late. We're already there."

"No, we're not. We can help Normals accept us; we just have to go about it the right way."

"When are you going to wake up, Caitlyn? The world's full of hate." He shakes his head. *"You're not stupid. I don't understand why you're opposing me."*

Because I'm human? Because I care? I push the thoughts down hard.

"Don't say I didn't warn you...see you in class," he sends ominously. Daniel closes his mind to me and walks off without looking back.

I shake myself and walk the other way.

A door at the end of the hall grates open, and a tall, thin boy stumbles into the hall, a woman supporting him.

Alex.

My breath flutters in my throat like a trapped butterfly.

Alex's head snaps up, his gaze meeting mine. *"Caitlyn!"*

I feel happy and sick, all at the same time.

"I don't trust some high school nurse," the woman is saying. "You're going to let Dr. Matthews check you over. And if—and only if—he says you're okay, are you coming back here."

Alex nods, but he's not really listening. All his attention is focused on me. *"Caitlyn, I'm sorry I was such an ass."*

"You just believed the propaganda. But you came around pretty fast. I was proud of you."

Alex snorts. *"Well, thanks. But you're the amazing*

one—getting that close to me when I was spewing all that crap."

"That's over now. I know"—I hesitate—*"I think you're on my side. . . ."*

"Of course I am!" Alex and the woman—it must be his mother—are almost level with me.

"Good. But Alex, I have to know—are you going to turn me in?"

"God, no! What do you take me for?"

"Believing in Para-rights is one thing. Meeting a real live Para is another."

"You can count on me to protect your secret, I promise. I will never betray you."

Relief floods me like a drug, smoothing all the tension away.

"I'm sorry for every stupid thing I said before. Forgive me?"

I can feel how much he means it. I want to laugh at the rightness of the moment. *"Yes!"* God, yes. Happiness warms me like the sun.

And then I feel the stiffness in his body, the soreness and bruising, the pain that's still in his lungs. *"Alex!"*

"I'm all right. Really." He grimaces.

This close, Alex's skin looks soft and smooth, marred only by the darkened swelling around his cheekbones and nose.

Alex's springy black curls lie enticingly against his forehead. I want to reach out and touch his face, but I don't dare do it, not with his mother here.

I feel him laugh.

My face burns. I can't believe I projected my thoughts. I have to get a grip.

Alex's eyes are so intense, it's as if I'm the only one that exists for him. I used to feel that way with my dad, and with Daniel, too. Pain tears through my chest.

I wrench my gaze away from Alex's. I don't know Daniel anymore. For him to have done this to Alex, just to get to me. . . .

Alex grips my arm. *"You know who did this? Wait, do you think he wants to hurt you?"*

The warmth of his fingers seeps through my sleeve.

I jerk my arm away, my breath shaky. I have to shield my thoughts more. *"I can't tell you. Don't try to find out, Alex. It's too risky for you."*

"No. Not *finding out is what's risky. Let me help."*

"This is the girl who found me, Mom," Alex says loudly. *. . . the girl I'm falling for . . .*

I want to laugh, to shout with the joy of it. Alex really likes me! Even knowing what I am. *Who* I am.

The woman smiles at me, her teeth almost as white as the pearls around her neck. "Thank you for saving my boy. I'm in your debt."

"Mo-om." Alex's cheeks darken. "Don't be so dramatic."

"She's not always like this—I swear."

"I like her. She loves you a lot, you know."

"I know."

His mother clasps my hand before I can back away.

Her hand is gentle, her ring finger ringless. "You're welcome at our home anytime." . . . *thank god she found him* . . . *seem to really like each other* . . .

I reach up to brush my hair from my face, breaking contact. "Thank you. It was nice meeting you, but I've gotta get to class." I look at Alex. I want to hold him, know he's okay. "See you later."

"See ya."

I walk down the hall, then sneak a peek over my shoulder. Alex and his mom wave.

I laugh and wave back.

It could work out between Alex and me, if we're careful. If Daniel doesn't mess everything up.

CHAPTER 18

I walk up the three flights of stairs to English, red paint chips from the banister sticking to my palm like scars. I'm crazy to still be in this town when Daniel's adding to the hate. But how can I leave Alex or Rachel—my first real friends in years? And how can I leave, knowing what Daniel is planning? Knowing the people he'll hurt.

My skin prickles.

I turn casually, like I'm looking at the brick stairwell. No one's there.

I'm just jittery. I plod down the hall to Mr. Arnold's classroom. I wish I could skip his class completely. I hesitate, my hand on the doorknob, then jerk the door open and walk in.

Mr. Arnold stops talking, midsentence. "Well, well, if it isn't Ms. Ellis. Come in." I quickly walk to my seat.

"Good. Now, where were we?"

I sense Mr. Arnold zeroing in on me. I look up at him, all attentive. He scowls and picks another student to answer the question.

The others' thoughts slice through my head so loud it's

hard to think. . . . *did you see? . . . how did she know? . . . who would hurt Alex? . . .*

I press the tips of my fingers against my lips. I can't believe Daniel hurt Alex to get to me. And I can't *believe* I let Alex know I'm a Para. That's three people who know about me when no one should. Make that four.

Maybe I can do a mass memory-erase, make them forget it ever happened.

Shit. I pinch my bottom lip. I'm no better than the ParaWatch say we are if I misuse my power like that.

Even in self-defense? a small voice inside me whispers. *Even if it doesn't hurt them—if it just keeps you safe?*

No. I won't mess with people's heads. I won't do what Daniel's done. Not even to protect myself. I'm better than that.

Then I think of Mr. Temple and I'm filled with shame.

Rachel waits for me at the end of class. "You've got to be careful, Caitlyn," she hisses. "Mr. Temple suspects you."

My heart clenches, then releases. *"How do you know?"*

Rachel starts down the hall. I join her, my shoulder brushing against the wall.

Rachel stares ahead.

"He wants me to watch you," Rachel thinks. *"Said there was something suspicious about the way you found Alex."*

So my "persuasion" didn't last long. Relief mixes with

my fear. *"He practically accused me of being a Para until I told him to get a trooper in. He must have fingered two Normals in a row."*

Rachel shifts her backpack.

"That sounds like him. He hates Paras so much he can hardly think past the hate."

"Yeah . . ."

"But?" Rachel prompts.

"I think it's something more."

Rachel scrunches up her nose. "What more?"

I feel again the way Mr. Temple blocked me, smell the metallic scent beneath his thoughts, see the way Daniel looked at me in the hall. I am sure Daniel did something to him. Maybe even made Mr. Temple suspect me. "What did you say to him?"

"I told him it didn't feel right, and I wouldn't do it," Rachel says unevenly. "He looked like he wanted to hurt me—but then he sat back and smiled this horrible smile, and said that loyalty was a good quality in a friend, but that I should be careful who my friends are."

I suck in my breath. "It sounds like he was threatening you."

"Yeah. Like a villain in a bad movie." Rachel laughs shakily.

I feel weighed down. "First Alex gets hurt, and then you get threatened. You should keep your distance from me for your own safety."

Rachel punches my arm. "I'm not going anywhere. I've faced homophobes and bullies who wanted to beat me to death. And I'm still here."

But this could be more dangerous than that. Paras have abilities that Normals don't.

The crush of bodies and thoughts is overpowering. I flinch and pull myself inward, trying to deflect the mind-noise.

"Your defenses still down?" Rachel asks.

"Yeah." An uneasiness creeps over me. Somehow Daniel is playing with my talent. It's like he trained himself to use his power to hurt others, while I trained myself to protect others. He has the sword, while I have the shield. How can I fight with only a shield?

CHAPTER 19

Alex is waiting for me outside my next class. Even with his face puffy and bruised, he is still beautiful.

"You're back!" I touch his chest tentatively. "You okay?"

"Yep. Now let's go find that a-hole who's got it in for you. Daniel, right?"

I look away. "Let's just drop it."

"Can you still hear me? What if he exposes you? You have to find a way to shut him up."

"I don't know if I can."

Alex crosses his arms. "There's something you're not telling me."

I swallow. *"I—I already tried."* I flush with heat. *"Mr. Temple told me he suspects me. And I made him forget."*

"You made him?"

I nod, bracing myself.

"Good!"

My mouth opens. *"Good?"* I can't believe he's not freaking out.

"Good! Then he can't tell anyone."

"Well . . . the effect already wore off."

"It wore off—and he can finger you anytime."

"Yeah. And that's not everything. I don't think it'll work on Daniel; he's a Para, like me." I feel a giggle push up inside my chest, even though nothing's funny. *"Daniel's my brother. He was taken years ago; we never found him. But he's shown up here—he's a Para-slave. He hates Normals for what they did to him, and he's trying to convince me to oppress them, the way they've oppressed us. He's the one who did this to you."*

"So your brother—he's a power-hungry fanatic."

"I wouldn't say that. He's hurting, Alex."

"Okay, he's hurting. And he wants to hurt back. And what will he do if you don't join him? Will he finger you?" There's a dangerous note to his thoughts.

I suck in my lower lip. *"I don't think he wants to inform on me. He wants to bring me over to his side. But if I don't . . . yeah, he might turn me in."*

"But damn it, he has to know what it's like, he has to know how bad it would be for you. If he cares about you at all, he wouldn't go there." Alex clenches his hands into strong fists. *"Tell me where he is. I'll talk some sense into him, one way or another."*

"Alex—no."

"He wants to hurt you. And he already hurt me."

I wrap my arms around him, not caring who sees us, not caring that it blocks people's way as they rush to class. *"I'm sorry,"* I send.

Alex arches back to look at me. His eyes focus on my lips. I have just seconds to think that I don't know how to kiss, don't want to be clumsy, am not sure I'm ready though I want it so much, before his lips touch mine, soft and gentle. I shiver, and press up against him harder. His kisses me again, and again.

I can't believe how good it feels. How right. I've never even kissed anyone. Never wanted to. But this—it's better than I thought it could be.

Alex pulls back to look at my face, and I follow him, draw him back to me.

. . . get a room! . . .

The thought thrown at us is angry, jealous, but it can't pierce my happiness. *This* is what it's like to be in love—to feel like nothing else matters.

Alex pulls away, separating his body from mine, but I still feel the connection between us. He puts his lips to my ear. "You have to talk with your brother, make him promise not to inform on you."

"I know."

"Good." Alex nods firmly. "Now we just have to figure out where he is."

"He should be in my next class," I say reluctantly. "If he's still working undercover."

We rush there, but Daniel's not in the room. We wait in the hall, but he doesn't appear, not even when the bell rings.

"I need to get in there," I say.

"See you at lunch? We have some talking to do."

"Yes." I can barely get the word out.

Alex kisses me and leaves.

Daniel never shows up for class, but I don't expect him to.

◉

I close my locker, turn to Rachel. "I'm meeting Alex. We have to work some things out."

"Does he—*know*?"

"Yeah."

"Wow." Rachel whistles. "Good luck."

"He's changed! You've seen that."

"Uh-huh."

"He has!"

. . . the way my family "changed" to accept me?. . . piling on the platitudes but never comfortable with me anymore . . . never leaving me alone with another girl . . .

I want to tell her that it's not like that—want to tell her I'm sorry—but that would make her uncomfortable. I didn't mean to listen in; her thoughts were just so loud.

Warm happiness mingled with calm approaches me. Alex. I turn.

"You feel like getting a hotdog?" *. . . something that doesn't taste healthy . . . don't know how much longer I can take that place, even for her . . .* He smiles his easy smile at me.

"Sounds good!"

Rachel's sadness reaches me, her loneliness. But I know if I invite her, she'll feel even more left out. "Rachel—"

. . . she's happy . . . gotta be happy for her . . . Rachel makes shooing motions at me. "Go!"

"Come on." Alex grabs my hand and tugs me down

187

the hall and out into the sun. The tense, oppressive feeling of the school leaves me.

I wait for the overwhelming rush of thoughts and emotions that comes with skin contact, but I only feel happiness.

I feel it all the way to the vendor in the park, breathing in Alex's vanilla scent, feeling his strong hand in mine.

Alex gets a hotdog for him, a veggie dog for me. I take a bite, piled high with onions and tomatoes.

Suddenly I am ravenous. I gulp the veggie dog down.

Alex grins at me. "I like to see a girl eat."

"Then you can buy me another," I say, surprising myself.

Alex buys one more for me, and two for him, and we walk slowly through the park, the sun warming my skin.

Alex finishes his two in the time it takes me to eat my one. I laugh and wipe the mustard from his chin—a bold move for me. I act so different around him—but he makes it easy. He doesn't flood me with thoughts and emotions, yet I know he likes me. Really likes me.

Alex leans against a tree, pulling me up against his hard body. He leans forward to kiss me. His lips are soft and wet, and they feel so good against mine.

I press closer to him. His lips get firmer, more insistent, and my whole body feels alive.

I feel a rush of desire. I don't know if it's his or mine, and I don't care. I don't care about anything except the feel of his lips, his body rocking against mine gently, the heady scent of him—

No. We're going too fast. How do I know for sure I

can trust him with my life? I know what I sense from him, but it's hard to trust it, especially after everything with Daniel. I yank back.

Alex groans. . . . *why did she stop? . . . feels too good . . .*

"I know. But we haven't talked yet."

"Did you just—?"

"Sorry. I didn't mean to."

"Geez." Alex blows out his breath. "That'll take some getting used to."

I bite my lip. This isn't going to work. How could I have thought it would?

I wrench away from him.

"Hey," he says, catching my hand. "What's wrong? I thought you wanted—"

"I did! I do!" I'm practically shouting, but Alex doesn't pull away.

"Okay, so what's—"

"I'm not sure this is a good idea."

Alex looks at me steadily. "I am not going to betray you. I would never do that. Even if we broke up—and I hope we never will—I would never turn you in." His breath shudders in his throat. "A long time ago, I couldn't protect my mom. My dad almost killed her. And I swore"—his eyes are fierce—"I swore I would never do that to anyone, not ever. Never threaten anyone's life, and I would try to protect anyone who needs it."

"A hero complex, huh?" I say, my lips trembling.

"I'm serious, Caitlyn," he says.

"I know." I look away. "I'm just scared. I'm sorry." I

look up at the tree branches, trying to keep the tears from falling. One rolls down my cheek anyway.

Alex gently brushes it away. "I don't know how to convince you," he says and shakes his head. "I made a promise to myself years ago that I would never be in a relationship because I didn't want to be like my dad. But when I saw you, all that flew out of my head." He takes a shaky breath. "The way you really *see* me—and you still like who I am—no one's ever done that for me before. That's something I don't want to lose."

"I *do* see you," I say quietly. "And I love who you are. There is nothing in you that makes you like your dad."

Alex's eyes moisten. "And you can tell?"

"You know I can."

Alex blows out his breath. "Wow. Don't you see how special you are? To see into me like that? With or without your . . . talent, you see me, you believe in me. I know I'm just a—a Normal . . . but I promise I'll protect you and your secret. I won't let you down."

His gaze sharpens. "If you can see into me with your gift, can't you find out if I'm telling the truth?"

I nod.

"Then do it," he says simply. "I'm all yours." He holds out his hands.

I grasp them and a rush of emotions flood over me. Love. Awe. Respect. Guilt that he couldn't protect his mom. Hope that he can protect me. Determination that he will. Nervousness and relief that I can read his thoughts, that I could have an early-warning signal if he ever starts turning into his father.

I let go of his hands. "Thank you."

"I won't betray you," he says again.

"I know."

I see the tenderness in his eyes, the deep love and sweetness. No one has ever looked at me like that before, like I'm someone they want. Damn it. I feel too good around Alex to fight it anymore. "Okay," I whisper, knowing it's a mistake, knowing I'm already falling in love with him and I can't stop it.

Alex grins widely. He tugs at the copper bracelets on his wrist and slides one off. "I want you to have this," he says.

I slide my hand through and the warm bracelet against my skin feels like a promise.

◉

As soon as I walk back into the school, my senses overload, the lights too bright, the sounds too loud, people's thoughts rushing at me harder than before. My eyes water, and I am grateful for my dark glasses.

I feel it again—someone watching me, stalking me, hiding inside others' minds. Daniel.

I reach toward the faint hum, and it vanishes.

I stumble to science class, get out my notebook, and stare at the Bunsen burner on my desk while Mr. Kinley drones on about electrons and ions. None of it means anything to me. I wish he'd teach something that matters—like how to create a mind shield against Para-haters or people who think they're doing good when they're not.

I try to focus more in my next class, and the one after that, but I can't stop reaching for Daniel. Every time I find him, he disconnects. It's like he's having fun eluding me. Taunting me. Showing me that he's more powerful. I have to make him see that Normals are important, too. That no one group is better than another. But I still haven't figured out how to convince him by the time the last bell rings.

In the hall, boys run past me, hollering at each other. A huddle of girls squeal together, their laughter reverberating in the air.

All around me lockers slam shut, books are tossed in bags or backpacks, gossip is whispered. Most people are ready to head home or go to their afterschool activities. But I'm still waiting for Daniel's next move.

If Daniel can get into my head—sometimes without my even realizing it—why can't I get into his? There has to be a technique.

I head for the library so I can think. Mrs. Vespa looks up from her desk and smiles when she sees me. "Caitlyn."

"Mrs. Vespa—you going to be open for a while? I need a quiet place."

"Of course. Why don't you use that nook I showed you the other day?"

I nod gratefully, and make my way there.

I heave my backpack onto the floor and perch on the empty chair. I'm used to going into Normals' minds unnoticed. But other Paras? It's like a crime. It's an unspoken etiquette to announce your presence, to not misuse your gift. And another Para would sense me. So how does Daniel do it? How does he get around my awareness?

I chew on a piece of cuticle sticking up from my finger and rip it off with my teeth. Maybe it doesn't matter how he does it. I have to find my own way.

I close my eyes, breathing evenly, and notice the rigidity of the chair against my butt, the solid floor beneath my shoes, grounding myself in my surroundings.

I visualize my mind-voice being invisible—no weight, no sound, no emotion. I visualize it until I believe it.

Then I picture Daniel as I last saw him—the coldness in his eyes, the firmness of his jaw, the hardness in his core. I pull up each detail—the steel blue of his eyes, the sweep of his blond hair—until I can almost see him in front of me.

I breathe slowly, focusing on him until I can feel his chest rise and fall with breath, can feel the rage and pain warring inside him. I layer that on top of my own thoughts, try to think like him. *"Stupid Normals think they're so superior."* Then, like a wisp of air, I slip into his mind.

I let his thoughts vibrate through me. . . . *am more powerful than anyone* . . . Deep beneath that fierce bravado, under hardened layers of scar tissue, I feel the hurt, quaking boy I once knew.

This is my chance to find out why he did what he did. I think I already know, but I want to be sure. And I've got to do it without letting him sense me.

"When I beat Alex up, stuffed him in the locker . . . ," I send, layering my thoughts with his own thought pattern.

I wait. Nothing.

I try again. *"When I beat Alex up . . ."*

. . . *gave me the biggest rush!* . . . *making a Normal cower*—Caitlyn's *Normal* . . . *never saw us coming* . . .

I feel sick deep in the pit of my stomach. *"Me and . . . Zack and those three Normals I convinced to help us. They are so gullible. Like Caitlyn's loverboy could ever have a talent. Man, we gave that Normal a beating he'll never forget. Serves him right, sucking her face like he's one of us . . .*

I swallow back a minipuke. If I needed any more proof that I should run, this is it. But I can't leave now. Daniel won't stop hating Alex and Rachel just because I've left.

I want to rest my head on my knees and weep, or punch my fist into the chair. But I don't do either. I just sit there, letting his thoughts wash over me.

. . . stupid Caitlyn, doesn't even know what's coming . . .

I want to scream. *"What's coming?"*

"What? Caitlyn?" I feel him reach for me, malevolent energy ready to strike, just as I leap out of his mind. I pull myself back to the library, to the hardness of the chair, the firmness of the floor beneath my feet. I slap shields around myself, blocking him out as best as I can.

I got into Daniel's mind unnoticed! At least until he sensed me.

I rub a shaky hand over my face. Daniel may think he's more powerful than anyone, but deep down, he's insecure and frightened. And the Daniel I once knew—he's still there under the layers of hardness. But the hardness has become more who he is. It's who he wants to be. Who he must have felt he needed to be to survive.

I stretch and look around. The library is deserted— chairs resting upside down on tables, students and their

bags all gone, a hollow, listening feeling to the room —
though the lights are still on.

A door in the back of the library opens, and Mrs. Vespa
walks in, a stack of books in her arms. "Ah, you're back.
Did you figure out whatever it was you had to figure out?"

"What do you mean?" I ask, my heart quickening.

Mrs. Vespa smiles wryly. "I've seen '. . . *Paras, my
grandmother, my best friend. . .*' creative, intelligent people
zone out like that before. Usually when they're trying to
figure out a solution to a problem."

She knows! God, she knows! But I force my heart to
slow, keep my breathing even. She's been around Paras her
whole life. She's loved some Paras. She would never turn
one in.

I force a laugh. "You got me. Yeah, I think I figured it
out."

"Good." Mrs. Vespa nods smartly. She sets her books
down on the table carefully, not looking at me. "If you ever
need help figuring out . . . a problem, I hope you'll feel you
can turn to me." She casually tents her hands to form a P.

Relief floods me. She's part of the Underground, a
Para-supporter. I make the symbol back, and she nods, just
the smallest movement of her head.

I leave the library feeling happier, safer. But then I start
to think how I told myself I wasn't going to connect with
the Underground until I knew who the rat was. What if Mrs.
Vespa is the one after me? But I don't recognize her mind-
voice, and I don't think she recognized mine. She just saw
something that reminded her of the Paras she's loved. And
she doesn't feel malevolent, not on any level.

I push open the school doors and step out into the late afternoon sun. I think I can trust her. I'm going to until I see something that tells me otherwise.

Alex jumps off the staircase railing, landing gracefully on the asphalt beside me. "Caitlyn."

"Were you waiting for me?"

"No. Yes. I mean—all right, I was." He smiles sheepishly. "You wanna do something? Take a walk?" He holds out his hand.

I tentatively put my hand in his, waiting for the explosion of thoughts, but all I feel is happiness.

We walk down the street together, our legs moving in synchronicity, our palms warming each other's. It's so intimate, holding someone else's hand. Letting their skin warm yours.

As we walk, I take in the green leaves on the trees, the vivid blue of the sky, the strength of Alex's hand. There is so much beauty in the world, even when there's pain and fear. It's the beauty that wraps around me now. We pass stores and apartments, until I realize I'm leading us back to the motel.

I stop. "You feel like a swim? It's a bit grungy, though."

Alex smiles a slow, easy grin. "I'm game for anything."

I push through the entrance, nodding to the motel owner who watches us curiously, then lead Alex out back to the pool. Leaves and garbage float along the surface.

Alex whistles. "You weren't kidding about the grungy part."

"I know. But it's still a pool." Already I can feel the lure of the water, the blessed silence.

"Yeah." Alex walks around the edge, looking in.

My cheeks burn. What was I thinking of, bringing him here?

Alex strips off his shorts and T-shirt, his bathing suit underneath, and cannonballs into the pool, T-shirt in hand. He walks down the length, swimming in the deep end, dragging his T-shirt behind him like a net to collect all the debris. In just a few laps, the pool looks better. Swimmable. Shareable.

"Come on in!" he calls.

I strip down to my bathing suit, then slide into the pool. The cool water closes over me, the buzz of thoughts disappearing. I swim to Alex. He pulls me up against him, then squeezes my butt.

I shriek and splash him. He pulls away, laughing.

I wish he could connect with me the way I connect with him. I'm just going to have to vocalize more.

"You look serious all of a sudden," he says and closes the distance, kissing me again. "What are you thinking?"

I burst out laughing. Maybe he doesn't need telepathy. "That I need to tell you things when they come up, instead of wishing you could hear them."

"Damn right you do. I'm at a disadvantage here," he says, splashing me again.

I splash him back.

Alex grabs my hand, his eyes suddenly serious, cutting off my laughter. "I feel so good with you, Caitlyn, in a way that I don't with anyone else."

Goose bumps rise on my skin. "I feel that way, too." And I do. When I'm with Alex, it's like we're two bowls nestled inside each other. No sharp edges, just a perfect fit. Like home. I haven't felt that way since Dad died.

Alex pulls me to him, then lifts me up in both his arms, the water holding most of my weight. I wrap my arms around his neck, resting my cheek against his shoulder, the water gently lapping at us. I feel weightless in Alex's embrace, almost like I can fly. I raise my head and kiss him, not able to get enough of him. I even like the taste of chlorine and salt because it's on him.

Between the water and Alex, all the mind-noise is gone. I could float on this feeling forever.

I kiss him again and he kisses me back, his warm breath sending shivers through me.

There's an electricity between us, a current that connects us. I touch his chest, the muscles firm, and feel his heart pounding. His breath is coming faster now.

Alex's lips find mine again and warmth bursts through me. I've never felt this good right through my whole body, or felt this close to anyone without connecting mind-to-mind. It's probably the closest Normals can come to telepathy.

We kiss until my lips feel bruised and then I pull away.

I feel so much pent-up energy inside me that I don't know what to do.

"Race you!" I call, twisting away. Then I surge forward.

I hear him leap after me, feel the movement in the

water. I swim hard and deep, keeping my legs straight and giving it all I've got.

Alex moves up beside me. Just as I get close to the edge he passes me, slapping the tile and laughing.

He shakes his head, spraying water everywhere. "Damn, girl, you sure can swim! You'd be our secret weapon on the team."

"Next year," I say, knowing even as I say it that I probably won't be here anymore.

CHAPTER 20

I pull myself up out of the pool and Alex comes up behind me, dripping cold water on me. I squeal and reach for my towel. When I turn around, the delight seeps out of me.

There are dark bruises all over Alex's stomach and legs. Alex towels off like there's nothing wrong. "I've had worse, believe me."

"That doesn't make it okay."

I touch my fingers to a bruise on his chest. I made this happen. I put him in danger by being seen with him—

No. I didn't do this. Daniel and his buddies did.

"There were five of them," I say, keeping my voice steady. "Daniel, another Para, and three Normals he coerced. They jumped you from behind."

Alex stiffens. "How do you—?"

"I got it from Daniel—from his thoughts."

"You went into his thoughts?" Alex lowers his voice, even though there's no one else here. "Isn't that dangerous?"

"Not if he doesn't catch me."

"But he has it in for you," Alex says flatly. He towels off his hair. "How are we going to stop him?"

"I don't know."

Alex shakes his head. "You can't just leave it like that. He could destroy you."

Alex is right. I rub my aching chest. But I don't have a solution.

I sit and stare at the wall in our motel room, my body heavy. Alex left hours ago and I still can't make myself move. I know I should do something, anything. Get my homework done. Make supper before Mom gets home. But I can't think clearly. I'm having trouble even caring. There's just so much wrong and I don't know how to fix any of it.

A key turns in the lock. I get up slowly, feeling worn out, using the back of the chair for support.

"Sorry I'm late!" Mom calls. "I brought pizza." She closes the door with her foot, holding the cardboard box in front of her.

I breathe in the rich scent of cheese and tomato sauce and stare at her. Then I take out our plates before she realizes what she's giving me—all that unhealthy fat.

Mom sits heavily at the dresser that acts as our table. I give us each a slice top-heavy with mushrooms, broccoli, zucchini, spinach, and onion—her attempt at making it healthy—and push a plate toward her.

"Thanks, sweetheart." Mom kicks off her shoes and sighs heavily.

I sit down across from her, seeing the stress of all the years on her face. "Long day?"

"Yes," Mom says. "How was yours?"

I take a bite of my pizza, the cheese burning the inside of my mouth, and try to think of something happy to tell her. "A friend of mine came over after school. It was fun."

"That's good." A watchful look comes onto her face.

I know she's going to tell me not to get too attached. I plunge in before she can. "Mom—"

"What is it, honey?"

"Did Dad ever teach you how to defend against other Paranormals' attacks? Or how to counter them?"

Mom drops her half-eaten pizza slice. "Did someone attack you?"

"No," I say, keeping my face as neutral as I can. *He attacked Alex. I don't know for sure that Daniel attacked me. Yeah, right.*

Mom's gazing at me intensely, as if she stares at me hard enough, she'll be able to hear what I'm thinking again.

I take another bite of pizza, knowing I have to tell her something. I chew slowly, swallow. "I want to stop running, Mom. If we could just stand up to the Government Paras, maybe we wouldn't have to keep running."

"Oh, Caitlyn." Mom reaches for my hand. "I know it's been rough on you. I never wanted to bring you up like this. But you know it's not safe to engage with them. They'll know exactly where you are."

"Unless I cloak myself with a shield of positive energy," I say. "Dad taught me that once. Before the riots."

Mom's face seems to get thinner. "That was to protect

you from Normals. There weren't Government Paranormals back then, and there weren't hunters. Another Paranormal can sense you right through the energy. No, you'd have to hide your thoughts, the ones that identify you as you."

That's what I instinctively did with Daniel the first time I tried not to let him know that I was in his head. I hid my own pattern of thought. He only felt me when I started questioning him as me. So I can't let myself break out of his thoughts next time.

"Thanks, Mom!" I jump up and kiss her. "Gotta finish my homework."

I grab my slice of pizza and take it with me into my room. Then I lie down, stretching out to make myself comfortable, and close my eyes.

The first time I tried this, I wrapped a bit of Daniel's thought-pattern around my own. He must be expecting me to try that again. I have to do something more—I'll have to make myself "be" Daniel.

I reach for the vibrating hate that I know is him. It fills me, fogging my mind. But underneath it, I feel the Daniel I once knew and I move toward him. Suddenly I'm back at the riots, the woman pulling us from the crowd, telling us she knows we have a gift. Telling me—no, telling Caitlyn—that she'll make sure she's safe.

And then I am viewing the mob from a different angle. I am seeing myself—seeing Caitlyn's white face—and Ilene smiling down at us with her big eyes. I feel myself not trusting her, yet being drawn to her.

She touches my cheek. "I wouldn't forget you, Daniel. *I know you're special. More special than any of them.*" I stand taller, reach for her hand. The woman pulls us forward and then the mob surrounds us like a human wave, tugging at us from all angles. Caitlyn's and my hands are ripped apart and I push her hard. "Run!" I yell and grip the woman's hand to keep her with me, to keep her away from Caitlyn.

The woman's mouth tightens. Cold pain splinters through my head, making me scream. The woman drags me deeper into the crowd, toward Dad, who's standing on a milk crate, trying to calm the mob. But it's too late. I know it, and the woman knows it. But still he keeps trying. I can't breathe and don't want to look. Mom stands next to him, begging people to listen.

The woman grips me tight, pain clawing my flesh. She looks more beautiful than ever. There's something about her that draws every gaze hungrily to her even before she speaks.

"This man is a traitor!" she yells, pointing at Dad, and somehow her voice rises above the shouts and noise of the crowd, and hovers there, echoing. "This man is a Para, and he's planning on murdering you all! Murdering every one of you who is not like him!"

"No!" Dad shouts. "That's a lie! We're peaceful!"

"Run!" I want to scream at him. "Get away from her!" But it's too late. Even I can feel the pull of her thoughts, like a giant magnet, wiping out all other thoughts beyond the one that vibrates through the air. *"Kill him!"* she sends.

The mob surges forward like a tsunami, descending on Dad with bats and knives, their voices hoarse with kill-lust. Dad collapses beneath them.

"No, please!" Mom screams.

I can't bear to watch. I close my eyes as hot blood spatters my cheek. I feel the sudden emptiness as Dad leaves, feel Caitlyn's pain thread through my own. And then I feel nothing as the woman drags me forward—not one other Para in the entire world. It is a silence, a loneliness that I've never known. I wonder if this is the way Dad felt just before he died.

I gasp and sit upright, tears streaming from my eyes. "Daddy!" I scream, my voice coming out in a whisper. It's too horrible to see. But Daniel saw it all. Daniel and Mom. I sob into my pillow, trying not to let her hear. And Daniel—he was trying to save me. I never knew that. I cry until there are no tears left.

Shafts of light pierce my curtains.

It's morning already.

CHAPTER 21

I grab my dark glasses and ram them on, shutting out the blinding light. I hold my head in my hands. The way Dad died—it's horrible. How did Daniel ever stay with Ilene, let himself be trained by her after what she did? I shudder. I know he didn't have a choice, not as a child. But now? Why is he still with her now? Has he been so brainwashed by her that he truly believes she's right? Or has he become like her, to survive?

I know I should tell Mom everything. But it's become a heavy, dark secret that I cannot form into words.

Mom's already got the coffee on when I come out, the cream of wheat bubbling on the hotplate, the chunks of apple cut up, the brown sugar set out on the dresser top. No matter where we are, what new place we've come to, she tries to give me a sense of home.

My throat tightens.

I watch her from the doorway. There are deep shadows under her eyes, and her hair looks untidy—like maybe she didn't sleep well either.

I try to draw calmness to me, then walk in.

Mom tousles my hair. "Well, good morning!"

Nothing comes from inside her—no happy thoughts, no turmoil or exhaustion, not even her love wrapped around me, warmer than a hug. I can't believe I still look for it.

"Morning." I pour myself half a mug of coffee under her frowning gaze, fill the rest of the mug with milk and a spoonful of sugar.

Mom sets a steaming bowl of cereal down in front of me, then sits across from me, her face not giving away how she's feeling. She never used to shut me out before Dad died.

I pick up my spoon. Maybe that's why Mr. Temple can shut me out—some hidden trauma. But if that was true, half the world would be able to shut me out. And I've rarely met anyone who can.

"You going to eat that or let it congeal?" Mom asks.

"Eat it." I pinch some brown sugar and sprinkle it on my cereal, the golden brown grains sticking to my fingers. I lick them clean, the sweetness melting against my tongue.

Mom takes a sip of her coffee, then sits there cupping her mug in both hands as if she's cold. "You cried out in your sleep again."

I brush at my fingers.

Say it. Just say it. "I dreamed about Dad. About the riots. There was a woman who led the mob, wasn't there?"

Mom sets down her mug unsteadily, coffee sloshing onto the dresser top. "Why would you bring that up?" Her eyes grow shiny with unspilled tears and her nose reddens.

She presses her fingers against her lips, like she's holding something in. Hiding something. But then, so am I.

I shove a spoonful of steaming cereal into my mouth. "Hot hot hot!" I cry, fanning myself.

Mom jumps up and pours me a glass of cold orange juice. "Here."

I gulp it down.

"I don't know why you do that." She shakes her head at me.

I do. *Distraction*.

Mom smoothes back my hair. There is nothing, not even a wisp of emotion through her touch—just a nothing-ness that divides us.

I don't know how Normals do it. How they trust each other, understand each other without truly *being* with each other.

Mom's hand leaves my head. She moves back to the dresser and cuts open two pitas, her movements brisk and stiff. She always keeps busy, never gives herself time to feel.

"Mom—"

She turns to look at me. "What is it, Caitlyn?"

"I . . ." *I wish you'd let me in. Wish you'd talk about Dad. Wish you'd tell me everything will be all right.*

"I love you," I say.

"Honey, I love you, too." Her hand hovers over the pitas. "Is something wrong? Do you think someone's sensed you?"

One more little lie won't hurt. "No."

"Good." Mom turns back to the counter and wraps our

pita sandwiches in plastic wrap. She puts one in a reusable lunch bag for each of us, then adds little packs of apple-sauce, carrots, and molasses-sweetened cookies.

I could do all that myself on the days I don't eat at the grill, but whenever I suggest it, she acts like I'm taking something away from her. And maybe I would be. Maybe this is her way of telling me she loves me.

Mom turns around, wiping her hands on a dish towel. "I'm sorry. I didn't mean to shut you out. That was just such a horrible day. I try not to think about it."

"I know."

"Yes," Mom says softly. "You do."

I try to connect with her, but I bounce right off her mind.

Mom rubs her forehead, frowning. "I have this weird feeling—"

"Yeah?" I look at her eagerly.

She shakes her head. "It's probably nothing. I don't have anything to base it on. But I can't shake the feeling that we're being watched."

I grow still.

Somehow she knows about Daniel. Has he been watching her, too?

I have to tell her. "Mom—"

"Look at the time! You're going to be late for school. And I'll be late for work." She kisses me on the cheek. "If you need me, call."

With my disposable cell phone so that no one can trace us. But I shouldn't have to call her.

I half turn away so she can't see my eyes. "I will."

I pass the bakery where Paul lived. It's still closed up, the windows darkened, the building with a deserted, unused feeling to it, yellow police tape over the door. I hope Paul's okay, wherever he is. Hope his family is, too.

The closer I get to school, the tighter the skin feels around my head. I get that sick, weak feeling again as my natural barriers break apart and people's thoughts grow to a roar. But this time I'm prepared. I pull white light around me, imagining it as a barrier.

The tension and pain recede, the thoughts retreating back to a normal level. I get past the ParaTrooper and make my way to my locker, wondering if Daniel's watching me, waiting for me to join his side—or if he's watching Alex or Rachel. I swallow dryly.

Rachel's at my locker talking to another girl, their heads almost touching. There's an excitement in them both, barely contained, and a tension spiraling upward. They are entranced in each other, drawn in on every level. I hesitate, and the girl facing me notices me, nudges Rachel. Rachel turns around, her face flushed. "Caitlyn!" Her eyes sparkle, and her voice has a breathless quality to it. "This is Emily. Emily, Caitlyn."

I see the way Emily's touching Rachel's arm, can feel how much Rachel wants to kiss Emily's hand, her neck, her lips, and I grin. "Hey."

"I should get to class," Emily says. "Nice meeting you, Caitlyn. Rachel's told me all about you." She rushes off.

I look at Rachel, eyebrows raised.

"Nothing secret, I swear," she says quickly.

"I know." I grin wider. My head aches again, the skin around my eyes too tight, but for a moment, watching Rachel and Emily, I barely noticed it.

Rachel waits impatiently. "So?" she bursts out.

"So?" I say, as if puzzled, laughter bubbling up inside me.

"So what did you think of her?" Rachel leans closer to me. "And what did you pick up?"

"She likes you, full out. She's as excited about you as you are about her. I like her."

Rachel laughs and hugs me. "Thank you!"

The bell rings. I fiddle with my lock, taking out some books, then slam my locker shut. "Later!" I rush to math class.

Away from Rachel and her excited happiness, my headache gets stronger. Even my teeth hurt. I slouch into my desk and pull out my binder. Seeing Rachel and Emily reminds me of Daniel and Ilene—only there's no cleanness in Daniel and Ilene's relationship, no lightness, just a twisted, jagged energy.

The quiet, stealthy way Daniel and Ilene managed to mind-speak—outside of even my awareness—scares me. There's more he's not telling me. Something he knows would put me off. I've got to find out what.

The math problems on the smartboard swim in front of my eyes. I can't make sense of them. I stare at the board, letting my eyes unfocus, and go inward. I remember Daniel's and Ilene's whispering voices, the feel of their energy before they bounced me out. I pull myself there, layer by layer—past the surface thoughts, the emotion, the consciousness, to the private plane I felt them on. Reach for the vibration that is Daniel.

"They have no idea what's coming."

"I can't wait for it to happen," Ilene's higher, sharper mind-voice sends eagerly.

"We'll cleanse the earth."

I pull out, fast. They're talking about murdering every single Normal. How can I possibly stop this? I'm just one person. . . .

I think of all the Normals who've helped us, who've been kind when they didn't have to be—Netta, Mrs. Vespa, Alex, and Rachel, and so many others. I can't let them die.

CHAPTER **22**

I've got to convince Daniel to rethink this. To feel. *"Daniel,"* I send. *"Don't do this. You are not like Ilene. You're not a murderer."*

"Ah. You eavesdropped on us, did you? I should have known you'd find a way. You're like me. Powerful."

"I'm nothing like you—not if you're going to kill. Daniel, please—you can stop this."

"I don't get it," Daniel sends. The classroom disappears from around me as his rage fills my head. *"Why are you wasting your time on Normals who'd hate you if they knew you?"*

"Daniel, what happened to you? Where did all this hate come from?"

He doesn't respond. I feel him sifting through my memories, trying to find my most vulnerable places. Things he can use to manipulate me.

I shove him out of my head and slam a barrier up around me as hard as I can. I feel bereft, like I've lost him all over again. And maybe I have. Maybe the Daniel I remember—the Daniel I feel deep inside him—doesn't exist anymore. Not enough of him, anyway, to make a difference. I hug my arms around myself.

I keep up my barrier the entire day. I can't afford to let Daniel find a way to hurt me. But the barrier takes effort; after an hour I feel even more tired than when I woke up. By lunchtime I have a headache so bad I want to cut my head open to ease the pain. By the last bell, I've had three nosebleeds and so much pain in my head that it's hard to focus.

I can't keep this up.

◉

Alex is waiting for me at my locker after the last bell. "I feel like I haven't seen you all day."

"Me either." He pulls me close. I breathe in his sweetness, and the pain in my head lessens, then eases all together. I relax for the first time today. That has to mean something, doesn't it? That we're meant to be together?

I smile into his eyes and kiss him gently. Someone clears their throat.

We jump apart and Mr. Temple's standing there, looking cold and menacing. "The hallway is not your personal make-out spot," he says crisply. "Move along."

"Sorry," I say, my face heating up. I don't know why I'm apologizing.

"Come on," Alex says, grabbing my hand. "I'll walk you home."

We walk together through the streets, the sun shining down on us, my head hardly hurting any more. Somehow the day doesn't seem so awful now, the ParaTroopers not so intimidating.

When we reach the motel, Alex holds me tight. He doesn't want to let me go; I can feel it. It's such a high to know he wants me as much as I want him.

"You want to come up for a bit?" I ask, trying not to feel embarrassed about the dingy motel. "My mom won't be back yet."

Alex strokes my cheek, and I lean into his touch. "Sounds good."

The motel owner swings open the door before we even reach it, her eyes taking us in. Alex's hand tightens on mine.

"This your boyfriend?" the woman asks abruptly.

"I—uh—"

"Yes," Alex says firmly.

The woman looks him up and down, like she's measuring his worth. She turns to me. "Looks like you picked a good one. Not like my Henry. Good fer you." She squints at me. "Does yer mom know you're bringing him back here?"

"She won't mind," I say in a rush, though I'm not sure that's true.

The motel owner raises her eyebrow. "Guess that's not fer me to say. Just don't be getting up to any hanky panky upstairs. I don't want no trouble here."

My face heats up like an oven. "No, we just—"

"Ah, go on with you!" the woman says, pushing us toward the elevator. She's obviously recovered from her shame at me seeing her broken and sobbing. I wonder if she's trying to get some feeling of power back.

I tug Alex past her and we step into the elevator, the doors closing behind us. Alex looks at me on the ride up, wagging his eyebrows. *"Hanky panky?"* he asks, and then we're both laughing. Alex kisses me again, catching me mid laugh, and suddenly I'm all serious, wanting more. I fumble with the lock on the door as Alex breathes into my ear, his warm breath sending shivers through me, making it hard to concentrate.

"Stop it!" I swat him, but I don't really mean it.

I push open the door—and Mom's standing there, looking awkward. "Mom! Hi. Mom, this is Alex. Alex, this is my mom."

"Hi, Mrs. Ellis, good to meet you," Alex says, holding out his broad hand.

Mom smiles at him. "Why don't you have a seat in there? Caitlyn will be with you in a minute."

"Sure—uh—I'll be right in here." *"Now we're in for it."*

Mom pulls me into my room, closing the door, her face creased with worry. "I had a feeling I should come home early."

A feeling?

"It's a mom thing," she says quickly. "Listen, Caitlyn—I'm glad you're happy. But don't let yourself get too attached. You know it will only hurt more when we leave."

"Why do we have to move again? Some Paras never do."

"Some Paras aren't so powerful as you. They're not so visible. You wouldn't have any kind of life if they took you in."

I look away. I know she's right. Being tracked everywhere I go, electroshock when I don't do something well enough or fast enough for my trooper, and being forced to turn on my own kind.

Mom brushes my hair out of my face. "I know it's hard, sweetheart, but I think you should pull back. It'd be kinder to him; he obviously likes you. And I don't want to see your heart get broken."

"I know. I know! Okay?" I step toward the door, wanting the conversation to be over.

Mom sighs. After a moment, she reaches around me and opens the door, and I start back toward Alex.

I don't want to have to distance myself from him. I don't want to have to leave Alex at all. Right now, I don't want to be a Para.

◉

Alex and I sit stiffly beside each other until Mom takes pity on us. "Why don't you two go to Caitlyn's room? You'll be more comfortable there."

I grab Alex's hand and drag him into my room, shutting the door.

"Leave the door open!" Mom calls.

I open the door a crack, grinning at Alex.

Alex rubs his neck. "That was awkward, wasn't it?"

"Yeah."

"Your mom's pretty cool. Mine would never let me go into a bedroom with a girl, even if the door was open."

"It's not like we have anything else here but bedrooms," I say, laughing. I sober up. "It's not cool, though. She doesn't want me to get attached to you, because we might have to run."

"She's trying to look out for you. She doesn't want you to get hurt."

"She can't stop it! If we have to run—" I feel like I'm inhaling mud. "I can't stand it."

"I won't be able to stand it either."

Alex pulls me down onto the bed with him. He traces his fingers over my face, my lips, watching me intently, like he's trying to memorize my face.

Tears prick my eyes.

Alex kisses my eyelids gently, then my cheeks. "We have to keep your brother from turning you in. And we have to keep you off of Mr. Temple's radar. Maybe if we do that, you won't have to leave."

I clasp his face in my hands and try not to cry. I can't believe how much Alex cares about me. How much he's willing to risk. I kiss his soft, full lips. I feel so safe with Alex—deeper than a childhood safe. A belonging safe. A rightness I've never felt before. I breathe in his smell.

I kiss him again, and then I am lost in our kissing, in the shivery sweetness of it. We kiss harder, faster, and I press myself against him, feeling him against me.

"Caitlyn," he whispers.

I want to feel his body, and the weight of him. I roll over, pulling him with me.

"Your mother!" Alex hisses.

"I don't care!"

Sweat clings to his forehead. I pull him closer and we roll again—right off the bed with a thump.

I snort back my laughter.

"Everything okay in there?" Mom calls, her voice getting louder, like she's walking toward us.

We leap up.

I run my hands through my hair, tug on my shirt to straighten it. "Everything's fine, Mom! Really." *Don't come in, don't come in . . .*

Her footsteps pause outside. The door opens. Mom pokes her head in. "Nothing broken?"

I roll my eyes. "We're okay."

Sweat rolls down Alex's cheek.

"All right. But Alex should be going home soon. You kids have school tomorrow."

"Yes, ma'am," Alex says, his voice strangled.

Mom nods rigidly, then leaves.

Alex and I look at each other. And then we're laughing, shh-ing each other, but our laughter only gets louder. I laugh until my stomach aches, but it's a good feeling, a release.

"I should get going," Alex says, glancing at my door.

I swallow another laugh. "See you tomorrow?"

"Count on it." Alex's eyes look darker, bigger, somehow. . . *don't want to go . . .*

I walk with him to the motel room door.

"Good night, Mrs. Ellis," he calls.

"Good night, Alex," Mom says, so close we jump.

Alex rushes out the doorway. I watch him until the elevator doors close. I see him like a snapshot, framed by the elevator, his gaze never leaving mine—like he, too, knows we might not have much time together.

Sadness clogs my throat and I turn to see Mom standing behind me, her lips pressed together so tight they almost disappear.

"I've got homework," I say, and edge around her.

Mom puts her hand on my arm. "Caitlyn—be careful."

I can't look at her. Was she careful when she was dating Dad?

"Cait—"

"Don't you even remember what it felt like to love Dad?" I shout. I run into my room and slam the door. I don't respond when she knocks. I can't; I'm too angry.

◉

In the morning, Mom's waiting for me, the cereal all laid out on the dresser we sit at, my bowl covered with my plate to keep it warm. I pour myself half a cup of coffee, topping it up with milk, and this time she doesn't even glance at it.

"I'm sorry about last night. But Caitlyn—you know we'll be going on the run again."

"Why? Why do we have to?" I shout, but I know why. Because of me! Because of my stupid talent. "I don't want it anymore!" I yell, pushing back my chair. "I hate this life. Tell me how to get rid of it, like you did. Then we can just be two happy Normals who never have to move. And who talk and lie to each other with words."

"Caitlyn!" Mom's eyes widen, her face blanching. "I

didn't get rid of my talent. And you shouldn't try to; it feels like I'm missing a lung."

I sit back. "But you never mind-speak to me! I never sense anything from you at all, not even like I would from a Normal. It's worse than living with a Normal; it's so lonely I can't stand it."

"I didn't realize what it was like for you. But I should have," Mom says softly. She grabs my hand. "I'm not shutting you out on purpose. I think my ability is still there; sometimes I can almost feel it. But I can't get to it, not even a little. It's been that way from the moment your dad died."

"Oh," I say. She's not trying to distance herself from me at all, or trying to become a Normal. I think about what I saw in Daniel's memory, of how she saw Dad die, how she stood right beside him trying to stop it, and I shudder. Maybe trauma *can* do that to a person—push everything vital so far down that it can't be reached.

"I'm sorry," I say, feeling sick and hot. All these years I felt rejected by her, felt so much anger toward her, and she wasn't doing it on purpose. If only we'd talked. "I didn't mean—"

"No, *I'm* sorry, Cait," Mom says, reaching for my hand. "I'm sorry you felt so alone. Sorry I've leaned on you so much for what I'm missing. I love you just as much as I always have—maybe even more."

My lips quiver, though I fight to hold them still. "I love you, too," I whisper. And I do.

Mom kisses my forehead, smoothing back my hair. "I know you do." She hesitates. "Caitlyn—I want you to be extra careful today. I keep feeling like something bad's going to happen."

My stomach knots. I push my cereal away. Maybe she's wrong. Maybe her precognition really is coming back. But if it was, surely I would feel it. I glare at my cereal. Is this a warning I should be listening to or not?

◉

I slow down when I near the bakery where Paul and his family used to live. The yellow police tape is gone now, but there's a government FOR SALE sign on the door. They're going to profit from Paul's family fleeing and pocket the money to fund more anti-Para activities. I grind my teeth. At least Paul's mother and grandfather are free. And maybe, somehow, Paul will find a way to escape. Though I know I'm only telling myself that to feel better.

I'm almost used to the school ParaTrooper by now, but I know that's stupid of me. He still pulls students aside every day—and a few of them have been Paras. I shove at him with my mind when he questions me, telling him to overlook me—but the other Paras, they can't do that. I swallow my heavy guilt and step through the gate.

Alex is waiting for me at my locker. "You okay?"

I lean into him, glad for the closeness of it, and he wraps his arms around me. "Aside from knowing my brother's planning a rebellion? Sure."

"Talk to him again," Alex says. "See if you can reason with him."

But I know he won't listen.

"Hey, you two. Bell's about to ring," Rachel says from behind me.

I reluctantly pull away from Alex and turn around. "Be careful, okay? Watch out for Daniel, both of you."

"I will. Quit worrying," Alex says. "He's not going to come after me again. That'd be too obvious."

He doesn't know Daniel.

"We'll be careful," Rachel says.

Emily strides up to Rachel and reaches for her hand. Rachel's face lights up.

"What will you be careful of?" Emily asks.

"Careful to . . . watch out for homophobes," Rachel says.

"But why . . . ?" Emily scrunches up her nose as she looks at me and Alex, then back at Rachel.

"Didn't I tell you how Caitlyn put that homophobe Becca in her place in front of all her peeps?"

"Yeah!" Emily beams at me. "You were super."

I shake my head. "Rachel's helped me lots of times, too. Without her, I would've been lost my first few days here."

Emily tilts her head, looks at me seriously. "Not everyone would do what you did, you know. Stand up for us. Most people look the other way or join in."

The way people do to Paras. But I can't say that.

The loudspeaker crackles. "Attention students. You'll be happy to know that our resident ParaTrooper, Mr. White, has caught three more Paras. We now have the highest catch rate in the country! We are safer because of him."

Rachel's face pales. Alex squeezes my arm, empathy

and worry for me in his touch. I jerk away, not wanting to fall apart where people can see me and put it together.

"Caitlyn—"

"No! Leave me alone!" I break away from them. "Gotta get to class." I yank out my phone. Anyone sees me, they'll probably think I'm texting the good news. I log onto my anonymizer, then to my blog. "People you know are getting taken away. Your neighbors, your friends, your family. Are you really going to let this happen? Yes, *you!* You can make a difference. Speak out before it's too late."

◉

First period, Ms. Edwards's class. I approach the room slowly. Mr. Temple's at the front, the wall in shadow behind him. Students sit quietly, not laughing or talking, their backs straight against their chairs, their heads bowed. What is Mr. Temple doing here? And why is everyone so quiet? It feels wrong—worse than yesterday.

Do the others really care about Paras? Or are they just scared that an avid ParaWatch member will mistakenly finger them?

I open myself up to the room. People are starting to feel uneasy. Many of them never knew an illegal Para, never saw someone they knew be taken away until the last few days. But that's not the only uneasiness. There's something more—some feeling of danger.

Do I go in and pretend everything's all right? I peek in again. I recognize the back of that blond head, sitting right behind my chair—Daniel.

Mr. Temple looks up sharply. His mouth smiles, but his eyes stay cold. He gestures to the video camera sitting on his desk. It's pointed at me, its red light steady and unblinking.

I walk slowly down the aisle to my seat. Mr. Temple repositions the camera so that I'm caught in its view.

"Caitlyn, be careful!" Rachel thinks at me.

"Ah, how touching. One of your little Normal friends wants to protect you," Daniel sends. *"At least until her life is threatened. Or her family's."*

"Sir, is that a video camera?" Rachel asks, her voice barely polite.

"Yes, Rachel, it is," Mr. Temple says. "Each row will be taped for several weeks this term." His gaze fastens on mine. "It's a new *experimental* method of teaching, one that I hope will bring results."

My skin tightens. Mr. Temple's not even bothering to hide his suspicions about me. But it looks like he won't finger me and risk the fine without getting proof. It almost makes me want to laugh. It's not like my talent can show up on camera. What does he think he's going to catch?

"Isn't that against our constitutional rights?" a boy asks. "Don't you have to get our permission—*sir*—before taping us?"

I beam at the boy. He reminds me of Paul. An undercurrent of rebellion fills the room, laced with a growing sympathy for what Paras go through. I sit up straighter.

"It's just a few brave words in a classroom. Don't fool yourself. You should align yourself with your true allies. There's still time to join us."

I don't respond.

"You are just as stubborn as Dad was!"

Mr. Temple steeples his fingers together, looking down his nose at the boy who spoke. "Of course it's not an infringement of your rights, not when it's part of an educational program. Now take out your textbooks and read chapter forty-two, then complete the assignment at the end."

"But sir—you're not going to keep teaching Ms. Edwards's class, are you?" the girl next to me says, chewing on the ends of her hair. "I mean, I know you said she was out sick, but usually we get a sub." . . . *don't think I can stand being taught much longer by a toad like you . . . not that you're actually teaching us anything . . .*

Laughter bubbles up inside me. I bite the inside of my cheek, try to keep my face blank.

Mr. Temple taps his pen against the edge of his desk. "Yes, I will continue to teach you until Ms. Edwards is feeling well enough to resume her duties." He looks at me, the corners of his mouth turning upward, his cheeks barely moving. "Though I don't think it will be for quite a while."

"Oh, maaaan," someone groans.

"Enough! Open your textbooks and read silently."

The girl next to me slaps her books onto her desk.

I open my textbook and stare at the page, moving my gaze across the words but not taking them in.

I don't like the way Mr. Temple answered the question, as if it was a private joke between the two of us. Having Mr. Temple so close to me makes me uneasy—like having a razorblade in my pocket. One wrong move, and the blood could be mine.

I glance up at Mr. Temple. He's watching me from the shadows, expressionless, like he's waiting for something.

"Para-lovers won't survive the revolution," Daniel sends urgently, his words ripping through me. His mind-voice grows louder than the roar of a train. *"We're the only ones who can help you. Don't throw it away, Caitlyn!"*

Pain splinters through my head, gouging into my eyes.

I stare blindly at the page and visualize an invisible shield of light enclosing my mind, separating me from Daniel.

"You can try to shut me out, but I know you can still hear me. I hate this—but if you won't join me, I'll let them destroy you. Your Normal friends won't try to protect you; they'll be too scared."

"You can't just kill people because they're afraid."

"I can't let them enslave and kill us anymore. I don't understand how you can. But maybe you don't know the hell it is because you haven't lived it."

Pain explodes through my head, as if someone threw a handful of marbles at my exposed brain.

I reach for Daniel, but he's not trying to hurt me, not right now. He really is trying to convince me to join his side.

I scowl at my textbook. I've been reading the same sentence over and over. But it's hard to care about social studies when my world is falling apart.

Mr. Temple steps out of the shadows, his dark gaze on me. I stare at the page until my vision blurs.

My head is pounding, bright pain behind my eyes.

I have to figure out what Daniel is up to. How he plans on killing Normals. If the pain is coming from him . . . if he's hurting someone now . . .

I reach out toward him again. Rage and fear roar like a tornado. But not pain.

I yank away. The pain and pressure keep getting worse. I get that full feeling that comes before a nosebleed. I have to make the pain stop.

I press my fingers to my temples. My scalp is hot, itchy with sweat, the pain so bad it feels like my head will explode.

Terror nips at the edges of my mind.

I shove it away, but it comes back stronger. It's not Daniel; I am sure of it. He's not this afraid.

I let down my shield. Screams rush in, and a burst of heat engulfs me. There's a crackling, roaring sound as the heat licks at me.

Fire! Someone's trapped in a fire!

CHAPTER **23**

My pen skids across the page.

Mr. Temple steps toward me.

I drop my textbook on the floor, then bend down to pick it up, shielding my face from Mr. Temple.

"Something wrong?" Daniel sends, his voice mocking.

The screams are so loud I can barely concentrate. My throat tightens as if the terror is my own.

People are trapped, right here in this school. And they're going to die if someone doesn't save them.

They cry for help with every atom of their panic-crazed minds. Their fear gives them a volume that's piercing.

I have to force myself to stay in my seat, to not rush out to find them. The camera is still recording, and I can feel Daniel and Mr. Temple waiting for me to break. I have to find another way to save the students. And I have to hurry.

Mr. Temple walks down the aisle, coming to a stop beside me. "Are you feeling all right, Ms. Ellis?"

I look right back at him. "I'm fine."

"You seem to be sweating."

"Something I ate."

"Ah." Mr. Temple smiles a thin smile. "Do you need to be excused?" His excitement crackles through me like electricity, sharp and painful.

It's the perfect excuse for me to slip away—but it feels wrong.

Mr. Temple knows about the fire, I'm sure of it. Maybe he even wants to use it to prove that I'm a Para. That I sensed something.

"No, thank you, sir," I say.

Mr. Temple looks disappointed. "Then get back to work." He stands there until I start writing out the assignment. Then he walks to the front of the room.

I'm shaking all over now, the panic so bad it's a struggle to breathe. I force myself to draw air into my lungs, then pull up a feeling of calm. I direct it toward the fear, honing in on one person, trying to make my thought-voice sound like theirs. *"I have to stay calm. Where am I?"*

. . . the auditorium . . . drama class is always here . . . Mr. Michaels, he said . . . but the fire . . . it's too late now . . . we're all going to die . . .

"No, we're not. Someone will hear us—"

. . . no one will hear us! . . . too far from the other classrooms . . . Tom's been hammering on that door . . . no one comes . . . our cells can't get a signal . . . please god, help me and I'll be a better person, I swear . . . I don't want to die . . . it's too soon, I'm not ready! I only just found someone I love! And we haven't even . . .

I break contact. The voice—it felt familiar. Emily's voice. Rachel's Emily. I shudder.

Two boys are snickering behind me. I want to scream at them—"Don't you know people could die?" But of course they don't—how could they?

Pens scratch against paper, keyboard keys click. The wall clock ticks loudly, counting out each second.

Sweat beads on my forehead. I don't know what to do. I can't help anyone if the ParaTroopers take me away. But asking Alex and Rachel to help means putting them in danger.

I smell burning hair.

I reach out to Alex and Rachel. *"The auditorium's on fire—people are trapped inside. Will you help? It could mean people suspect you—"*

"I'm in," Alex thinks at me. *"Just tell me what to do."*

"Of course I'll help," Rachel adds. *"Wait, the auditorium? But that's where Emily has drama!"* Panic fills her.

"She's there. She's okay so far. But if you're going to help her, you need to stay calm, okay, Rachel? You need to get out of class. Rachel, pull the fire alarm. Alex, run as fast as you can to the auditorium. Something's blocking the doors. I'll meet you there."

My vision blurs, white spots dancing in front of me.

I squeeze my eyes shut, focus on the kids in the auditorium. Heat beats at my body, pressing me down.

"Mr. Temple? Mr. Temple?" Rachel waves her hand wildly.

Mr. Temple frowns at her. "Yes, Ms. Levy?"

"I need to be excused. Got to go to the bathroom."

Mr. Temple sighs. "Now, right this minute? Is it really that urgent? You can't hold it for another thirty minutes?"

"No, sir."

Mr. Temple shakes his head, muttering under his breath.

Rachel makes a tiny whimpering sound.

"All right, go," Mr. Temple says, turning his back on her.

"Thank you, sir." Rachel rushes out of the room.

Mr. Temple's staring at me again.

I scribble words in my notebook, not caring if they don't make sense, just wanting to look like I'm writing.

The seconds tick by, agonizingly slowly.

My lungs feel clogged with smoke. I cough, deep and hard.

"Something troubling you?" Daniel sends.

"Daniel! They're people, just like you and me. Help them!"

"Help who? I don't hear anyone."

I stifle my coughing. Come on, Rachel! What's taking so long?

The heat is almost unbearable, flames licking against my skin. I *have* to free them.

I grab my books—

The fire alarm clangs, piercingly loud.

Students cheer and jump up, scraping back chairs and scattering desks.

Mr. Temple's lips tighten into a thin line. "Get up quietly, class, and walk to the door in an orderly manner. You are high school students, not kindergarteners."

I push my way into the lineup.

Daniel hovers behind me like a shadow.

Mr. Temple looks at me hard as he passes us. "Daniel, stay close to Ms. Ellis, please. She may need assistance." He grips the doorknob. "All right, class, you may exit!" he shouts. "Stick together now."

He opens the door, and we stumble out, the clanging louder. The hall surges with students, most of them excited to be missing class. I blink sweat out of my eyes.

Daniel grips my arm, his mouth tight and grim. *"You know what you have to do to make this stop."*

I jerk my arm out of his grasp.

I have to lose him, fast.

CHAPTER **24**

I plunge into the crush of students surging forward.

*. . . got outta that test . . . look on Mrs. Emerson's face
. . . is it real? . . .*

The hall seems to narrow and shift before my eyes, the
insistent shrill of the bell drilling through my skull. I dodge
ahead, but Daniel jerks me back like our wrists are cuffed
together, his rage so bright it almost blinds me.

"I'm not going to let you save them."

I slam a shield around myself, dampening the intensity of his thoughts and the students around me, but not
shutting them out. I have to listen for the others.

"Hurry!" I urge the crowd in front of me. They're too
slow.

The screams pull me down the hall.

How can they not hear them? I squeeze past people
like a minnow darting between fingers. Daniel squeezes
right behind me.

"You're not going to lose me," Daniel shouts in my
ear. *"I'm sorry, but that's the way it is."*

My heart aches. *"Daniel—let them go. They did nothing to you."*

"Maybe not yet—but they will. And some have already turned us in. Why can't you see it?" His mind-voice almost pleads with me.

I try to make him forget, but I am being buffeted from all sides. The clogged, sooty feeling fills my chest, choking the air away. My breath comes in tiny, rasping gasps.

Why haven't Alex and Rachel let them out? *"Alex—"*

"It's locked! We can't get it open!"

"The key—it's not in the office!" Rachel sobs.

Daniel. Of course.

Punishing me. Showing me how powerful he is. Or setting an elaborate trap for me.

But I can't let people die. Not even Normals. *"I'll be there as fast as I can."*

I look at Daniel. As powerful as he is, he still has the weakness that every guy has. *"I'm sorry, Daniel,"* I send, even as I bring my knee up hard to his crotch.

I don't wait to see him double over. I push past people, ignoring the angry grunts, the bombardment of thoughts. I race down the stairwell, not caring who I bump against, just knowing I have to get there.

The cries are more desperate now, urging me on, the aching feeling of smoke in my lungs making it hard to breathe.

I reach out as I run, try to touch all the frightened voices at once. "Get down on the ground, facedown. Get yourself away from the smoke."

Their terror almost stops me moving. Blackness blurs the edges of my vision.

I force my legs to keep running, my lungs to keep pumping. I push past students moving in the opposite direction, trying to get out. I don't know if the trapped students listened to me or not.

It feels like it's taking forever—so many people in my way. I want to scream.

Down one more flight, then two, the acrid smell of smoke burning my nostrils, my throat, my eyes tearing up, my body sweating from the heat. My head aches, the pressure building inside my skull. People shimmer in front of me.

"Help is coming," I send, as loudly as I can. The screams lessen.

I don't need to know where the auditorium is; I'm being pulled right to it. I plunge through the students exiting and run down the hall, past the trophy cases, around the corner—

My chest aches, my breath short and heavy, but I push myself on.

There's a thump behind me, like someone landed hard.

. . . almost got her . . .

I run faster.

Daniel slams me against the wall.

Pain shudders through my bones.

"You're not getting away that easy." Daniel pushes his face close to mine, his breath like rotten eggs. "You will watch them burn, and know you could have saved them, if only you'd joined us."

"No!" I dodge to the right.

Daniel blocks me.

I try to stay calm. I can smell the smoke now, and not just through other people. It's in every breath I take. I can almost see it around us—a slight mist, blurring the door at the end of the hall. "You're more powerful than they are; they don't even have a chance. It's cruel."

Daniel used to care. I pull up a memory: Dad walking with us down the street. We hear a girl cry out; Daniel and I both feel the terror. Daniel breaks into a run toward the group of older boys crowding the girl. Dad runs after him. "Let that girl go!" he roars, as Daniel kicks one of the boy's shins. The boys turn and scatter. The girl, her blouse torn, her face dirty, bursts into tears. Daniel and I send her calm while Dad talks to her in a soothing voice. We walk the girl home.

"Those boys, they used their power over this girl. You must never use your talent to hurt people weaker than you are," Dad sends. *"That's just cruel. Understand?"* Daniel and I nod firmly. "I'm proud of you, son," Dad says, clapping Daniel on the shoulder. Daniel walks taller.

I throw the memory at Daniel.

Behind me he stumbles, off balance.

I run. The terror is subdued, now, the heavy, choking feeling like my lungs are filled with ash.

Rachel is standing outside the auditorium, tears streaming down her cheeks, her eyes reddened. She runs to me as soon as she sees me. "We can't get them out!"

I yank on the door handle. The metal burns hot.

"We tried that! What can we do?" Her voice rises in a wail.

Thick smoke pours out of the cracks around the doors.

I pound on the door. "Help is coming!"

Alex runs up, a crowbar in his hand. "Maybe this'll work!" he yells over the clanging of the bell.

He wrenches the bar between the doors and yanks. The doors barely move. They're old, heavy doors, built to last.

Alex yanks the bar again. Strong as he is, the doors don't budge.

Daniel. He did this; he'll have the answer.

I grit my teeth, reaching out toward him—and feel the glee at all these weak Normals panicking, not even guessing they're just part of a larger plan. . . . *Caitlyn is doing better than even I thought she would. She is a worthy ally, one I can be proud to have by my side in the long months to come* . . .

I wrench out of his thoughts, feeling sick. But I still don't know how to open the doors. I've got to enter his mind.

I close my eyes, pull glee and power-lust around me, and enter. *"Locked the auditorium door . . ."* I fold my thoughts into his.

. . . the look on her face when she did it—like she enjoyed it as much as I did . . .

I see a flash of Ilene, her large doe eyes shining with excitement.

I leap out of his head. The people trapped in the fire are weakening, getting close to passing out. Rachel stares at me, her face drained of blood. "You can do something, can't you?" she begs.

I reach for Ilene and sense a coldness so deep it's hard to think. I dip into that low, thrumming cold, wrapping myself in it. I shudder. "After I locked the door . . ."

. . . I dropped the key in the trophy case; no one'll ever find it. Caitlyn will see that she needs us if she wants to do anything in this world. She'll see she could have avoided their deaths if only she'd asked for our help. Though why she cares about those Normals, I can't fathom . . .

I push myself off the wall, my legs suddenly weak. "The key's inside the trophy case!"

Rachel spins around and races down the hall.

I press my palm to the hot door. *"Help is coming, just hold on. Keep your faces close to the floor. Crawl to the hall exit if you can."*

Rachel comes back panting, holding out the key, her face hopeful and scared.

I jam it into the lock and turn it, tugging at the doors. They resist me, then bang open, gray smoke billowing out. The heat hits me like a kiln, searing all the moisture from my flesh.

CHAPTER **25**

Students stagger out of the auditorium, coughing and gagging, tears streaming from their eyes.

Rachel rushes in. "Emily!" she cries. "Emily, where are you?" I start forward.

Alex grabs my arm. "Get outside with everyone else. This *has* to be a setup. There's no way this door should've been locked from the outside—"

"I'm not leaving. I have to know everyone's okay." Their fear is mine now.

Alex looks at me, sees the set of my shoulders, the determination in my mouth. "Fine. Just—don't go in there."

I stand back, feeling useless as Alex rushes forward to help.

"Thank god, thank god!" a boy with a soot-blackened face says, stumbling and crying.

"We couldn't get out!" a girl wails, tears streaming down her sooty cheeks.

"You're all right now. Just get outside," I say.

Their stunned, frightened faces nod.

Rachel comes stumbling out, Emily leaning heavily on

her, both their faces black with soot. Alex follows, helping a girl who can't stop crying.

The ragged line of students dwindles. Sirens wail in the distance, getting closer.

. . . help me . . .

Someone's still trapped inside, someone who's not coming out with the others. Someone who can't!

I run back in. The heat roars at me like a hungry beast, drying my eyes, cracking the inside of my nose.

"Caitlyn, come back!" Alex calls.

I cover my nose and mouth and bend over as I rush down the aisle. A wall of flame and smoke consumes the stage, the curtains, licking toward the ceiling. The heat presses down on me, the fire roaring with hunger. My lungs clench, rebelling against the hot, thick air. I cough deeply, struggling to breathe.

I reach out toward the flickering energy. It's weak, but I can still feel it. I'm almost there. I trip over something — a shoe — and then I am dragging the man back toward the door. The flames roar louder, as if they don't want me to escape. The man is too heavy. I suck in smoke and fall to my knees, coughing raggedly.

And then Alex and Rachel are there, lifting the weight of the teacher from me, half dragging, half carrying him to the door.

The three of us carry him down the hall and out into the cool air. Students and teachers, frozen in wide-eyed clusters, turn to look.

Fire trucks roar up to the doors, lights flashing, sirens wailing. Firefighters leap out, fastening the hose to the hydrant, running into the school, coats flapping around their waists, masks dangling from their faces, oxygen tanks strapped to their backs, axes and crowbars in their hands. Shouts, then a hose is dragged into the building.

"Move back, people, away from the school," a firefighter shouts, motioning us back.

The sky is a deep brooding gray, as if it knows what happened inside.

Paramedics rush to take the teacher from us and put him on a stretcher, slap an oxygen mask onto his face.

I slip into the crowd, Alex close behind me. Rachel turns to Emily and holds her tight.

I can feel Daniel's gaze on me, the anger prickling at my scalp. *Do you really think no one will notice?"*

Mr. Temple is watching me, too, darkness pouring from him in waves.

"You all right?" Alex asks, his voice soft and urgent.

I nod.

He wraps his arms around me. I feel his heart beating against my chest, breathe in his sweet smell, still there beneath the acrid scent of the fire.

"Scared me . . ." He brushes his lips against my hair. "At least nothing bad happened. Nothing seriously bad." *"You're all right."*

"Daniel did this."

Alex's arms tighten. "Daniel."

"Yeah."

"What is he playing at?"

"Young man, we need to talk to you." A paramedic.

"Later," Alex says, not even turning to look.

"Son," the paramedic says. "Come on."

"Go." I push Alex away. His chin raises, stubbornly, and I know he's going to argue.

"It's better not to draw attention," I send firmly.

Alex sighs. "You need me, you call. Got it?"

"Yeah. Now go."

He walks away with the paramedic.

Fear and rage, as loud as a shout, punch into me. I whirl around. Mr. Temple is jabbing his finger at Daniel, his face pushed up close, his shoulders hunched furtively. He looks over his shoulder, then harshly whispers. I can't hear what he's saying, but I can feel it.

I reach for Mr. Temple's mind.

. . . But you said! . . . only Para kids at risk . . . could lose my job . . . protect Normal kids, not hurt them! . . . can't trust . . .

And then I feel the wave of Daniel's power wrapping around Mr. Temple, calming him down, making him realize that Daniel knew Caitlyn would save them, that the Normals were at no risk, that the only way to get rid of the Para-freaks is to follow Daniel's lead.

Mr. Temple's arm drops, and he blinks, then looks at Daniel and smiles blankly.

My skin ripples. I inch backward, deeper into the crowd, away from them.

People are standing in hushed clumps, faces pale and still. Some girls are crying, others are shaking. The boys look like robots that have been unplugged.

Mrs. Vespa moves through the crowd toward me. "Caitlyn—are you okay?"

"Yeah."

"Your face . . ." She motions.

I scrunch up my nose. "What about it?"

She pulls a compact out of her purse. I open it and stare. My face is covered with soot, my eyes blinking out like an owl.

"Do you have a tissue or something?"

Mrs. Vespa digs a packaged Handy Wipe out of her purse and hands it to me.

I scrub my face and hands, the white wipe becoming black, leaving streaks along my skin.

"I assume you had something to do with the rescue."

"Yeah—but don't go thinking I'm a hero." *There's a renegade Para here, with a thing against Normals. He's trying to get me to join him—by force.*

Mrs. Vespa harrumphs. *"Stay away from him. You don't want to get mixed up in that."* She touches my arm. "If there's any way I can help—and I mean any—you let me know."

My eyes tear up. "Thank you."

Mrs. Vespa squeezes my arm. *"Call to me if you need me,"* she thinks at me, waiting until I nod to show her I heard her. Then she slips back into the crowd.

A hand clenches my shoulder from behind and I stifle a scream.

"Where do you think you're going?" Daniel says.

I didn't sense him behind me until he touched me. How can that be? I turn, slowly.

His face is smooth as a mask, but a muscle twitches in

his square jaw. His faded blue eyes are almost gray, like dirty cement. I can't see into them.

"I'm going home. Mom—she'll be worried. She'll have heard about the fire on the news."

Daniel looks over his shoulder.

Mr. Temple starts toward us, as if beckoned. "No student is allowed to leave the school property without parental consent."

Shit. Shit. Shit.

I reach out to Mom as hard as I can. *"Mom, I need you to come pick me up—right now. At school."*

I can't sense her. I don't even know if she's heard me; she's been cut off from me for so long, I can't tell. I reach for my cell, but it's gone.

The school trooper comes to join us, and behind him, another trooper. One I've never seen before, pulling a Para-Controller out of his breast pocket.

"My appendage. My handler." Daniel curves his lips into a predatory smile, his bone white teeth gleaming.

"Don't go anywhere. Those reporters are going to want to talk to you," Daniel says.

I glance at the TV and radio vans pulling into the parking lot, the reporters and crew spilling out. Car doors slam, cameras are hefted onto shoulders.

"Why are you doing this?" I send. *"You know I can out you just as easily as you can out me."*

"I'm already in their servitude; what difference would that make? The reason they put me undercover here was to catch you." Daniel shakes his head with a fake-sad

smile. *"Come, now—I thought you liked Normals. I thought they were your friends."*

"Why would the reporters want to talk to me? I didn't do anything," I say.

"Oh, no?" Mr. Temple arches one eyebrow and stares pointedly at the traces of soot on my hands.

My chest is too tight. I cough. "It was another student—two of them, actually—who are the heroes. I just tagged along."

I send this to Rachel and Alex.

"That's bullshit," Daniel says, too loudly.

People turn to look.

"Daniel—"

"I saw you in there," Daniel says, his face impassive, his eyes bright.

People gather around. . . . *saved us . . . what's happening? . . .*

I have to stop this. But I don't know how. I'm too tired to think it through. Even my brain feels mired in soot.

"I'm right here, Caitlyn. Tell me what to do and I'll do it," Alex thinks at me.

"Stay close."

I reach out to Daniel, sending waves of confusion, but I am too late.

"She's the one who got them to unlock the auditorium door," Daniel says, pointing at me. "She went straight to the fire before anyone even knew there was one. And that was from three floors up. It's like she knew what would happen—before it did."

My hands grow cold, even though my skin's burning.

Daniel's eyes open, falsely wide. "Maybe she's the one who set it. Unless—"

The school ParaTrooper looks back and forth between us. Daniel's trooper rests his hand on his gun and keeps looking between Daniel and me and the ParaController in his hand.

Daniel's about to say I'm a Para. I open my mouth but nothing comes out.

Alex bursts through the ring of people, knocking into Daniel. "Caitlyn is the last person who'd do that! I think that's more your kind of thing. Setting people up like that." He puts his arm around my shoulders.

A reporter strides toward us like she smells a story, the camera operator close behind.

Daniel's trooper turns to him. "Fallon, have you got something to tell me?"

That's not our last name! So Daniel did try to protect us, once upon a time.

"I don't know yet," Daniel says.

His trooper glances down at the ParaController, then shrugs.

"You see how good I am?" Daniel smiles at me. *"I can fool even my own handler when I want to. I don't think there's another Para who has the talent to do that. Except maybe you."*

Rachel shoves through the crowd to stand on my other side, with Emily close behind her. "I'm the one who pulled the fire alarm."

"Then how did Caitlyn know where the fire was?" Daniel asks, triumphantly.

Everyone's looking at me. I turn so the reporter can't see my face, and lower my voice an octave. "I could smell it." *"Come get me, Mom! Now!"*

"So could I. That's why I pulled the alarm," Rachel says, her voice rising.

Mr. Temple turns his head sharply toward Daniel, like he's listening to something no one else can hear. Then he looks at Rachel. "And your classroom was on *what* floor?"

"The fourth," Rachel says miserably, squeezing her eyes shut. *"I'm sorry, Caitlyn."*

"It's not your fault."

"I think I'll go get checked out by a medic," I say, wiping at my forehead. "I don't feel so good."

"You stay where you are," Daniel's handler says, pulling out his gun and pointing it at me.

"Afraid the Normals will know what you really are?" Daniel sends. *"But they're your friends."*

"Can you tell me what happened here?" The reporter thrusts her microphone toward me.

"Yes, Caitlyn, do tell them. Your face will be all over the news. But you've got nothing to be afraid of, right? Normals are such reasonable people."

I shake my head.

"Answer the question," Daniel's handler growls.

The school's floor plans flash through my head. "I just know I smelled the smoke. I'm sure that if you look at the blueprints, you'll see that the auditorium vent connects to the classroom I was in."

Daniel's handler narrows his eyes.

The school trooper barks at Mr. Temple to show him the blueprints.

"Oooh, good save," Daniel sends.

The school trooper and Mr. Temple walk toward the school office while Daniel's handler watches me through slitted eyes.

"Your cries to the poor victims almost left me deaf," Daniel sends, *"And your plea to Mom gave me a splitting headache. Your talent is going to such a waste."*

"Mom, where are you?!"

Right on cue, our beaten-up car screeches to the curb. Mom runs toward the crowd of students, her hair flying behind her, her hand clutching her purse-strap with white fingers. Her eyes frantically search for me.

CHAPTER **26**

"I'm okay, Mom." I focus on sending only to her, but sending as hard as I can.

Mom's head snaps around, her gaze fastening on mine. She changes direction and strides toward me, her purse banging against her hip. "Oh, Caitlyn, I was so worried!"

"Daniel's alive! He's here. But he's turned," I send quickly, shielding my thoughts. *"His trooper's here, too. There was a fire; they know I saved the others. We have to be careful."*

I worry the shock will be too much for her, but she manages a half smile. Her gaze passes over Alex, Rachel, Emily, and the reporter, then rests on Daniel, her eyelids flickering. Mom looks at Daniel's handler, then back to me. "When I heard about the fire on the news, I came right over—"

"And what station would that be, ma'am?" Daniel asks, unsmiling, and steps forward. "Odd, isn't it, that none of the other parents are here?"

Mom's skin pales, her breath catching in her throat.

"My god," she says and I can see the restraint it takes to not say his name.

Daniel's eyes don't waver. He reaches out his hand to shake hers. "I'm Daniel Fallon. And you're *Caitlyn's* mom."

There's a low rumbling, like a monster clearing his throat, and the sky turns dark.

"That's right," Mom says, her voice wavering. "I'm Caitlyn's mom." She pulls me to her, putting her arm around me. Her eyes are caverns of pain.

I lean into her, trying to give her strength. With her beside me I can think more clearly. *"This story is going nowhere,"* I send the reporter, using my persuasion. *"There's a more interesting story going on by the stairs. Don't want to get scooped!"*

The reporter wavers, then half turns.

But Daniel clears his throat and the reporter turns back to him.

"I'm curious how the radio station got the news so soon," Daniel says, stuffing his hands in his pockets and rocking back and forth on his heels. "The reporters just got here."

"Oh, you know newscasters," Mom says, not even blinking. "Always listening in on the police scanners—and a good thing for us!" She squeezes my shoulder. "I'm going to get my daughter home. I can see she's had quite an experience. . . . I think you should get yourself home, too, young man."

Daniel gulps and I see he knows that Mom was telling

him she loves him and wants him with us. But that would mean we'd be enslaved, too. He couldn't come back to us without his handler knowing.

"Do we have something here, Fallon, or not?" Daniel's handler taps the screen of his ParaController again.

A small shudder passes through Daniel, jerking his body, the pain making his face gaunt.

Mom gasps and starts to reach toward them but I grab her arm. Beside me, Alex clenches his hands, unable to do anything. Rachel looks away, her eyes wet. I can see the pain still shuddering through Daniel. I bite my lip until I taste blood.

"Not," Daniel says through gritted teeth, his gaze on me.

I want to tear the ParaController out of the trooper's hands, turn the electroshock on him and wipe that smug look off his face. And I want to hold Daniel, to take away his pain. But I can't do either. Not if I want to stay free. Just thinking that weighs me down with guilt.

Scattered drops of rain plunk on my face and arms, and a raindrop slides down Daniel's cheek like a tear.

A girl shrieks at the rain, half laughing. Others hold their books and backpacks over their heads. The sound breaks up the stillness of our group.

"I don't think you have any cause to shock your young charge," Mom snaps at the trooper. "It looked to me like he was cooperating."

"Yeah? You wanna make an issue out of it?" the trooper says, chomping on his gum. "Maybe you need to be questioned, too. I'd be happy to give you a once-over."

Mom glances pointedly at the camera operator, then the reporter. "You getting all this?" she asks. "Here are our tax dollars at work—brutality and misuse of power."

"Yeah!" Rachel shouts. "Trooper brutality."

Alex loudly agrees. The reporter focuses on them, then back at the trooper and Daniel, who is still writhing in pain.

"Hey, now wait a minute—," the trooper says. He looks at the reporter, then back at Mom. He taps the screen again and Daniel stops shuddering. My brother breathes in small gulps of air and I want to cry.

"Daniel, I'm so sorry."

"That was nothing."

Mom turns me with her, and we start to walk away. I've never been more proud of her.

But Daniel's handler blocks us. "I'm afraid I have to ask you to wait. I want to question this girl."

Mom squares her shoulders, her grip on me tightening. "Are you seriously suggesting my daughter had anything to do with this? Are you accusing her?"

"She appeared to know the students were in trouble before anyone else did," the trooper huffs.

"I heard the fire alarm and I smelled the smoke. I made the connection," I say, keeping my face as flat and as empty of emotion as I can.

The rain is coming down faster now, the fat drops sliding down my face and neck, soaking my T-shirt.

"Are you accusing her?" Mom asks again.

"She ran right to the fire, when nearby classrooms—," the trooper starts.

"You heard my daughter," Mom says, shielding her head from the downpour with her purse. "If you or your colleagues have any more questions for her, you can question her at home. Because that's where she'll be. Come on, Caitlyn. Let's get out of this rain." She steers me around the trooper and this time he doesn't try to stop us.

We walk to the car with Mom's arm around my shoulders. I haven't felt this happy to see her in a long time. "Thank you—"

"Get in the car," she says.

I get in and buckle my seatbelt, shivering in my soggy T-shirt and jeans. Mom doesn't look at me; she just starts the engine with a trembling hand. Then she drives onto the road, the windshield wipers thunking back and forth.

"Your seatbelt," I say.

She buckles it up with one hand, her gaze firmly on the road. "Why didn't you tell me Daniel was here? How long have you known?"

I swallow. I don't know what to say. "Mom—"

"He's a Government Paranormal," Mom says quietly. "Daniel—my Daniel—is a government tool."

"It's true," I say.

Mom clenches the steering wheel in a death grip. "He endured torture to protect you—to protect us both."

It's not that simple, but I can't tell her that. I still don't even know how to sort it out myself. I keep seeing his body jerk as electricity coursed through him, his teeth gritted against the pain.

I lean against the cold glass of the window and let my

head bump against it. I know Mom's taking us back to the motel to pack and run.

"We can't leave yet, Mom," I say. "I have friends here—"

"Friends?" Mom says. "This is your *life*—all our lives—that we're talking about. Friends don't matter. And Daniel—oh, Daniel—" She hits the steering wheel, her voice breaking. "You knew Daniel was here, didn't you? You knew."

She turns to look at me.

I wish she'd keep her gaze on the road.

"How long have you known?" she repeats.

"A—About a week."

Huge gusts of wind shake our car, battering us from side to side.

"A week?" Mom stares out the windshield. "A whole *week*! I cannot believe you didn't tell me! I have the right to know, Caitlyn. He's my son!" She pounds the steering wheel again. "It's that boy, isn't it? You're willing to risk everything for that boy."

"Alex has nothing to do with this! I didn't *know* it was Daniel, not at first—and once I found out, he begged me not to tell you." It sounds bad, I know it does. "I wanted to tell you. But Mom—Daniel's changed. He's not . . . sweet anymore. He's not . . . on our side."

Mom makes a choking noise and I'm afraid to look at her. "Of course they trained him," she says. "But he's still our Daniel." Her voice is uncertain.

"He's not, Mom," I say quietly.

"He endured torture for you!" Mom says again.

"And he put doubt about me into his handler's mind. He called attention to me, too."

"Damn it, Caitlyn—how do you expect me to trust you after this?" Her voice quivers.

"I don't know." I scrunch down lower in my seat. She's so angry, she's trembling. Yet only a few seconds ago, her pain was so raw I could almost taste it. I wonder if she's using her anger to protect herself. To keep from falling apart.

"Is there anything else you're not telling me?" Mom asks in a clipped voice.

I swallow hard. "The principal—Mr. Temple—suspects that I'm a Para."

"This just gets better and better," Mom mutters. "And yet you somehow want to convince me that we should stay."

"He hasn't turned me in. I—I made him forget." *Even though he's already remembered it again.* That knowledge sits like a chunk of ice in my stomach.

"You *made* him—?" Mom shakes her head. "How did you do that? This isn't you, Caitlyn. I don't know you!"

There's a coldness in her voice that I haven't heard before. It makes me struggle to breathe. "Mom—"

"No. I don't want to hear it. I'm too angry with you right now."

The rain is pelting down in sheets and Mom slows the car to a crawl. She leans forward, peering out the windshield. The thunk of the wipers is loud in the silence.

I'm shivering hard now, my clothes heavy and cold.

Mom glances at me, then turns the heater on.

Tears burn down my cheeks. "I'm sorry I didn't tell you. I didn't want to hurt you. But Daniel is mixed up in some bad stuff."

Mom's lips tighten. "What kind of 'stuff'? Worse than hunting down his own kind?"

"He thinks we're better than Normals. That Normals don't matter. He's planning a rebellion and he doesn't care if he kills Normals while putting Paras in control."

Mom is silently crying now, too.

My tears come faster, stinging my eyes and nose, seeping into my mouth.

Mom pulls over to the side of the road and turns off the engine. She bows her head as rain drums on the roof of the car.

"We can't stay here, Caitlyn. Not now—though I can't bear to leave Daniel again." She sighs heavily. "I know how much you like Alex. But it's not living if you're always at the mercy of other people. What kind of a life is it if you're a slave who doesn't get to choose what she does or who she hurts? Do you understand what I'm saying?"

I nod, too full of emotion to speak.

How can I ever leave Alex? But I know I have to. If I stay and they arrest me, they might arrest Alex, too. And Rachel. And maybe even Mrs. Vespa.

No. We have to leave. My chest aches.

I push the grief down to a cold, hard place inside of me.

"I'm sorry," I send to Alex, to Rachel. Then I shut myself off from them completely.

CHAPTER 27

We're carrying our duffel bags to the car when Rachel and Alex run panting up the street.

. . . *She's been crying* . . . "See? I told you something was wrong," Alex says.

"What are you doing? You're not leaving, are you?" Rachel asks, wrapping her arms around herself.

The sun beats down on us, steam rising from the glistening wet road as I drop my duffel bag into the trunk of the car. I can't look at them, but I have to. I turn to Rachel. "I'm sorry I didn't connect you to your dad. If you focus on him, maybe I can do it before—"

Rachel shakes her head, her eyes filling with tears.

"Are you leaving?" Alex asks, louder.

Mom sets her duffel bag firmly down on top of mine. "Yes."

"Because of Daniel?"

Mom puts her hands on her hips and looks back and forth between us. "I see you told them."

"They're good people, Mom," I say dully. "If you'd just listen—"

"Good people can make mistakes. If they slip up and tell your secret, *they* don't have to pay." Mom slams the trunk shut. "And that trooper was sniffing around. He really wanted to find something."

"Mrs. Ellis—I'd never betray Caitlyn. I care about her. And she *saved* a lot of people today," Alex says. "You should be proud of her."

"I'm happy they're alive, but she put herself in danger by helping them. And she knew that's what she was doing."

"The trooper let me go, Mom!"

"For now. But you know it's only a matter of time before he catches on. Daniel knows that. We're risking ourselves—and him—by staying here. If his handler finds out he was protecting us . . . " She turns her face away.

Torture. We'd be inflicting torture on Daniel. But if we're found out, we're the ones who'll be tortured. And if I don't stop Daniel, it could mean the death of an entire population—all the Normals, including many innocent people.

"You're not alone," Rachel says earnestly. "There are people here who want to protect you. Give us a chance."

"How are you going to protect us from the government?" Mom takes out her keys and presses a button to unlock the car doors. "How are you going to protect us from the ParaTroopers, or even the ParaWatch? One phone call—that's all it takes. You want to help, then please don't tell anyone you saw us."

"But no one's made the call!" I say, desperately. "Mr. Temple isn't going to; he's already fingered two Normals. And both troopers backed off when I mentioned the blueprints. They have no proof, and Daniel wasn't revealing anything." I know I should get in the car, but I don't move. I can't.

"It doesn't matter." Mom jingles her keys. "We have to get out of here."

"I hate this!" I cry. "It's like *we're* the criminals."

Mom clasps my face in her hands. "I know, baby. But the alternative is far, far worse. And you have nothing to be ashamed of." She kisses my forehead and lets me go.

"Mom—Daniel shielded himself from me *completely*. I didn't even feel him until he touched me. No one's ever managed to do that before—"

"Except your dad," Mom says, her eyes sad.

And you. "There's got to be a way that I can do that, too. Disappear right off his radar. Or at the very least, I can shut down like you did. Wall him out."

A look of pain, like a wound cracking open, passes across Mom's face. "It's like losing your soul," she says softly, so softly I almost don't hear her.

"But what kind of life do we have if we're always running? Sometimes it feels like I might as well be dead."

There. I said it. The thing I swore I'd never say.

The silence around me vibrates, as if my words are echoing between us.

A bus roars by a few streets over. Kids shout as they play in the street. I steel myself and look at Mom. Her eyes are full of shadows and pain.

"I didn't know you felt that badly. I've been trying to *give* you a life, not take it away. But honey—we have to go."

"If you're leaving, I want to go with you," Alex says, his chest swelling out. "Mrs. Ellis, I love your daughter. I don't want to lose her."

Hope flutters inside me.

Mom laughs. "A Normal—on the run with two Para-normals?"

"A person who loves another person. Period."

"What happens when you have a lover's spat? What happens when you realize how much power you hold over Caitlyn? Over me? I'm sorry, but it just won't work."

"I wouldn't do that," Alex says.

"You don't know what you'll do until you're actually faced with it. What if they threatened your family? Or killed them? Would you give us up then?"

Alex goes silent.

Mom holds up her hands. "I wouldn't expect you to make that kind of sacrifice. I'm just pointing out the reality—"

"I wouldn't betray you," Alex says quietly.

Mom nods slowly at Alex. "You care about her. I can see that. But—"

"There has to be something we can do!" Rachel says. "We have huge Para-support here, the strongest in the country!"

"And a strong anti-Paranormal movement, too," Mom says.

Listening to them, I feel like I'm waking up. "I can make Mr. Temple forget again—and the two troopers. And I don't think Daniel actually wants to turn us in. Not while

261

he's trying to convince me to be on his side. We should be safe for a little while at least."

Mom looks over the top of the car at me, raising one eyebrow. "What do you mean, convince you to be on his side?"

My face grows hot. "Daniel wants me to help him purge the world of Normals. Make it for Paras only."

"The Authority!" Mom says, dropping her keys.

"The *what*?" I ask.

The lines on Mom's face grow deeper, her eyes filling with despair. She leans a hand on the hood of the car for support.

Alex goes over to her. "Mrs. Ellis—maybe you should sit down." He picks up her keys and hands them to her. She takes them with a shaking hand.

"Mom?" I say.

"The Authority has him," she says hopelessly.

"What are you talking about?" I ask, my stomach clenching.

"The Authority! They're an organized group of Para-normals who want to conquer Normals. They hated your father for trying to make peace and they murdered him for it."

Ilene! Ilene is part of the Authority. And that means Daniel must be, too.

Now Mom leans both hands on the car's hood, like it's the only thing keeping her up. "I've heard they've been growing in strength and that they finally got a Paranormal with a lot of talent. Not the one they were searching for, but a powerful one. If Daniel's part of the Authority . . ." Her eyes look sunken, her face old. She reaches out and touches my cheek. "I'm afraid you're the one they're looking for, Caitlyn. I've been trying to keep you safe from them for years. That settles it. Get in the car—we're leaving right now!" Mom opens the car door.

"But someone's got to stop them." The words pop out of my mouth.

They all turn to stare at me.

I shift uneasily. "We can't let the Authority take over the world and murder all the Normals. *We're* the only ones who can stop other Paras. Normals won't even know what's happening until it's too late."

They stare at me, shocked, but what I said feels right. "Mom, we have to *do* something. Not just for Normals, but for *all* of us."

"She's right," Alex says hoarsely. "No way do I want to risk Caitlyn getting hurt. But if a Para doesn't stand up to this, there might not be anything left, not for anyone. And Caitlyn's the strongest person I know."

I feel a small glow of warmth at his words.

"Oh god." Mom covers her mouth with her hands. "I was afraid of this."

"Huh?" I stare at her stupidly.

"You don't know how much you're like your dad. You've always had such a strong sense of justice, even when it put you in danger." She rubs her cheek with the back of her hand. "But maybe you're right."

"I'll practice shielding until Daniel can't detect me. If Dad could do it, and Daniel can, then so can I. I just need a little more time. You know I have to try, Mom. We can't let a massacre happen. Even if Daniel's the one leading it. Especially if he's leading it."

I plead with Mom with my eyes. I don't bother shielding my despair; I send it, along with my trembling hope.

Mom's lips tighten and she looks haggard. Then she says, "One more day. And if anyone comes sniffing around, we run. Agreed?"

"Agreed." I laugh through my tears.

I still don't know how to defeat Daniel. But I know that it'll help if he can't sense me.

I have to learn how—by tomorrow morning.

CHAPTER **28**

Mom stands in my doorway, the shadows wrapping around her. "You can't just hide—you have to shield yourself from Daniel completely." Her voice catches.

"I know." I sit up, making space for her.

The bed sags as she sits beside me. Her shoulders sag, too. "I don't know how to help you with this. I never needed to hide my talents—and you're far more powerful than I ever was."

I rub the back of my neck. "I've been thinking about that. Daniel said he heard me twice when I didn't intend him to: when I sent to you, and when I sent to the kids in the fire. Both times, I was sending as hard as I could."

"Because I've been shut off from you." Mom pushes my hair away from my forehead. "It must have been so hard—"

You don't know how hard. I squeeze my eyes shut, clamp down on the thought. "I know it was really bad for you when Dad died. . . ."

"But it must have been horrible to suddenly be cut off from me like that—to lose your connection to both your

Dad and me." Mom's voice wobbles. She puts her arm around me.

I lean into her softness, but my mind is racing, trying to figure out how to do this. "I think I have to focus on connecting to one person at a time, and reduce my volume and intensity. But there must be something else I'm missing."

Mom pulls back. "I wish I could help you more, honey. I feel so useless. But you are smart and talented and brave, and I believe in you." She stands. "Don't stay up too late trying to figure this thing out. You'll need energy tomorrow, trying to shield."

"I know." I try to smile, but I can feel it slipping, fear close beneath.

Mom hesitates in the doorway. "If there's any way I can help . . ."

I want to ask her to open up to me so she can tell me when my shields are working, but I know she can't control it. Know that my asking would cause her pain. The words stick in my throat. "You help, Mom. More than you know."

She shakes her head and smiles a lopsided smile, then leaves.

I sit up straighter. I have to make this work.

My head aches from all the mind-noise, the constant fight to shut it out.

I pull the curtains together tighter, then turn the light off. The dimness eases the pain.

I lie back against my pillow, stretch my legs out, knocking clothes to the floor.

How did Daniel hide himself completely? Even today? It can't be water—it rained on us all. Dad could do it.

Daniel can do it. What connects them? I chew on my lower lip.

What is it about Alex that makes his mind-voice so quiet? Why doesn't he overwhelm me? It's not just that he's calm and happy. There's something more. Something that connects him up with Dad and Daniel. I just can't see it.

Something they all eat? Something they think? Something they visualize? I slap the bed. No.

Okay. Back to what I do know. Being immersed in water shields me from people's mind-voices, quiets them. Water is an element—something you can actually see and touch. Something natural. What if there's something else that Daniel's discovered that he can carry or wear or eat that shields him?

I Google "water" and "properties" on my cell phone. I read and read until I stumble over "nonmagnetic." Magnetic. Our brain activity, our thoughts, create electromagnetic energy. I remember learning that in some science class. What if water, being nonmagnetic, helps block or even repel some of that energy?

I search "nonmagnetic substances." They include water, copper, and aluminum. I sit up. That must be why the basement ceiling where Daniel and Ilene meet is covered in aluminum! And Dad's watch—the one Daniel wears—is copper. Dad loved its reddish brown richness, its warmth. He used to say it made him feel good.

And Alex. The bracelets he wears, that look so good against his skin—they're copper! I touch the one he gave me.

But if copper helps shield thoughts, why isn't the bracelet I'm wearing enough?

I close my eyes. Alex wears a lot of bracelets. I'm only wearing one—a thin one. Dad's watch—Daniel's now—is thick and wide. Maybe I need more copper.

I leap up, run to my doorway. "Mom—do you have any copper jewelry? Or anything made of copper?"

Mom turns to look at me, puzzled. "I have a necklace your dad gave me. And your dad's favorite ring—aside from his wedding band—was a copper ring he designed."

Did Dad know what copper could do? If he did, why didn't he tell me? "Could I borrow them?" I ask.

Mom's face tightens.

"I promise I'll give them back. It's important."

Mom slowly opens her purse, then a small velvet pouch, and pours some jewelry into her hand. "I was keeping his ring for Daniel, for if we ever—" Her voice breaks off.

"He's got Dad's watch," I say.

"He does?" Mom looks startled. "Well then, I guess your dad's ring should be yours. He used to wear it on his pinky finger, so it just might fit. . . ."

She holds it out to me.

I slip it on. It fits perfectly over my thumb, like it was meant to be there. The pain in my head lessens.

Mom's still holding out the jewelry. The necklace Dad gave her—I remember it now. It has coils of copper twisted into interconnected spirals. Like us, Dad said. I lift it up around my neck. It's heavier than it looks.

"Here, let me help you with that," Mom says.

I turn, and she fastens the clasp around my neck.

The pain recedes to a dull, nagging throb. The mind-voices are quieter, now; even the light seems less harsh. My shoulders drop. I hadn't even realized I was hunching them.

Mom turns me around, holding my shoulders as she looks at me, smiling, her eyes glistening. I can see the love in her eyes, even if I can't feel it, mind-to-mind. For a moment, everything feels right. And then I remember Daniel and his plan.

"How's your practice going?" Mom asks.

"I'm figuring it out. Got some more thinking to do though."

"Don't stay up too late," Mom says, brushing back my hair.

"No," I say. But I will if I have to.

Back on my bed, I stare at the ceiling again. The copper helps, but not enough. There must be something I'm still missing.

I go back to my cell phone, to the page on nonmagnetic properties. And then it hits me: if there are substances that are nonmagnetic, of course there are things that are magnetic.

And what if Daniel knows that, too? What if he used it against me? I've been having more trouble than usual shutting out people's mind-voices, and I've been in a lot more pain since we came to this new school. Ever since I found Daniel—or he found me.

I grab my backpack and dump everything out. I sort through my things—textbooks, binders, pens and pencils, a calculator, favorite books, a browned, half-eaten apple in a Baggie, my family photo—nothing I don't recognize. I put everything back except the apple, which I toss in the garbage. I feel guilty. How could I have suspected Daniel would do something so horrible?

I heft my backpack up to toss it to the floor, and my hands hit a hard lump in the side pocket. Even though I tell myself I'm being paranoid, I reach into the pocket and touch something cold. I pull it out.

A gray slab of metal almost the size of my hand, its surface rough and dimpled, sits in my palm. My breath catches. I'm pretty sure I know what it is, but I go back to the web page to check. Yep, cobalt. One of the most highly magnetic metals that exists. And I certainly didn't put it there.

Sadness pushes at my chest. Daniel had to know that it would cause me pain if he weakened my barriers, that it would let the mind-voices crash in. He had to know it'd make it harder for me to blend in, and more likely that I'd be fingered as a Para. Yet he did it anyway.

I dump the cobalt down the garbage chute. In seconds, the mind-voices become a whisper, the pain almost a memory.

CHAPTER **29**

I snap awake, then lie there, not sure what woke me. Little pinpricks of sun pierce through the curtains. The pain isn't so bad as it's been lately, but it's still a relief to put my dark glasses on.

I stayed up into the early morning practicing shielding and trying to figure out how to deal with Daniel. I have some ideas, but I'm not sure how much further ahead I am. Except that knowledge is power—and I know now what Daniel was doing. I know how he made things harder for me—and that means I'm less vulnerable now. Unless he has something else he can use against me that I don't know about—which he probably does. I stagger to the bathroom and take a hot shower, where the water raining on my face wakes me up.

The sound of water against the tub is like a song. I let the water beat against my back, my neck. It's not so effective as deep water for shutting out the cacophony of people's thoughts, but it helps.

I'm drying myself off when I notice the silence. It's always quiet wherever we are; Mom makes sure of that—but this is a held-in silence. There's no breakfast smell, either—no coffee or hot cereal or toast.

I dress hurriedly, then stumble out to the main room. Mom's hunched over in her chair, her head against her hands, the newspaper spread out in front of her like an obituary notice.

"What is it?" I ask, hoarsely.

Mom looks up, her face bleak. "If the troopers didn't know we were here, they do now."

I pull out a chair, wood dragging against the thin carpet, and sit. Fear moves off Mom in waves, turning my stomach—and then it is gone, so fast I wonder if I imagined it. I clench my hands together. "What does it say?"

Mom picks up the paper, the sheets crackling in her hands. She clears her throat.

"Twenty-two students and one teacher at Normal Heights High School were saved from certain death yesterday when a mysterious voice told them what to do. 'I heard the voice of an angel,' Mariah Garcia, age 17, said, 'telling me to get close to the floor, to stay calm, and that someone would save us.' Mariah, who is suffering from smoke inhalation, would likely have died if she hadn't heard the voice telling her to lie facedown on the floor. 'We were all too scared to think,' Mariah admits."

My mouth is as dry as dust.

Mom keeps reading, her voice flat.

"Mariah wasn't the only one who heard a voice speak to her. All twenty-two students heard the voice advising them to keep calm. And this reporter has it on good authority that two of the students who helped rescue the others heard a voice telling them what to do."

The newspaper trembles in Mom's hands. She steadies it.

"This incident suggests that the voice was that of a powerful telepath—an unregistered Paranormal. 'There's nothing Normal about them,' Mr. Jarred Temple, principal of Normal Heights High School, says. 'And if I have one of them hiding at my school, I'm going to root them out with the help of our resident ParaTrooper. Paras are a perversion of human nature."

Not everyone would agree with Mr. Temple. Some see Paranormals as a higher evolved human being. Others see them as a freak of nature. Whatever people's opinion, the fact is that it's illegal to be an unregistered Para. No one knows just how many Paranormals live unregistered in the city, though it's thought that the number is low since the inception of Government Paras. But whether it was mass hallucination, the voice of an angel or God, or an unregistered Paranormal student, it looks like Normal Heights High School has its very own hero. On the eve of Para Cleansing Day, this gives us all something to think about."

Mom sets the paper down as carefully as if it's going to explode. "I know I promised you one more day, but—"

"We can use this! I can say I heard the voice, too. Then I'm not a suspect."

"I want you to get your stuff together."

"Mom." I lean toward her. "We have to stop the Authority. The whole country will be worse off if we don't.

And it's different this time. We have people on our side. Please, just give me today."

"It's not a risk I want to take. You know Normals get zealous this time of year. It will be even harder to leave tomorrow."

"No one would expect two Paranormals to travel on Para Cleansing Day."

Mom crosses her arms. "That's because it's crazy!"

"It's the right thing to do, and you know it!" I shout.

There's a long silence. Mom bites her lip. "All right, Cait. We'll stay. Just today."

Somehow, I've got to pull off a miracle.

Out on the street, people's thoughts stab into my head like shards of glass. Fear and excitement coil and thread through people, vibrating into me. Normals are hyper-alert, trying to spot anyone who's not in synch with them. I touch Mom's copper necklace, the bracelet I wear, and the voices retreat into static.

Already the streets are strung with red-and-black lights, signifying the blood and deaths that occurred during the Para Cleansing. Para massacre. Cantaloupes are piled high in barrels, ready for people to smash onto the streets the way Para skulls were smashed. It makes me sick that people can celebrate the murder of others, can enjoy reenacting it. Hotdog vendors are setting up along the sides of the road. Tomorrow there will be even more vendors—French fry, pretzel, ice cream, cotton candy, and souvenir vendors, all wanting to make a buck off Paras' deaths.

I reach out to Alex, then Rachel, visualizing my thoughts touching only theirs. *"Did you read this morning's paper?"*

"That stupid reporter!" Alex thinks at me. *"Didn't she know what she was doing, putting the troopers on you like that?"*

"I'm not letting it stop me. I've got to take Daniel down." Today.

I feel Alex smile, like a warm hand on my heart. *"Good . . . but be careful. I want you safe. You're half my heart. . . ."*

"And you're mine."

"I hate to interrupt" —Rachel hesitates— *"but are you sure that's a good idea?"* Her thoughts shudder.

"Rachel, what is it? Did something happen?"

"Some troopers came to our apartment last night. They kept questioning me about the fire, about how I knew."

My stomach clenches. *"What did you tell them?"*

"That I smelled it. I used your excuse of the connecting vents. They didn't believe me; they kept threatening to take me and my family in. So I told them that I heard a voice, but that I didn't know who it was. I'm so sorry, Caitlin."

"No—you had to. Thank you for not giving up my name."

"I would never!"

But how long can she last if she and her family are taken to government lockup? I have to end this—fast.

CHAPTER **30**

Before I even reach the school, I sense them—minds trying to probe me, dig into my thoughts, and home in on my location. Not just one mind—three, maybe four, all reaching for me. Daniel, Ilene—I recognize her coldness now—and a Para-slave. And troopers stalking me like hunters after prey.

I glance at the store windows as I pass, trying to ignore the black-and-red decorations, the jarring fear.

There. A ParaTrooper—I'd recognize him anywhere, even when he's trying to be in disguise by wearing a regular suit and tie. His civilian clothes don't hide his training, his I-own-the-world stance, legs parted, hand at his waist where his gun is probably hidden, his gaze raking every passerby.

I keep my pace steady. The dirty gray sidewalk shifts like bones beneath my feet.

I could run. But I feel troopers gathering around the school, and in the streets behind me, the streets ahead. They're caging me in. I won't desert Alex and Rachel, won't let them fend for themselves against Daniel. And I won't leave without my mom.

I can almost see her sitting in her cubicle, her head in her hands, waiting for the phone to ring.

"I'm sorry I got us into this," I tell her. I try to swallow down the fear lodged in my throat. I'm afraid I'll never see her again.

No. I clench my fists. I *will*. We'll get out of this together, like we always have.

I march toward the school even though I know Daniel and the troopers are waiting for me there. Even though I know it's a trap.

◉

I sense the reporters before I see them, feel their frenzied energy.

. . . unregistered Para . . . the day before the Para Cleansing . . . need this for my ratings . . .

I stand outside the fence. Reporters are scattered around the school yard and clustered around the front steps with their recorders and microphones, leaning in to capture every word. Students pose, excited to have their opinions heard.

ParaTroopers pace the grounds. I can see them staked out along the edges, watching, waiting. I feel them in the school windows above. And outside the school grounds, two separate groups of picketers march—a large group of anti-Para picketers, and a smaller group of pro-Para picketers. It's the second group that surprises me.

Paras with any sense won't be here today. But some will try to blend in. Like me.

I don't see any way out of this except to use what Daniel taught me.

As I enter the yard, attention shifts to me. I reach out, slowly, directing the troopers' and reporters' attention back to the mass of students. *"I'm nothing. Just a dull student, a shadow, wasn't even at school yesterday. I'm not worth noticing."*

And one by one, I feel their minds drop from me.

My body vibrates deep inside. I'm using parts of myself that I've rarely used. I clench my teeth, jaw aching. I've got to hold my focus a little longer. Past the troopers, two reporters, the cameras picking me up as I walk by, the lineup, the door, then in past the resident ParaTrooper.

As the trooper waves me through, I let their minds go. The trembling inside me stops.

The hall is full of chaotic energy—girls clumped together, talking loudly, boys throwing dirty sneakers and books to each other, a teacher marching past, the secretary glaring out into the hall.

"That was very impressive, Caitlyn."

The screech of Daniel's thoughts is like metal on metal.

How did he get into my mind, when I built my defenses so carefully against him? When I'm wearing so much copper?

I look around, but I don't see him anywhere.

I want to chuck him out of my head, but some instinct stops me.

"I only just taught you, and already you can use mass suggestion. What did you tell them? That they couldn't see you? That you don't exist? You're powerful, Cait. Just think what you could do with the right people to back you up. You could make any law or break it. You'd be unstoppable."

There is such longing in his voice, but it's not for me. It's for the power I'd give him. I touch Mom's copper necklace, Dad's ring, Alex's bracelet.

"I can offer you the world. You hear me, Caitlyn?"

He's not in my mind; he can't be. He must be sending his thoughts out like a net throughout the school, trying to catch me and reel me in. He can't hear me, not completely. If he could, he wouldn't have needed to ask what I'd done. The copper works!

I walk down the hall, then peer around the corner.

A big ParaTrooper keeps flicking his gaze between the photo he's holding and the students passing by. Girl students.

I pull back. These guys will be easy to avoid—at least until they come storming into the classrooms.

. . . dirty Para-lover . . . standing against the wall like it'll protect her . . . send her flying . . .

I look up. Becca's charging toward me, a fierce look on her reddened face, hands ready to shove me.

I dodge to the side, and Becca slams into the wall where I'd been.

"Are you all right?" I say, my voice dripping with fake concern.

Becca clutches her wrist to her chest, her teeth gritted together. "You—you!"

I shouldn't have done that. She looks like she wants to claw my face. But I don't have time to deal with people like her. *"Walk away,"* I suggest, focusing only on her.

Becca glares at me, then whirls around and stalks away. I peek around the corner. The trooper's still there, eyeing Becca like he likes what he sees.

Down the other hallway, I feel another trooper watching students. And two floors above me, there's a new Para—a Government Para urgently trying to sense me so she'll avoid the torture that comes with failure, especially for a quarry this big.

She's a midlevel Para, with enough power to sense me.

I chew on my lip. Maybe it wasn't such a great idea to come to school today after all.

CHAPTER 31

I walk away from the closest trooper, merging back into the surge of students, the shouting and pushing and laughter, the cell phones trilling, the boys punching each other on their shoulders.

I need somewhere to hide while I try to take down Daniel, Ilene, and the Government Para. I don't want to face all three in their lair where they outnumber me, physically and mentally.

I head for the safest place I can think of. The library.

I sense them before I see them. The darkness with a bite.

I fumble in my backpack, jerk my compact out. I check my nonexistent makeup while I try to spot them.

There, in the stairwell. One trooper, hands held behind his back, legs splayed in a stiff stance. Another, staring at the display case, using my trick. And a Para-slave beside them, searching, reaching for me. Not the powerful one I sensed a few floors above; this one is more like an annoying gnat. But even a gnat can zone in on something to devour.

I snap my mirror shut, touch my copper necklace, then walk toward them. The trooper at the case stiffens, turns.

I focus on him and the Para-slave. *"I'm just a boring Normal, not the one you're looking for."*

The trooper is facing me now, his gaze fastened on mine, his hand coming up to his ear piece. The Para-slave turns his head sharply, like he's sensed me.

I push harder, feeling the strain. Have to be careful not to let the Para-slave sense me. Not to use too much power, but still use enough. *"I am the most normal Normal you've ever seen. Yawningly normal. Nothing like the target."*

The trooper rubs his forehead and blinks. His gaze slides from mine.

The Para-slave looks at me, his gaze lingering, then narrowing. He might be a low-level Para, but he senses something familiar in me and his eyes gleam. He takes a step toward me, a satisfied smile on his face, knowing he's caught a big fish. He'll get rewarded well for this.

"I am a Normal," I send like an arrow at his skull.

He reaches for the trooper beside him.

My heart beats hard. Maybe the suggestion shouldn't be about me; maybe it should be about him. *"Go home. You don't want to be here, betraying your own kind,"* I send, with all my power behind it.

The Para-slave stops, shaking his head and blinking. Then he turns and walks down the hall, away from his handler.

"Hey! Where you going?" the trooper shouts.

"Home," the Para-slave says over his shoulder. "I don't belong here."

"The hell you don't!" the trooper yells, yanking his ParaController out of his pocket. Students turn to watch, wide-eyed, frozen like statues. "Get your ass back here!"

The Para-slave shakes his head and keeps walking. The trooper taps his screen twice. The Para-slave jolts, his body tightening, then vibrating as the shock passes through him. His eyes widen, his mouth opening in a noiseless scream.

I edge back through the crowd, feeling sick. I had to keep myself safe, didn't I? So much is depending on me. And I'm not the one who shocked him. But guilt fills my chest.

"Had enough yet? Get back here!" the trooper yells.

The Para-slave shakes his head and the trooper shocks him again. White foam bubbles from the Para-slave's mouth. The trooper must have upped the volts.

I close my eyes. Even though the Para-slave was going to turn me in, I can't let him be tortured like this. *"Stay and do your job,"* I send him. But I am too late. His mind is fading. The shock was too much. The Para-slave collapses, body hitting the floor with a thud, still vibrating.

I'm shaking, sick to my stomach as I walk down the stairwell. How could all those Normals stand by and watch? Why doesn't anyone do anything?

But I know why. The government is too big, too powerful, and they use fear to control people. Fear, punishment, and reward.

I push open the library door.

Mrs. Vespa looks up, her face lined with tension. The silk scarf knotted around her neck looks like it's choking her. "Caitlyn, it's good to see you." *"There are troopers in* the building, and at least one Government Para. We have to get you out of here."

"It's good to see you, too." *"But I'm not leaving. Alex and Rachel are in danger. And so are you!"*

Mrs. Vespa takes off her glasses, lets them hang from the chain around her neck. They gently bump against her large chest. She picks a book up off the counter. "See if this interests you." She hands me the book. *"How so? You're the one they're after."*

I pretend to read the back cover. *"That Para who wants to kill Normals—I think he's planning to act today, just as soon as he can get me out of the way. I'm going to stop him."* At least, I'm going to try.

"How can I help?"

I turn the book over in my hands. "Looks good." I feel too exposed, just standing there. *"I need somewhere quiet where I can focus. Somewhere no one will see me. I thought I could hide out here—if you don't mind the risk,"* I send.

"My office would be the best place," she thinks at me. "I've got another book to show you, if you like that one," Mrs. Vespa says. "One that just came in."

I nod and follow her, breathing easier once the shelves hide me from the windows.

The library door swings open. Dark energy fills the room.

I jerk around, peeking past the shelves. A trooper with a gun.

Mrs. Vespa's nostrils flare, her head rising. *"I'll get rid of him. Don't you worry."*

She marches toward the man, looking formidable. I stealthily slip the knapsack off my shoulder, then press myself up against the shelf. I stand there, ready to nudge the trooper's thoughts if he gets suspicious. Book spines poke my back, the cold metal of the shelf biting into my neck as I strain to listen.

"Can I help you?" Mrs. Vespa asks, as if she doesn't really want to.

"You seen this girl?" a deep male voice rumbles.

"Why no, no, I haven't."

I reach out toward the other exit. A dark presence stands there, waiting. I bite my lower lip.

"This is a respectable school," Mrs. Vespa says haughtily, as if she's offended. "We've cleaned out all the Paras."

"Newspaper says differently. And you had a few Paras hiding among you even last week. They're tricky buggers to spot—look just like the rest of us. But don't worry; we'll find them."

Heavy footsteps clump toward me.

I clench my fists. *"There is no one here. No one but the librarian."*

I pour all my energy into it, repeating it over and over as the footsteps pause, then start down my aisle. Let this work; please let this work. *"Just another empty aisle."*

I don't dare move, don't dare turn my head to look at him, just keep pouring it on.

I smell cigarettes, feel the floor trembling under the trooper's weight, the books shaking—

I look out of the corner of my eye.

I see the gun first—a long, narrow muzzle, smelling

of oil. Then a thick, meaty hand on the grip, the fingers roughened, the nails blunt. Black uniform with a red stripe down its sides, red-and-black ParaTrooper badge on his chest, wide shoulders, a square chin, flinty eyes. The trooper turns his head back and forth as he scans the shelves.

He's almost upon me. I press myself harder against the shelf, books like bony fingers digging into me. The illusion will fall apart if he brushes up against me, or feels my breath on his skin.

"All you can see are rows of dusty old books," I send with force. I hold my breath, wishing I was thinner, flatter. *Don't let him notice me.*

He walks past me, his sleeve almost grazing my chest.

My lungs burn. The pressure in my head sparks bright cold pain behind my eyes.

The man trips, stumbles over my backpack, joggling it hard, shaking my arm as I hang onto it.

God, no!

He turns back, squinting at the floor just past my feet. I let my bag go.

The man's forehead furrows. . . .*what the—?*. . . He snatches up my backpack, his bristly crew cut almost scraping my face.

"Someone left the bag behind. All the students are gone," I send fervently. My lungs are going to burst.

"Whose backpack is this?" the man barks.

"Walk toward the end of the shelves," I send desperately.

The man does, without seeming to notice what he's doing.

Bright spots dance in front of my eyes. I crack open my lips, let a tiny breath escape, and suck in an even smaller amount.

Mrs. Vespa appears at the end of the stack, her gaze flitting to me, then to the trooper. She covers her mouth with her hand.

The trooper spins around.

"The aisle behind you is empty!" I send.

His gaze passes right through me. He frowns and turns back to Mrs. Vespa.

Mrs. Vespa rests her hands on her hips, looking stern again. "Put that gun away, young man. I do not allow guns in my library."

You go, Mrs. Vespa.

"I *said*—whose backpack is this?" The trooper holds my bag up in the air, his frustration slamming into me.

My lungs shake. I let out a tiny bit more air, draw in another sip.

"It must be one of the students with a free period."

"I want to see them all in front of me," the trooper snaps. "Now." He turns and walks down the aisle toward me.

I press back harder against the shelf.

A book shifts beneath my shoulder blades.

The trooper's eyes narrow. He stalks toward me—

"Scream!" I think at Mrs. Vespa. *"Please scream."*

And she does. Long and loud and high.

The trooper drops my backpack and whips around to face Mrs. Vespa, aiming his gun at her head.

Mrs. Vespa shrieks louder, raising her hands.

I let my breath out.

"What is it?" the trooper shouts. He looks over his shoulder at me.

"Books. You only see books," I send, tears streaming from my eyes; I can hardly see through the blur of pain. Liquid drips onto my shoe. Blood.

Oh shit.

Mrs. Vespa keeps screaming.

The man takes a step toward her. "What are you screeching about?"

"I'm sorry. I thought I saw something," Mrs. Vespa says, sounding flustered.

I slowly raise my hand to my nose and hold it closed, willing the bleeding to stop. But it keeps running out, spattering onto the dark carpet. *"There is nothing here for you to see. Nothing at all. You were mistaken."*

"Where?" the trooper barks.

"Outside."

The trooper sighs. "That's one of my men. Nothing to be afraid of, ma'am."

He marches down the length of the library, looking between each shelving unit, peering at the remaining students. Finally he signals to his partner, and they leave.

I let go of my concentration.

My legs flutter like grass in the wind. I sink to my knees, blood gushing from my nose.

CHAPTER 32

Mrs. Vespa appears at the end of the aisle, her hand on her heaving chest. "Why couldn't he see you? My god— Caitlyn!" She rips off her scarf and holds it firmly against my nose to stanch the flow. The pink silk blooms into a deep red.

I'm using too much of myself, and I haven't even faced Daniel yet. How am I going to get through this?

Mrs. Vespa makes worried sounds as she holds the scarf against my nose. I push it away.

"I'm all right." I hate that my voice shakes.

"Does this happen often?" Mrs. Vespa asks.

I shake my head, then stop, dizzy. "No, just lately, when I . . . do too much." Then I realize what she said. "You *saw* me?" Was the trooper stringing me along the whole time? But there was too much frustration in him for his actions to not be real.

"Of course I did. You were standing right there. But why couldn't the trooper?"

If he wasn't faking it, why didn't it work on Mrs. Vespa?

I reach for her mind. I don't sense any psychic gifts. She isn't wearing copper. So why?

I look at the books around me. "Mrs. Vespa, you read a lot, don't you?"

"Of course, dear. But what's that got to do with anything?" Mrs. Vespa studies me. "And why did you expect me not to see you?"

I pull on my lip. Maybe books help everyone, not just Paras. I focus just on her. *"I used my mind to—well, to suggest that the trooper couldn't see me."*

Mrs. Vespa's eyes widen. *"I heard a faint voice telling me that there was no one there—but it was like elevator music, insistent and irritating. So I tuned it out."*

I stare at her. She heard me giving her a suggestion. Other than my dad and mom in training, and Daniel since he reappeared, no one ever has. And Mrs. Vespa's a Normal.

"It's all the reading you do," I say. "It has to be." *"It looks like books help Normals, too, not just Paras."*

"What do you mean?"

"Reading strengthens your mind, makes you less susceptible to Paras. To any influence."

Mrs. Vespa puts the earpiece of her glasses into her mouth, sucking on it thoughtfully. *"Yet another reason to read more. Not that I needed one."* She takes the glasses out of her mouth. *"You may have eluded the troopers for now, but I doubt they'll give up that easily."*

"I know."

The loudspeaker crackles. Mr. Temple's voice booms out. "Caitlyn Ellis report to the principal's office. Immediately. Caitlyn Ellis."

Right on cue. I wipe the sweat off my upper lip. *"Mr. Temple sure hates Paras."*

"That he does. I think his ex-wife was one." "Now, let's get you that book."

I follow her down the length of the library, feeling exposed by the windows opening into the hall. We walk past students sitting at work tables, reading, writing, texting, whispering to each other. A few turn toward us— *"Don't recognize me. Don't look at me."* —and then turn back around.

The red exit sign blinks at me like a warning.

I reach out with my mind as I walk. The midlevel Government Para felt the surge of power I sent to the trooper. She is narrowing in on me, but she hasn't located me yet.

Every step I expect to hear a shout and have hands grab me.

. . . want to die . . . going to do it . . .

The despair is so strong I stop. A girl is sitting as still as if she's part of the wall, her arms around her knees, her lowered face hidden by her hair.

Mrs. Vespa follows my gaze. *"She often hides in here. I think there's something wrong at home, but she won't open up."*

"Somebody's got to get through to her. She's planning on killing herself. Soon."

"I'll talk with her again. I'll make sure of it." *. . . should have done more . . .*

"You helped make a safe place for her. She comes here, doesn't she?"

"I suppose. Now let's get you safe." Mrs. Vespa tugs me forward.

I look back over my shoulder. The hunched-over girl hasn't moved. I send her comfort, as strong as I can.

Rage laced with the scent of metal shrieks through my skull, making my teeth vibrate.

Daniel must have been waiting for me to use my talent again.

I focus on the copper I'm wearing, draw it like armor around me. The shriek fades, but I know Daniel sensed me.

I feel a leopard-like presence nearby; the troopers are only a classroom or two away. I push up close behind Mrs. Vespa, so close I'm almost touching her back with my nose, as if her wide body will protect me.

I follow her into a room I hadn't noticed before, opening off the back wall.

Mrs. Vespa flicks on the light. "It's all yours." *"I'll let you know if anyone comes looking for you."*

I don't remind her that I'll know first.

She leaves, closing the door behind her.

The room is small and cramped, with a clunky, outdated computer, a water cooler, and stacks of papers and books fighting for space on every surface, even crowding around the pot of a giant aloe vera. Everything looks old or in need of repair; even the chair is stained and faded, echoing the years of librarians who used it.

I sink down on the squeaky chair. Pain bores through my skull.

They are searching every room in the school. They already checked the library. But once they finish and come up empty, they'll start all over again. And Daniel—he's planning something; I can feel it, in the pressure building against my skull. I think he's planning on setting off the revolt today. It makes a sick kind of sense. To so many others, the Para Cleansing is just a holiday, but to Paras, it's a day of grief. To strike back today would be to make tomorrow different. But I don't want his kind of different.

I draw my knees up to my chest. Daniel has strong allies, and they've all trained a lot longer than I have. I have no doubt that Daniel knows many more techniques that can be used as weapons, ones he didn't bother to teach me, but I have to find out what he's doing.

But it's a fine line between becoming aware of him and letting him become aware of me, or of tipping off the Government Para, with all the ParaTroopers waiting on the sidelines. I have to do this carefully, like the gentlest caress of a breeze, while I'm protected by my copper armor.

I lightly reach out for Daniel. The lust for power shudders all around me; the air itself has become heavy with it.

He's trying to pinpoint where I am, sending surges of his power outward. He's furious at my ability to hide from him, and he briskly maneuvers the troopers, suggesting they go here and there, all in the hopes of flushing me out.

I'm scared I'll alert him to my presence, but I have to know what he's planning. I push deeper.

Daniel's seething rage tears through me. His desire to swallow my power and use it for himself almost overwhelms me.

. . . The two of us could have been so great—with our combined power, we could have made the entire world safe,

not just our country. But I'm not ready to give up on Cait-lyn yet . . . .

. . . maybe if I give her another taste of the power, the thrill of it . . . and if not, I'm willing to hurt whoever I have to, to make her see the way . . . perhaps that Normal boy she likes; that's her most vulnerable link . . .

I want to fly screaming from Daniel's mind. But I force myself to stay longer. "Hurt Alex . . . ," I prompt softly.

. . . choke off his air from the inside, make him die a slow death. Make her watch the things I can do to that Normal, make Caitlyn beg to join me. Gotta send a Para-Trooper to pick him up, get him within my range . . .

I pull out of Daniel's head, gasping, and visualize pricking a hole in my copper armor. *"Alex?"*

"Damn it, where have you been? I thought you were going to listen for me!"

"Alex—you need to leave the school! Get away from here! Daniel's sending troopers after you. He wants to kill you."

"I'm not leaving you here to fend for yourself. You know that. Besides, what can the troopers do to me? I'm a Normal."

"They can torture you, kill you! You know that—any-one suspected of helping a Para can be tortured. You have to leave now!"

"No!" The answer is hard. Definite, coming from deep inside him.

"Okay, then at least make sure you don't get stopped by the troopers."

"Now that I know they're coming, I'll be okay," Alex thinks. *"They won't want a Normal. You're the one who needs to get out of here."*

"No. Daniel wants you; weren't you listening? He wants to kill you and make me watch."

"To get to you. To force you to join him. You're the one who needs to get out of here, Caitlyn. Get someplace safe."

"I can't; not before I stop him."

"So what're you going to do—just wait for them to find you?"

"I've faced these guys before. I'll be all right."

"Damned right you will. I'll make sure of it," Alex thinks, shoving confidence at me. Fear threads beneath it.

"Alex, no. I can handle it."

"You can't. You're holed up somewhere, and you're scared and hurting."

Shit. I can't believe I let him see that. *"I'm fine. I don't want you to—"*

"Help you, the way you helped me? Protect you? Show you I love you? Too late."

He closes himself off from me.

"Alex, what are you going to do? ALEX?"

CHAPTER **33**

"Damn it, Alex, talk to me!"

But all I can hear is a kind of chant—*it's all good, it's all good*—and nothing beneath it. He's shut me out of his thoughts.

I pound the arm of the chair. I can force myself into Alex's mind, but that might hurt him. And I can't go screaming for him, not without tipping Daniel off. Daniel and the Government Para.

I make another pinprick in my copper armor. *"Rachel, have you seen Alex? I think he's about to do something stupid."*

"He got a rest room pass; he just left."

Shit! *"Can you stop him? He's got this crazy idea that he's going to save me, but he doesn't know what Daniel's like. He could really get hurt."* Or worse.

"I'll try. . . ."

How can I ask her to put herself in danger for someone she doesn't even like? *"Forget it, I shouldn't have asked. I'll find another way."*

"It's all right; I've got a pass."

I grip the chair arms. *"Don't draw attention to yourself. And Rachel—watch out for the troopers. Daniel might send them after you, too."*

Rachel gasps. *"Troopers are running down the hall! They're heading for the stairs—"*

Cold sweat beads on my skin. Did Daniel hone in on my location after all? I hear their boots thundering on the stairs and feel the floor vibrate beneath them as they near the library.

And then I feel them running past, hear them shout, their radios squawking. Their voices grow fainter. The floor stops vibrating.

I can't breathe in. *"Do you see Alex?"*

"No."

Damn and double damn. I take a breath, then another, forcing myself to be calm. Alex knows there's danger. He'll be careful.

"Emily saw Alex, though. She went screaming to the troopers that she saw you run outside; Alex asked her to. He got other students all doing the same thing, but with different locations to different troopers. Some troopers are interviewing us now, and they're really confused. They've never seen anything like it." She giggles.

I don't know what to say. *"Thank you. Tell Alex—tell them all—thank you."* That's blown my cover. But it's given me more time. Time that I must use wisely.

I clench and unclench my hands. I don't know what to do, don't know if I should look for Alex, focus on Daniel, or figure out what to do about the Government Para.

I strengthen my visualization of copper armor, then reach for the midlevel Para-slave.

She's scouring the school for other Paras. I feel the urgency of the Para's search, the fear of being tortured, of never seeing her family again. I coat my own thoughts with hers, then reach deeper.

. . . Found two low-level Paras, and one midlevel—strong enough for that power surge earlier—but no high-level Para like the girl would have to be to send thoughts to that many at once. Don't know why they thought she'd still be here. I hate this!. . .

I feel her stiffen, feel her catch awareness of another Para—because she's looking for me. Feel her focus on a boy I've nodded to before in the halls.

I dig my nails into my hand. I have to divert the Government Para's attention from this boy. But how?

Daniel edges into my mind, his lust for power so strong that it blots everything else out for a moment.

That's it! I pull Daniel's lust for power forward, and push the Para student's back, dimming his energy with my copper shield.

The Government Para is still intent on the student. I yank Daniel's presence into her mind with every ounce of energy I have.

She gasps at the strength of his gift, the overwhelming essence of it. I can feel her choking on it, can feel Daniel become aware of her—of me—

I pull back even further until I am as far above them as I can be and still observe.

"You have been hiding what you are truly capable of!" the Government Para scolds. *"I must report—"*

"No!" Daniel's voice sounds like rifle fire. He reaches into her mind, crushing her memory. She falters, and I know he's thinking of killing her.

I gather up my energy to strike, but Daniel retreats like mist. The Government Para staggers, not remembering why she is here.

I reach inside her, knit her fragile strands together until they vibrate again the way they should. She gasps, remembers her name, her lost family—but she does not remember Alex, or Daniel, or me. She walks unsteadily out of the school.

I pull back to the room around me. I wince away from the torture I know she'll endure. I feel guilty for setting Daniel on her—but I couldn't let her take another Para. Not because of me.

I lean back in the chair. Daniel's been able to fool Government Paras into thinking his talent isn't so strong as it is. He's more powerful than I even thought.

I reach toward him again—lightly, so he won't sense my presence. Lust and power and glee rush through me like a drug. Daniel is feeding off energy from the Paras that the Government Para already caught, sucking their energy out of them so fast that they shudder in shock, their legs unable to support them anymore. I feel them age faster than should be possible as Daniel ingests their life force, draining it completely.

CHAPTER **34**

My god. I yank back, staring at the wall without seeing. Daniel is the Para-Reaper! My stomach heaves. He's
the one murdering them. He drains their energy so completely, so suddenly, it kills them.

A keening sound tears from my throat. I don't want to
believe it. But deep down, I know it's true. My brother is a
murderer. And he enjoys it.

I slide down from the chair, curl myself up tight, rocking. I don't want to know it. I'm not sure I can bear it. The
brother I loved—he's gone. And in his place is a heartless
soul. An inhuman one.

Grief washes through me in waves so strong I shudder. Deep down, I'd hoped that someday we could be a
family again. That we could have that connection we used
to. But there's no going back from this. There is no way we
can ever be like we were.

I punch the floor and slowly sit up. Even if I can't bear
what he's become—*especially* because I can't bear it—I
have to make sure he doesn't succeed. I have to stop him.

I get back onto the chair, my jaw tight. I've got to try harder to make him see what he's done. Bring him back to humanity, if I can. This is not something I can talk him out of. It's not a simple difference in philosophy or opinion. This is a deep soul choice between good and evil—and he made his decision. I let the tears flow out with my pain.

Slowly I reach for Daniel again—feel the energy surging into him like adrenaline, leaving the others weak and dizzy, their bodies unable to compensate for the loss, while Daniel pulses with their life force. He laughs with exhilaration, his laughter vibrating through my bones.

I pull the copper armor up around me, then make a tiny pinprick to connect.

"Daniel." I pour all the grief, shock, and revulsion through me, and let it flood into him. His focus jerks, then fastens onto me.

"Caitlyn—you don't understand—"

"You killed them. You killed those other Paras."

"They died to help our cause. They weren't powerful enough by themselves to make a difference. So they gave me what I needed to remain powerful."

"What do you mean?"

"You don't think all the government does is track and torture us, do you? The metal trackers in our tongues dampen our energy, keep us from becoming too powerful, too unruly. I have to keep draining it from others just to gain my own strength back."

"Cobalt," I guess. *"They use cobalt in the trackers to weaken you."*

"Yes." Daniel sounds surprised.

"Like the cobalt you put in my backpack."

"You found that, huh?" He pauses. *"Did you find the cobalt I put in your locker? Or in your classrooms?"* He giggles.

"Why, Daniel? Why did you do that to me?"

"I needed you to need me."

"You're family. I loved you. I would have done so much for you. You didn't have to try to make me dependent on you or the things you were teaching me."

"I did. You have to be completely on our side, or you're not with us at all. And you see, I was right. Even with all I did, it wasn't enough."

"Lying to me, hurting me—that's not the way to get me on your side." And neither is killing someone. Many some-ones. Not because he was forced to, at the threat of his own life or the people he loves, but because he chose to—to gain power. No matter what Daniel says, I can never look at him the same way again.

But something doesn't add up. *"The killings, the Para-Reaper—it only started a few months ago. That's what you told me. So why—?"*

Daniel's laugh echoes through my mind. *"I've been doing it for years. But I didn't used to need so much energy. I control more people now."*

I close my heart off from Daniel. *"I can't believe you're willing to kill, after what they did to Dad."*

"It's because *of what they did to Dad! I don't want any of us to ever be that vulnerable again."*

I can't believe his thinking is so twisted that he actually believes murder helps. *"You can stop this, Daniel, be-fore anyone else gets hurt. You have the power to."*

"I can't. It's already begun."

I've been so focused on our conversation, on trying to convince Daniel, that I didn't notice the undercurrent draining energy from us. Daniel's drawing on the others, using them. But it's more than just the Paras who were captured—he's also drawing on Normals, on students and teachers who have nothing to do with this, on people working in stores and offices for blocks around, and he's steadily reaching outward.

The energy drain is subtle—just a light bleeding of energy—not enough for anyone to notice, aside from a slight tiredness. But it's there. It's happening.

His reach is extending over the city like a storm. And he's not going to stop.

I feel the weight of the people's lives, the fragments of who they are passing through me—the laughter and tears, the scheming and pleading, the loving and praying. So many people, all just trying to live their lives.

Their faces flash through me, Netta's among them—and then Mom is there, looking up from her desk, her face pale—like she's just seen Dad.

"Mom!" I cry. *"I need you!"*

And then her face is gone. All the faces disappear.

I reach along the energy flowing directly into Daniel, and from him into a small network of Paras—Ilene, Zack, and a few others I don't know. The Paras revere Daniel; he's the only one who can do his—take energy from others and funnel some of it to any Para he chooses.

I close my eyes and focus on seeing through Daniel's eyes.

They're seated in a circle in a dimly lit room—I'm sure it's the basement room of the school, the aluminum helping to protect them, giving them barriers. Somehow, the circle increases Daniel's power, like it completes the circuit. He's drawing on Ilene's and Zack's talents to drain the Normals. He's already funneling some of the energy to Paras throughout the city, Paras who before could only control one Normal, maybe two at a time, but now, with this boost of energy, can control many more. It's like Daniel's a power station, absorbing energy and sending it out wherever he wants, strengthening the entire system rather than having many small, individual batteries working on their own. He's the heart of the entire network, and he's what will make the takeover of our city—maybe even our entire country—happen. And he's not going to stop there. He wants to control the world.

I yank myself out of his mind, shivering. Daniel has far outgrown Ilene. I wonder if she knows? I wonder, too, if this rebellion was Daniel's idea, or if he's just capitalizing on it.

I hold my head in my hands, feeling surprisingly weak. I look inward and my talent is at a low ebb. Daniel must have drawn on it while we were talking. It means my time is running out, just as it's running out for all of us.

I grip my hair in my fists. *How do I stop Daniel?*

I could pull the fire alarm. But that's not likely to budge them—they'll reach out and sense me, and they'll realize that there's no threat. And I don't want to expose myself to the troopers if I don't have to.

"Caitlyn." Alex's worry for me beats at my mind. He's been trying to reach me for a while now. *"Caitlyn, what's wrong?"*

I rub my face hard. I have to keep Alex safe, and Rachel and Emily, and Mrs. Vespa—and the entire city. But I don't know how or where to start.

"Caitlyn?"

"It's Daniel. He's draining Normals for miles around to replenish his own power. He's going to kill them."

"What can I do? Tell me how I can help."

I dig my nails into my scalp, trying to clear my mind. Daniel tried to weaken me by exposing me to cobalt—in my bag, my locker, and my classrooms—knowing something so highly magnetic would cut through all my barriers, like acid through steel. He knew how to make me vulnerable—probably because that's what the government did to him.

I don't know if I can find the hidden cobalt, not with all the ParaTroopers around. It's not like I can just walk into a store and ask for some. And even if I could, it might make him draw on the Normals even more in a desperate attempt to stop the energy leak. I lean back in the chair, my head heavy.

I can feel Alex's fear for me, and also Rachel's and Mrs. Vespa's. I can feel, too, how tired they're getting without understanding why; their eyelids growing heavy, their energy sapped. Even the ParaTroopers are getting weary.

Outside, a siren wails, then another, and another. I pull out my cell phone and log on to the Web to see if I can find out why. There are reports of troopers suddenly shooting each other. Normals are attacking trooper stations, and kidnapping judges, officials, and the police, locking them up. I shut off my phone, my hands shaking. This has to be Daniel's doing.

Daniel is growing steadily more powerful with all the energy he's draining from Normals and Paras alike. If I can find a way to break that connection, to interfere with Daniel's drawing on their power, I might be able to bring him back to my level so we'll be Para against Para, instead of many Paras against just me alone. Then I might have a chance at stopping him.

I chew my lip and try to think. Daniel lied to me over and over. I hadn't thought it was possible for a Para to lie to another Para; usually we're like open books to each other. But he did and it means he has talents that I don't even know about. But maybe I can mess with his head. One way to weaken a group is to make them doubt each other. If I can make him doubt one of his own group without letting him see the whole truth, maybe I'll have a chance.

I'm so weary my eyes are having trouble focusing. And the Normals around me are doing much worse. Some of the weaker ones stagger and collapse. I feel students lolling in their seats, their heads draped over their desks; I see students lying against lockers in the hallways, or else stumbling like drunks, their conversations forgotten and their words slurred. I've got to end this.

I wipe sweat off my forehead. Somehow I've got to make Daniel believe me. Just focus on my own truth, but don't let it through. . . .

I reach for Daniel.

He's there, sucking up people's energy and feeding on it. More and more people are falling into weary sleep.

"Caitlyn. Have you come to try and stop me again?" Daniel asks, his voice mocking.

"No. I wanted to warn you. You're still my brother."

"Warn me? About what?"

I feel Daniel's focus on me sharpen. I have to be careful. *"There's someone in your group who's plotting against you. They don't want you to succeed."* True. *I* don't. I push the thought away.

"How do you know?" Daniel asks, sounding suspicious.

He knows Paras can't lie to each other—it's strange that he even doubts me. Except he found a way to lie to me. And maybe he's figured out that I'm trying to do the same thing.

"I sensed it. How do you think?" I sensed it in myself. Still true . . .

"Who?" Daniel sends harshly.

"I don't know." Don't know if I'm the only one.

"What do you mean, you don't know?" His focus on the others wavers and the energy drain slows slightly.

I carefully direct some of the energy back toward the Normals he stole it from.

"There were a lot of voices in my head at the time.

Courtesy of you and your cobalt," I say. There *were* a lot of voices, confusing me, eating at me. . . .

"Fine. I'll look into it," Daniel snaps, and disconnects. No thank you, no warmth—but I hadn't really expected that from him, not anymore.

I reach out again and find Daniel probing the others in the room with him. He's wary, suspicious of everyone.

CHAPTER **35**

Outside, the sirens continue. It's getting hard to think.

There's a knock. Mrs. Vespa pushes open the door and shuffles in, her movements slow and weary. "I wanted to check on you," she says. She looks suddenly old—lines carved deep into her face, her cheeks hollowed out, wrinkles puckering up the veins on her hands. Wrinkles where none used to be.

I leap up. "I'm okay. But how are you?"

"Just fine. I'm awfully tired, though. I don't know how I can be at a time like this."

Her energy is at such a low ebb I'm surprised she's still standing. I've got to give her some of my own energy to keep her from collapsing—or worse. I've never done it before, but if Daniel can take energy and send it out to others, then so can I. It can't be that different from what I just did. I clasp both her hands in mine to give me more focus, then visualize directing some of my energy into her, filling her up with light.

I feel it draining out of me, filling her. My legs get weak. But I have so much more energy to spare. Sweat beads my upper lip and drips down the back of my neck. I keep sending more.

After a few long moments Mrs. Vespa straightens, shaking her head. "Goodness, how long were we standing like that? I must have had a catnap; I feel so much better now."

"Good!"

The lines on her face are lighter, almost nonexistent, the wrinkles gone from her hands. She doesn't look old anymore. I try to smile.

. . . Debbie said . . . Para-lover trash is back here . . . don't see her . . . maybe Mrs. Vespa . . .

I stiffen. *"Becca's coming! I can't let her know I'm here."*

Mrs. Vespa nods curtly. *"I'll take care of it."*

She steps out and eases the door closed behind her. "Becca, what are you doing back here?" Mrs. Vespa says, her voice muffled. "I thought you told me books were for geeks."

So Becca has some talent after all. No way could she stand the power drain otherwise. It's getting worse. Normals are collapsing under the strain and falling unconscious. Those with a bit of talent or who have stronger defenses through frequent reading hang on determinedly, but they're still moving as if they're walking through water.

I can't bleed my energy into them all. It'd kill me faster than Daniel's trying to. But I can give a few of them a boost to let them last a while longer. I reach for Alex, for Rachel, for Emily, and send them energy.

I feel shaky and weak, so weak I can hardly hold my head up.

"Caitlyn?" Alex says faintly. *"Where are you?"*

The strength of his vibrating worry surprises me, even with the energy I sent him. Could he be a Para, too? Or is the copper he wears protecting him?

"Caitlyn . . ." Alex sends forlornly.

I reach for him to answer but something stops me. The urgency in his mind, the amount of energy he has, the faint, metallic scent . . .

It's Daniel! He's talking to me through Alex, trying to get a lock onto me again, to drain me faster. But if I don't answer soon, he's going to get suspicious.

Got to make this quick. I cover myself with a few of Daniel's dark, ugly thoughts, then follow them. I let them pull me into the center of the raging power, ignoring the nausea in my stomach and the pain behind my eyes.

Just a little closer—

I make myself flatter, darker—and I'm there.

The crackling power flooding into Daniel is so strong he almost can't hold it. He sends some to Paras throughout the city to control the Normals around them, making them hurt each other and create chaos. And he sends small bits to Normals he wants to use to find me—Becca, Alex. His thoughts flood me.

. . . Eventually she'll have to give in; she has to be weakening. She doesn't have my influx of power. But she's more powerful than I thought; she's managing to elude me still . . .

311

The power rushes through his veins, leaving him high. He wants to hoot with joy, but he holds it in; he doesn't dare let the others know how much he's keeping from them. Especially Ilene.

I focus on her and, suddenly, she's aware of me, too.

I feel jangly inside, like I might shake apart, my muscles and veins tearing from my body.

Ilene likes this hunt, this caging and trapping other Paras. It makes her feel powerful. And she's taught Daniel to love it, too. She's laughing to herself, knowing I don't have much time left as Daniel hunts me down.

I pull inward. Black strands, the opposite of life, of energy, are writhing and snaking all around me, sucking up my life force faster than before. And mingled with the shrieking lust for power is a deep, thrumming cold, so cold it burns.

How could I not have noticed?

I dive through the narrowing gap, toward myself.

Something stings my neck as I fall. I tear off the dark strand and it bites into my hand.

I pull my copper shield to me, surrounding myself with it, and the strands dissolve. Then I'm back in Mrs. Vespa's office, a red welt on my palm and my neck burning with pain.

CHAPTER 36

"Caitlyn?" Alex's anxious voice, thin with exhaustion, reaches me. *"Why haven't you answered me? Damn it, if you don't answer me soon, I'm coming to find you."*

Just Alex this time.

"No, I'm okay." I break off a stalk of Mrs. Vespa's aloe vera, and squeeze the juice onto my neck. Its coolness eases the pain. *"Daniel was in your mind when you asked where I was. I think he was making you ask. I had to be careful."*

"Geez. I knew I felt off, like I was sick, but—Caitlyn, are you all right? Did he find you?"

"I'm fine!" Daniel could have killed me. He has more training than me, and with the power he's absorbing, it should have been easy. But he didn't.

Why didn't he?

Because he wants me to join him in taking over the world? I know he can't believe that I don't see how "right" it is.

I've got to stop him.

I remove all traces of the dark, metallic lust for power from Alex's mind, then wrap my copper shield around him, too, sealing him off from Daniel. I do the same with Rachel and Mrs. Vespa. I don't know how strong it'll be, or if it'll last, but it's a layer of defense that they didn't have before.

"Caitlyn?" Rachel reaches blindly for me, her worry boosting her fading energy.

"I'm here."

"Things are bad. People are dropping all around me. Do you know what—?"

"It's Daniel. I'm trying to stop him."

"Tell us what we can do to help," Alex says.

I hesitate. I just want to lie down and sleep. But I can't. And if I feel this way, how much worse must Rachel and Alex feel?

"Damn it, girl, don't hold out on us. Don't you trust us by now?"

"Of course I do. That's not it." I rub my aching head. *"I'm afraid."* Of Daniel. Of not being able to protect Alex and Rachel. But pretty soon I won't be able to protect anyone.

"Then let us help!"

"You can draw from us the way Daniel is drawing from the others, can't you?" Rachel says. *"You can use us to make you stronger."*

I bite my lip so hard my eyes water. *"I don't want to ask you to do that."* But deep down, I wish I could. If I'm going to stop Daniel, I need to have help. But how can I drain my friends? How can I put them at even greater risk?

"Damn it, girl, let us decide what we're willing to do!" Alex says.

I rub the back of my neck. I want to. I want to so badly. *"Tell us where you're at."*

Daniel's still draining people, funneling energy to other Paras close to him, then to some throughout the city, even the entire country. He's clearly been working on this for months. I feel his triumph as more and more Paras persuade Normals to turn on each other, kidnap law enforcers, mentally or telekinetically force ParaTroopers to shock or shoot each other. None of this would be happening without Daniel at the center, dispersing energy to others. But it is happening, and it's bigger than I realized.

"Caitlyn?" Rachel says.

"The library. I'm in the library. In Mrs. Vespa's office."

"We'll be right there," Alex says.

I send to Mrs. Vespa, letting her know they're coming, and then I try to look better than I feel.

Mrs. Vespa knocks. "I've brought your friends."

I open the door. The first face I see is Alex's, his warm brown eyes smiling at me. My heart jumps like a tambourine against my ribs.

They all crowd in, closing the door after them.

I want to wrap my arms around Alex, to feel the warmth of his body against mine.

Rachel smiles lopsidedly at me. "Things are pretty bad out there."

I nod.

Mrs. Vespa clutches at the door handle. "No sign of the enemy yet. Becca's long gone. But Jarred Temple mentioned that he has a video that proves you're a Para. Something about the fire. I haven't told him you're here." Her face is anxious. "Well, I'd better go; I don't want anyone to notice I'm gone." She leaves.

I push my glasses up. I have to focus.

"Hey! What happened?" Alex grabs my hand and turns it over, staring at the oozing welt on my palm.

I tug my hand out of his grasp. "It's nothing."

"I wouldn't call that nothing," Rachel says.

Alex grabs my hand again. "Caitlyn—"

"Daniel did it—with his mind. I told you this is serious stuff."

"Does it hurt?" Alex asks softly.

"I'm fine." I study them. "But this is what the power of the mind can do. So if you want to leave, I understand."

Alex shakes his head. "You're not getting rid of me that easy."

"Me either," Rachel says. "You're stuck with us."

Hope rushes through me, and with it, some energy I didn't know I had. "Good."

Alex lets go of me. "Tell us how to bring your brother down."

CHAPTER 37

Angry claws dig into my scalp. I whirl around as the door bursts open.

"I knew you were up to something!" Becca looks around at us. "I just *knew* it! Wait until I call the troopers down here!"

"You have no reason to call them. Not unless you want a fine," I say quickly. "They're not Paras."

Becca sneers at me. "But you are—right, new girl? I could smell you a mile away."

The room feels too small.

Alex crowds toward her. "I think you'd better leave."

"I'm not leaving until I have at least one of you to take in." Becca snaps the door shut behind her. "I'm collecting my reward."

"You're disgusting!" Rachel spits.

"Better than Para-lovers like you," Becca says. "At least I can sleep at night." She glares at me. "I won't let you hide your nasty self behind Normals anymore!"

Becca's anger drives itself like spikes through my

mind. I touch my necklace, pull my copper armor tighter around myself.

"What are you doing to her?" Alex asks, jabbing his finger in Becca's face.

"I'm not doing anything," she huffs.

"Yes, you are; I can feel it—hot needles in my scalp."

His words rock me so hard that I almost lose my balance. How can Alex feel what I feel? Normals can't do that. I stare at him, unable to make sense of this.

"You shouldn't be protecting her," Becca tells Alex snottily. "I didn't think you were that stupid. Don't you know how dangerous Paras are?" I can hear Daniel's metallic voice shuddering through hers.

"I'm not dangerous," I say, crossing my arms over my chest. "But the person you're working with is. Daniel, right? Or did he give you some other name?"

Becca's mouth slackens. "I don't know what you're talking about."

"Liar!" Alex shoves his face up near Becca's.

I touch Alex's arm. "It's okay." I look at Becca. "Do you know who you're helping?"

"Not you, you Para-freak!"

"She's not a freak!" Rachel says. "She's a better person than you are."

Becca laughs. "Then you don't know her. You've gotten sucked in by her lies. Did she tell you she can read minds?" She looks at their unblinking faces. "Reading minds is bad enough. But what this freak can do is worse. She can put things into your head like they were always there. Make you believe you're the one who thought them."

I shudder. "I'd never do that!" But Daniel has. Oh, Daniel. How could you?

"Yeah, you would. That's how you lure people into trusting you." Becca looks at Alex and Rachel, her mouth twisted in disgust. "Think about it—she comes here from god-knows-where, near the end of the school year. That alone should make her an outsider—yet suddenly you're all buddy-buddy with her. She's done a mind job on you. I'll bet Caitlyn Ellis isn't even her real name."

Uneasiness pours off Alex and Rachel, doubt and loyalty fighting each other. Alex looks at me sideways.

I feel like I'm breathing through a lungful of blood, drowning in it. "I didn't lie! Not about anything except my name—and that was only to protect my mom and me." I take a shaky breath. "I'm not using my power against you. That's not something Paras do. Well, not most of us. I didn't ask you to get involved. I don't want you to get hurt. The only time I used my gift on you was to protect you from Daniel."

Alex shoves his hands into his jeans pockets. "What's your real name?"

"Caitlyn *is* my real first name; I never changed that. But we had to keep changing our last name so the troopers wouldn't find us. My original birth certificate read Caitlyn Isobel Waters. But I'm still Caitlyn."

Becca throws back her head and fake-laughs. "What a load of--"

I reach for her arm.

"Hey! What're you—"

Fragments tumble through my brain—a younger

Becca, crying into her mother's empty nightgown; the minister droning on about the danger of Paras; Becca's father shouting that her mother was a freak.

I sift through the memories and draw the ones I need to me.

Mr. Temple, directing Becca into an empty classroom. "I know you're a loyal citizen, Becca. ParaWatch has been informed that a dangerous Para is coming to our school to recruit others. I need your help to stop her."

"I'll do anything," Becca says.

"Good. Now I'd like you to meet someone. He's going to work undercover at our school."

Daniel steps out of the shadows. "Hi, Becca. We're dealing with a perverted freak. Someone who manipulates innocent people the way your mother did. It could be dangerous. You sure you want to help?"

"You couldn't stop me."

"Okay, then. I want you to watch her, see who she befriends. Report directly to me or to Mr. Temple."

"Why not just turn her in?"

"She's too powerful, too sneaky. We have to go about this carefully. Listen—I want you to think angry thoughts at her, anytime you're around her—the angrier the better. Keep up a constant barrage."

Becca wrinkles her nose. "Why?"

"Trust me, it will hurt her. At the very least, it'll distract her. As a telepath, it's her biggest vulnerability."

Becca rubs her chin.

"If you don't think you can handle it—," Daniel says.

"No, I can do it."

I let go of Becca's arm. She staggers back, bumping her head against the door.

"Didn't you wonder how Mr. Temple knew about me ahead of time?" I ask. "The boy he introduced you to—he's not just a Government Para. He's a renegade Para who wants to destroy Normals. He's trying to take over the world. That's why he wants me."

"I don't believe you."

"Didn't you notice they knew exactly what to say to you? Daniel was feeding off your most painful memories to convince you to help him. He wanted you to help him before the other Government Para—the one who was actually assigned to this area—found out about me. Did Daniel push you to act fast?"

Becca's breath rasps loudly in the room.

"Well? *Did* he?"

"You're not natural!"

"I'm not *un*natural. I'm just different from you. And believe me, Becca—I'm not the bad guy here."

I feel Alex and Rachel relax. "Haven't you noticed people fainting, falling asleep? Or turning against each other, especially the troopers? That's Daniel's doing. You've been helping the wrong people, Becca. You've been helping renegade Paras." I send her a flash of Daniel, giving her a sense of his power.

Becca's lips turn pale. Then she slumps to the floor.

CHAPTER **38**

The metallic echo is gone. Daniel's taken his energy back from Becca. He must have felt her doubting him.

Rachel claps her hand over her mouth and stares at Becca on the floor. "Oh, my god. And I thought she was just a Para-hater and homophobe."

"What do we do with her?" Alex asks.

Darkness slithers across my mind, the lust for power curling through me. "We leave her. I have to stop Daniel."

"You said you can use us," Alex says. "Well, here we are."

I step over Becca, then lock the door. "I'll need you both to keep contact with me, help me amplify my gift."

I flop down on the chair, my legs trembling. Alex and Rachel drag boxes of books over and sit on either side of me. I grab Alex's hand, then Rachel's, ignoring the pain as her skin presses against the welt on my palm. "I'll need an anchor. Someone to pull me out if I stop breathing."

"Caitlyn!" Rachel cries. "You can't—"

"I *told* you it's dangerous. Daniel's got a lot of power. He's been trained to hurt others—maybe even kill them—

322

using his gift. And he *knows* me. He can use that to exploit my weaknesses."

"I'll be your anchor," Alex says quietly. "How do I pull you out?"

"Use my name, call to me, reach for me with all your heart and mind. Don't let go of me; I'm going to need your strength." *I don't even know if a Normal can be an anchor. But I have to try.*

"What should I do?" Rachel asks.

"Quiet your mind as much as you can. Focus on sending me copper light if you can imagine it. I'll do the rest."

"Caitlyn, are you sure—?"

"I'm sure," I say. "Try not to interrupt me unless you absolutely have to, okay?"

They both nod.

Alex leans over and brushes his lips against mine. His lips are warm and soft and smell like mint. "For luck," he says. *"And love,"* his mind-voice says. *"Come back safe. We need you. I need you."*

My lips tingle where his touched mine. "For luck," I say.

Rachel squeezes my hand gently, sadness mixing with her admiration for my courage. . . . *not sure I could do what she's doing* . . .

I close my eyes, breathing deeply, their weakening energy adding to mine. I drift up past all the voices, the cacophony of sound and emotion and shapes.

There! The shriek of almost uncontrolled power and the dark lust threaded with metallic scent—it's Daniel.

I've got to end this! I reach toward him.

The power pulls at me, snatching my breath. And then I am there, facing Daniel, seeing him as clearly as if we're in the same room together.

"*I knew you couldn't stay away,*" Daniel sends, smirking. "*You want the power, too. I know you do.*"

"*Stop draining them, Daniel. Let everyone go.*"

"*You know I won't. They don't deserve to live their little lives. But join me, Caitlyn, and I'll spare the lives of the Normals you love the most. Even Alex.*"

I bite my lip. I don't know how to stop him.

He looks at me sadly. "*Can't you see all the good we're doing? Haven't you heard the reports? Troopers shooting each other, ParaWatch members reporting themselves, officials resigning. We're making real change. We're taking back the city, the entire country, making it safe for Paras again!*"

I swallow. "*It's not real change, Daniel—not when you force someone to do it.*"

"*Sure it is. Freedom is freedom, however we get it. Normals have spilled too much of our blood. They owe us.*"

"*Daniel—this isn't you!*"

"*Isn't it? It's exactly who Mom thought I was. She sacrificed me for you.*"

"*What are you talking about? She loved you!*"

"*Yeah—loved me so much that she gave me to the enemy. Think about it, sis. You're the one who's been on the outside all these years. Not me. If she loved me so much, why didn't she come find me?*"

"*Mom and I looked for you for days, even though people were hunting us. And we never stopped looking for you—every town, every city, we'd look—and Mom would ask the Underground about you. She never gave up hope of finding you."*

Daniel's eyes flicker. *"You're lying."*

"I'm not. You're her son. My brother. And we loved you." I don't know if I can go on. I push the thoughts out painfully. *"It's my fault Ilene took you. I am so sorry. I'd do it all differently if I could."*

"Would you? You've had freedom. You haven't had to bow down to Paras and Normals who aren't so powerful or as smart as you—"

"No, I've just been on the run most of my life. With no home, no friends. No safety."

As we're talking, I can feel Normals' energy weakening for blocks around. I feel their life force being sucked out of them.

"Let them go. This isn't about them. This is about you and me."

Daniel laughs—an angry, unhappy sound. *"What do you care? You think they care? You think they even notice? They're just Normals. Not one of them has a gift, not like we do."*

He's trying to distract me from the power building up around me, making the air heavier.

I draw copper light up from my feet, feel it gather in my hands. *"No one deserves to be used. And that includes you."*

"You think I'm being used?" Daniel jabs his chest with his finger. *"I'm the one using them!"*

"You're making all the decisions?" I tilt my head, looking at him. *"What about Ilene? Don't you follow her orders?"*

"Ilene?" Daniel laughs. *"Ilene doesn't have a tenth of the power I do. She may have taught me, but she follows me now. I want you to join me, too. Together we'll be unstoppable. But if you won't join me, then I want you to suffer the way I have."*

Power is shuddering all around me, shaking with the energy Daniel's drawing from people. Strands of negative energy flow from Daniel toward me, coiling and uncoiling, getting ready to strike. To drain me.

A dark strand whips against my mouth, and I taste salty blood.

"Caitlyn!" Alex's voice.

I ignore him. Got to focus. Hope. Laughter. Love. The right of every living creature to live. Healing, community, the Normals who've helped us. I pull these toward me, and throw them at Daniel. Black shadows move in front of my eyes.

He blocks me with the strength of thousands, then sends his fury shrieking toward me.

Dark strands lash at me, slicing my flesh, trying to burrow inside me. They wrap around me, stinging through my clothes, crushing away my breath.

I scream as my skin splits open. Scream as darkness bursts through my mind. I keep sending love and healing to Daniel, reminding him of what he can be. Reminding him that Mom loves him, too, no matter what.

He jerks back like he's been bitten, but the love does not hurt him the way his draining of my power hurts me. Love is not going to stop him.

I can't see anymore; I can only feel the darkness as it shakes my body, squeezing at my heart. I gulp my own energy, struggling to breathe. I send my thoughts to Daniel to make him see—life matters. All life!

Darkness pushes into my chest and lungs.

"Caitlin!" Alex cries. *"Caitlin, come back!"*

His voice yanks me out of the darkness like a fish on the end of a line.

CHAPTER **39**

I'm lying on the rough carpet in Mrs. Vespa's office, choking on my own blood. My cheek burns. Daniel is so much stronger than me now.

Alex and Rachel crouch over me, their eyes frightened. Alex grips my shoulder.

I turn over on my side and cough up blood. *"Why did you do that? I wasn't finished!"* I send to Alex.

"You were killing yourself!" Alex shoves his hand in front of my face. "Look! That's your blood!"

I taste the saltiness of my blood, feel the burning of my open flesh. I know he's right, but I can't let Daniel and Ilene kill people.

Sirens wail in the distance, calling their distress. The chaos is worsening.

Something feels empty, out of place. I lift my head, ignoring the rush of pain. *"Where's Becca?"*

"She must have left when we were focused on you! Do you want me to—"

"No. There's no time." I sit up, my muscles shaking.

I won't look at Alex. I can't. I'm too angry at him, and too ashamed of myself.

"You were having convulsions," Rachel says. "Your nose was bleeding, and gashes started appearing on your skin. Alex did the right thing, stopping you."

"Thank you," I mutter.

But he pulled me out before I could stop Daniel. And now Daniel's going to kill all those Normals. Thousands of them. Maybe even millions.

Sirens wail louder, one after another.

I struggle to draw a breath. Darkness is closing around me, pulling at me.

I can't keep fighting Daniel this way—I'll lose. My ribs ache like they were kicked in, my skin is laced with blood, and I'm so exhausted, I can barely speak. I want to put my head on Alex's chest and cry. But that would be admitting defeat. So what that it didn't work to push light against dark. I just have to find another way.

"Alex—could I borrow your bracelets? The copper ones?"

Alex yanks them off and hands them to me without taking his gaze off me.

I slide the bracelets on my wrist, praying they give me enough of a shield from Daniel. I sit up straighter, keeping the pain out of my face.

"What are you doing?" Alex says.

"I'm going back in."

"You can't be serious! You'll kill yourself. I won't let you."

The darkness is swirling around us like a thick fog; I'm surprised they can't see it. *"Just hold on to me and don't let go, not for anything,"* I send. *"I have to finish this."*

Alex's warm hand wraps around my clenched one. Rachel grips my other hand. I close my eyes and fall into the darkness. It breathes around me, pushes my lungs up and down, tries to rip through my mind. I don't resist; I just follow it.

I let go until I am up out of my body and back into the blackness. It covers everything like a writhing carpet of snakes.

Daniel laughs. *"I knew you couldn't let them die."*

He's drawn Normals into a deep slumber, their bodies comatose, just human-shaped bumps under the carpet of black. Millions of them, right across the whole city, and spreading fast. They are in the sleep before death, the restful period of no-longer conscious. I send some of my energy to them, let them absorb it, even though I know he'll only feed off it.

I am so weary it's hard to focus.

"You can do it," Alex thinks at me.

I feel his warmth all around me, his presence buffering Daniel's, bringing me calm.

I turn to Daniel. *"I thought you wanted them to know what it's like to be us—to be hated and hunted. If you kill them, how can they?"*

"Oh, I'll keep a few around. But the rest—they don't deserve their little lives. They don't do anything to earn them. Not like we do. If you want to save a few, you know how."

No. I can't. *I won't.*

I think of Alex, of Rachel, of Mrs. Vespa and Netta, and all the people whose lives have touched mine; all the people who care, and I falter. If I fail, I'll lose them all.

I bow my head. What can I do to change his mind?

I think of a time when Daniel and I were laughing together, before all this started, and I send it to him.

Daniel relaxes his grip just for a moment. I dive deeper into his mind, pulling my copper armor tight around me.

I flip back through his memories as fast as I can, looking for the right one—his enjoyment at controlling people, his delight at lying to Ilene and shielding it from her, his pleasure at making a female officer think she wanted him. I'm getting closer.

There—I've found it. This one has power. I release the memory into Daniel's mind.

He's eight years old, tied to a chair in a darkened room, cold, joints aching, peed himself hours ago. And still the man in the uniform slaps his face.

"You can do better, Daniel. I know you can. Now make this soldier do something he doesn't want to do. Then we'll let you go."

I turn to him, feel him follow me into his mind. *"Did they let you go, Daniel? Did they show you mercy? The way you're showing people now?"*

"Get out of my head—or I swear to god I'll kill you."

The walls of his mind pulse. The darkness grows heavier. I struggle to move, or to even breathe, as I flip through the years. I can feel him gathering energy around me, draining people ever faster.

I hesitate over one of Daniel's memories. It is sealed—even from himself—but I can feel the pain seeping through. I break the seal and let the pain, the scarred memory, flow over me.

"Daniel." Ilene smiles down at him, strokes his soft cheek. "You're special, you know that? And one day you're going to win us the war. Don't you worry about those pigeons now."

Daniel screams, the walls of his mind vibrating. *"Turn it off! I don't want to see it!"*

The dark strands knock against my armor, cracking it, but I keep his memory flowing.

Daniel tries to keep his eyes on Ilene, on the love and praise she's giving him—he wants it so bad—but those pigeons are lying there so still, blood staining their beaks. Their hearts burst because he tried to make them do something they wouldn't—or couldn't—do.

The trooper sitting in the corner watching them yawns.

A dim pounding, shouting sound rises above the memory. I turn toward it. Mr. Temple and Becca are outside Mrs. Vespa's office, Becca gesturing wildly. The copper I'm wearing is burning into my flesh.

"Open the door this instant!"

"I'm sorry, you can't go in there," Mrs. Vespa says, pushing her firm body in front of Mr. Temple.

Mr. Temple shoves her aside and pounds harder, making the door shake, but he already looks years older.

Rachel stares wide-eyed at the door from the other side.

"Mom!" I send desperately. *"Mom! I need you!"*

I can't tell if she can even hear me. *"Mom!"* I scream, using all the strength of my mind.

The door shudders harder and a small gap appears between the frame and the door. Rachel drags boxes of books to the door, barricading it.

"Mr. Temple, that's my private office. I really have to ask you to leave," Mrs. Vespa says firmly. *"Caitlyn—just do what you have to do. I'll keep him out,"* she thinks at me.

Behind me, Daniel's still gathering people's energy, trying to rebuild his strength. The fragment of memory hit him hard.

I turn back to his memory, let it flow over us again. . . .

Ilene turns his face back to hers. "You and I are going to rule the world. Put all these Normals in their place. I know you've got the ability, the same as I do. And you've got the hunger. But you don't have control yet. You must practice."

Daniel wipes his face with his sleeve. "My dad—" His voice breaks. "My dad always told me we should never use our power against anyone weaker."

"Your dad was a dreamer. He wouldn't look at reality. And look what they did to him."

"But you—!"

The trooper in the corner stirs, gripping his rifle tighter.

"It's okay, Arnold," Ilene says, without turning around. "I've got this under control."

The trooper shrugs and yawns wider.

Ilene sets another cage of pigeons down in front of Daniel. "You need to focus. Practice. Get it right this time."

Daniel cries out again, the black strands piercing my skin.

I shudder with pain so strong it almost kicks me out of Daniel's mind. But I won't let it. I picture Mom, the love in her eyes. *"Hold on, baby. I'm coming."* And I keep unfolding Daniel's memory.

Ilene opens the cage and grabs the flapping pigeon.

"No, don't make me!"

"You have to learn some control, or you're of no use to me. Or to the government. Now make this pigeon dance."

"NO!" Daniel screams, all of his fear and anger going into the word like a giant fist.

Ilene ducks. Behind her, the trooper jerks, then sags back against his chair, pale and still, blood trickling from his mouth.

"I'm sorry, I'm sorry—don't hurt me!" Daniel cries.

"Hurt you? Daniel, I'm proud of you. Look at the power you already wield!" She shakes the dead trooper. Daniel recoils.

Daniel is crying now, along with his child self, and as he cries, the darkness inside him stretches and thins, the strands around me withering and pulling back. I draw my copper armor all around me again and the black strands hiss as they burn.

"It wasn't your fault," I say. *"You didn't know what would happen. You didn't understand."*

"I didn't mean to kill him," he cries.

"I know you didn't. But I think Ilene did. I think she wanted it to happen, and knew it probably would if she got you upset enough."

Daniel sinks, weeping, to his knees.

Rachel's cries slice through me. I stare down at my body and at the room.

The door is splintering as troopers pound it with their boots. Mr. Temple's urging them on like a madman.

And then a deep tranquility blankets everything, quieting the voices, slowing people's minds.

I know that mind-voice immediately, even though I haven't heard it in years. I know the way she can soothe people without saying a word.

Mom! She's here—and her abilities are back.

I'd cry if I had the energy.

By stopping the troopers, she's giving me more time. But even with that, I still don't know if I can defeat Daniel. He is so powerful, and he's got the power of many Paras linked up with him.

I'm only one Para trying to stop them. One Para with a strong talent, but still only one Para, drawing on the weak but willing energy of two Normals. Daniel's trained for years already. How can I even hope to surpass his power?

Despair and exhaustion weaken me.

"You'll win because you have to," Mom's calm mind-voice says. *"You'll win because it's right. And you're not the only Para you can draw on. You have me."*

As she sends this, I feel her bright energy meet mine, feel it coursing through my body like harnessed lightning, all of her fierce determination building up my own. *"Daniel may be my son and your brother, but he's lost his humanity. What he's trying to do is evil. And we cannot allow him to win. So get in there and fight—just this one last time. You can do this, Caitlyn. You're stronger than you know."*

Energy sizzles through me—hers and mine joined together, with Alex's and Rachel's woven in.

I take a deep breath and turn back to Daniel, to his dark strands that are still sucking the energy from people.

"You will not do this!" I shout, my mind-voice ringing out like a thunderclap, shaking the earth around us and making the air vibrate.

Daniel's dark strands shudder, becoming almost transparent, like gray ephemeral ribbons. His gaze locks on mine, his eyes so cold they make my bones hurt. *"You're not going to win,"* he says, his mind-voice mocking. The gray strands strengthen. *"You and your insignificant little group of Normals."*

"It's not just me and my Normal friends anymore," I say, gathering Mom's energy and my own up through my center.

Daniel's eyes widen. *"Mom?"* he mouths, looking almost like a vulnerable little boy—which he might resemble if it weren't for his dark threads still grasping, trying to devour everyone's life force.

I hold the energy inside me, bright and hot as the sun, and I hurl it at him, my mind-voice a command, stronger than any force of nature. *"You will stop this killing! You will stop! NOW!"*

Daniel freezes, his face draining to a pale twilight, the threads shrinking, becoming filmy cobwebs.

I tear at them with both hands, pouring in not just my energy, but my experiences, my soul. Love and pain, joy and sadness, compassion and fear all swirl together, pushing at the darkness. The strands fall away. The energy drain splutters, then stops. Paras and Normals alike disconnect from Daniel's grasp. Daniel's grief weighs him down so heavily, he doesn't seem to notice.

Throughout the city people sit up, blinking their eyes and shaking their heads to clear them. I pour my energy into them all, reversing the drain.

"It's all right," I tell them. *"It's all right now."*

And then darkness takes me.

CHAPTER 40

"Caitlyn." I smell lemon and tobacco. *"Caitlyn, wake up, honey. I have something you need to hear."*

Dad. I open my eyes to see him smiling down at me, his body glowing with light. He rubs his cheek against mine and I feel the rough bristles that used to make me laugh.

I smile, though I'm so weary my bones ache.

"You are not to blame for Daniel being kidnapped, or for my death. You couldn't have stopped the Authority, not then. And I was doing what every good father does. I was trying to make the world a better place for you to grow up in."

He pulls my chin up, makes me look at him. *"Ilene had her eye on you and Daniel both—but Daniel was flattered, and he was more malleable, so she chose him. It's not your fault."*

A lightness moves through me. *"Thank you,"* I whisper.

"You know I speak the truth. I love you, pumpkin. I'll always be watching out for you."

He looks over his shoulder, as if listening to something I can't hear. He turns back to me and touches my cheek with his roughened hand. *"It's time for you to go back now—so listen carefully. You saved a lot of lives today. I'm very proud of you. I want you to always remember that."*

"Caitlyn!" It's Mom's voice, scared, almost panicked.

Dad looks down past me, then back at me again, his eyes glistening. *"You have to go now."*

"But I have so much I want to say to you! So much I want to ask and find out."

"We'll talk another time, I promise. But you're worrying your mother." He clears his throat. *"Tell her I love her. I love you both."*

I put my arms around his neck and kiss his stubbly cheek. *"I love you, too."*

"I know you do, sweetheart. Now go."

He gently pushes me. The light sucks me down faster and faster, until I thump back into my body. Into the pain.

I gasp for air and groan, open my heavy eyelids.

Mom is leaning over me, her pale face weary, her bloodshot eyes terrified. "Oh Caitlyn!" she sobs, gripping my hand. Voices filter through the room but I can't make sense of them.

. . . "unexplained aging". . . "deaths and riots" . . .

Mom shuts off her radio and then there's silence.

"Dad says he loves you," I gasp out.

Mom's eyes well up, and a tear slides down her cheek. She squeezes my hand tighter, cramping it. *"Don't you ever scare me like that again. I need you here. The world needs you too much for you to use yourself up like that."*

I grin lopsidedly at her. *"Okay, Mom. I'll try not to."*

Her mind-voice is the sweetest music I ever heard and it's moving through my heart. I feel a total connectedness and love, and I don't know how I got through all that time without it.

Mom strokes my forehead with her cool hand. *"My love never went away. You just couldn't hear it."* Her touch pulls me the rest of the way back.

I'm exhausted from the battle and it's still hard to breathe; it's like having a gravestone on my chest. But I struggle not to let them see, to keep them from worrying too much. "We stopped him!" I croak, straining to see Alex and Rachel.

"*You* stopped him." Alex's voice is firm. "All we did was support you."

He lets go of my hand and I see that my dad's copper ring is cracked and red with my blood. It slides off and falls to the floor. Alex picks it up and, on one of his fingers, I notice a deep imprint the shape of my ring; his skin looks bubbly and pink.

"Alex, your hand!" I say.

He looks down. "All that copper you were wearing—your ring, the bracelets, the necklace—they burned so hot, they were glowing like the sun."

He cares about me so much he didn't let go, even though it must have hurt like hell. Gratitude and guilt fill me. "Alex, that must have hurt!"

I glance at my hand. There's a hole burned into my finger the shape of the ring—pulpy flesh carved away down to white bone, the skin around it seared black. My wrist looks as bad and I know my neck must, too, all from the copper that protected me even as it burned. It doesn't hurt, although I know it should. I swallow, look away.

Mom hands me three pain pills. "Swallow," she says. She gently draws the bracelets off me, trying not to hurt me, then the necklace, too. Then she takes a handkerchief out of her purse, soaks it at the water cooler, and lays it on my finger and wrist. Everyone is quiet—too quiet.

"What's wrong?" I ask. "What's everybody so glum about?"

"Besides the fact that you almost killed yourself?" Mom snaps, her fear and love fierce around me.

I'd missed our connection so much. Hot tears spill down my cheeks.

I'm happier than I've been in a long time. It's only the pain digging at my flesh that keeps me from laughing with relief. I actually did it! I stopped Daniel and the Authority. At least for now.

I'm so weary, I feel myself drift.

Voices filter through my mind, and then suddenly I hear Ilene's—sharp and cold. *"You stupid worthless incompetent failure! You were like my son! I gave you everything—and still you managed to mess this up."*

"You took me from my family!" Daniel yells. *"You tortured me!"*

"I trained you. Do you think you'd be half so powerful as you are if it weren't for me, you ungrateful sniveling twit? All I asked was that you bring your sister into the fold. And you couldn't even do that!"

"You'll never get her," Daniel says. *"She's stronger*

than you are. Stronger than any of us. Her soul's pure—unlike yours or mine."

"I can't believe I wasted years on you! You are not worthy of my sight. I forbid you to take the serum until you redeem yourself. Let's see how well you do without having your powers enhanced, especially once the pain of withdrawal sets in."

"Ilene, don't do this," Daniel pleads.

"It's better than you deserve," she snaps. *"Now be gone."*

Their voices waver, and then Daniel disappears.

Daniel, oh, Daniel. I want to cry again, but I am too tired and empty.

My mind aches and there's a fluttering sound in my ears.

Ilene appears before me, her eyes large and innocent, her mouth curved in a gentle smile. Love exudes from her like a perfume.

I look at the others, but I know no one else sees her.

I want to push her away and yell at her for the way she treated Daniel, but my mind feels fogged by her love.

She smiles wider, her eyes so intense I can't look away. Her steady gaze reminds me of the way my dad used to look at me, like I was the only one who mattered.

I know it isn't real. But I can't look away, can't stop the sudden longing for her acceptance and approval.

Ilene's eyes deepen to draw me in. *"You impress me, Caitlyn. You're more powerful than any of us thought. You stopped Daniel, at least for now, even after all my training. But you can make it right. Help us make the world a place where all Paras can live freely. As a token of our goodwill, we've destroyed the video that small-minded principal made."*

"Thank you. . . ." I can't seem to connect my thoughts. If I could just clear my head . . .

"You know your father wanted you to be just as free as the Normals. That was his vision." She reaches into her pocket and draws out a glowing vial and a syringe. *"But you're not powerful enough to do it on your own. If you want to save Paras and Normals—if you really care about other people as you say you do—then I can help you do that."*

The vial pulses in her hand like liquid starlight. It sings to me, a low humming like my dad humming me to sleep.

But it's not my dad. It doesn't sound like him.

I blink, shrinking back. *"Is that what made Daniel so strong?"* It must be the serum they were talking about.

Ilene strokes the vial with her fingertip. *"It enhances Paranormal power. We developed it ourselves."*

Her voice coats me like honey, sweet and thick, filling my mind.

"Join us and you'll be part of something much bigger than yourself. You'll be part of the new era. We have power beyond anything your father ever dreamed of. We have people in every government around the world, in every organization that matters. There's no end to what we can do."

Dad dreamed of a world where we could live freely— but he also taught me that *all* life is precious, Normal or Paranormal, and that we're all in this together. Not like the world Ilene and Daniel envision.

Ilene's eyes are almost glowing, like the vial is melting into her. I tear my gaze away and draw on my own energy.

I realize now that Ilene is an empath whose gift is enhanced by glamour. I don't know why I never realized that before. I saw, through Daniel, what she was capable of. I stare at her and suddenly I feel it—just the faint push to not question her, and to want her love. She's fine-tuned her technique, but she's not powerful. Not like Daniel and me.

When I look back, her smile is dimmer, her lips red slashes. And beneath the kindness in her eyes is a coldness deeper than the Arctic ocean, trying to pull me under.

I think about how desperate Daniel was, about those coiling strands that grew with his emotion, and about Ilene's coldness inside him.

"Your drug increases the user's power," I send, pointing to the glowing vial. *"But it also harnesses them to you, doesn't it? It gives the Authority some kind of control over the Paras who take it."*

Ilene blinks, a shutter snapping shut behind her eyes, and I know I'm right.

"I don't want it," I say firmly. *"Not now, not ever. I don't need your kind of power."*

"Oh, but you will, dear. You will," Ilene says, and then she's gone.

I shiver, staring at the place where she'd been, then rub my arms to warm myself. I know I made the right decision, but I'll have to train myself and get ready for when they come back. Because they *will* come back; I'm sure of it. And when they do, I'll fight them just as hard as I did today.

As long as I'm here—with all the people who helped me—they'll have fierce opponents.

I look at the faces around me—Mom, Alex, and Rachel—and feel the love and worry pouring off them.

"You didn't tell me what's wrong," I remind them.

"Daniel's gone," Mom says. "I felt him leave. Like he teleported out of here."

A Para with the ability to control people, charged up on some drug, and who can disappear at will—it's scary. But the Normals who warped his mind and soul—they're even more frightening. "At least everyone's all right. That's the most important thing."

Alex rubs his hand against the carpet and Rachel looks away.

"Everyone *is* all right?" I say.

"Honey, you were out for a while, and—"

"Mr. Arnold is dead," Alex says. *"I know you want the truth."* "Ten students and two teachers are in comas. Four had sudden bleeding and were taken to the hospital. People aged before our eyes—though after your ring burned bright, people began to look normal again. But who knows what the strain did to them. And that's just what happened here, in our school."

"And the news . . ." Rachel hesitates.

"Tell me," I say, my voice flat. I know some of it already.

"Troopers started gunning each other down—which I guess isn't a loss. But bystanders—just regular people—got caught in the crossfire all over the city and even farther away. A lot of people are injured . . . or dead. And that started the riots." Rachel looks down at the carpet.

"Riots?" I close my eyes. *Not again. I can't live through it again.* Regular people trying to kill us, not just troopers. Mom and me hiding in our car, living on hand-outs and in fear, not daring to stay in one place for even a few days.

"Someone told reporters that a Para in this school started it all," Mom says, expressionless; I know she's figured out that Daniel's the one who leaked that to the troopers and the press.

I can hear the helicopters now, their blades beating the air.

I feel numb inside.

No one should have died. And now there are riots again. I should have just given myself up—

"We all might be dead if you had," Mom sends. *"Don't you even go there, Caitlyn. You did the right thing. Daniel had to be stopped."*

I feel the pain in her mind-voice, and the great truth. I'm so grateful she sees him for who he is now.

"Emily—do you know how Emily is?" Rachel asks anxiously.

I reach for Emily's thought-patterns. She's tired, like everyone else, exhausted even, but her energy's starting to come back. Energy and worry. "She's okay," I rasp out. "She's worried about you."

Rachel squeezes my hand. *"Thank you."* Her gratitude and relief fill me.

Alex clears his throat. "Mr. Temple announced that more troopers are being brought in, and reporters are here to make sure everyone sees the big arrest. No one's been allowed to leave the school. And Mrs. Vespa heard that another Government Para is coming to hunt you down."

I straighten my shoulders.

This is the end we were running from.

CHAPTER 41

I heave myself to my feet. I always knew this day would come.

My chest aches like I've been stabbed. I know what I have to do, but god, I'll miss everything—my freedom, my mom, Alex, Rachel, Mrs. Vespa, Netta . . . even this school and that crummy pool at the motel.

"I'm not letting you go out there," Mom says, blocking the door with her body. "I'm not letting you get captured!"

"You can't stop it, Mom. They know I'm here. They're not going away until they get someone. You don't think we should let them capture someone else in my place, do you?"

"Not unless it's me."

I look away, angrily. "I'm the one who got us caught."

"No! You're the one who saved us. And you're my daughter! It is my right to sacrifice myself for you."

"Both of you stop it!" Alex says. "No one's getting captured. Rachel and I will help you escape."

They couldn't save us even if they tried. They'd only put themselves in danger. I shake my head, ignoring the pain. "I'm tired of running. Tired of hiding who I am. I'm sick of barely existing." I reach for the door handle with my good hand. "I'm going out there," I tell them.

"*Caitlyn—*" Mom reaches for me.

"*I'm old enough to make my own decisions, Mom. Let me have that freedom.*"

Her arm falls to her side.

I focus on Mr. Temple, Becca, and the troopers outside the door. It almost takes more effort than I have, but I manage to hold them in place like painted statues.

I walk out into the school yard, flanked by my mom, Alex, Rachel, and Mrs. Vespa. The trooper helicopters circle overhead. The school yard is blocked off by yellow police tape. Troopers in riot gear block off the yard, but still, people have pushed their way onto the grounds, shoving and yelling. Others surge against the metal fence and spill out into the street. There are anti-Para banners, of course, but I'm surprised to see just as many pro-Para signs bobbing up and down.

Reporters rush toward me shouting out their questions. Troopers get into firing position, training their guns on us. I take a bit more of my energy, my legs trembling so hard I can barely hold myself up, and freeze the rest of the troopers in place.

"Are you the Para they're looking for?"

"Did you turn troopers against each other?"

"Are you Teen Para?"

I hold up my hands and the school yard goes quiet. I can hear the traffic pass by a few streets away, can see the crowd swell as more people gather around. Microphones and digital recorders are shoved in my face, cameras trained on me. People in the crowd record me with their cell phones, watching me intently.

I lick my dry lips. "Yes, I am Teen Para, but I've never used my abilities to harm anyone. I did *not* turn troopers against each other. I value all life! I know what it's like to lose someone." The yard is eerily silent, people leaning forward to hear me. I raise my voice. "I am giving myself up to protect the people I love. My friends are innocent of anything except being good people. They didn't know my secret." Tears clog my throat, making my voice hoarse. People stare at me the way they gape at accident victims. I see Netta in the crowd, nodding at me. My head aches with the strain of holding back the troopers. Blood drips from my nose, but I go on.

"I wish no one had died today—trooper, Normal, or Para—but they did. I did not make this happen—but I beg you to end it, to care about your fellow human beings. I hope that tomorrow, before you begin to celebrate the holiday, you take a moment to think about all those who were murdered, and all the people who've lost someone they loved."

I release my hold on the troopers. They run toward me, rifles pointed at me. More troopers pour out of the school in a steady stream and I know that the only thing stopping them from shooting me on the spot is all the cameras pointed our way.

"Make sure you tell them you didn't know I was a Para," I tell Alex, Rachel, and Mrs. Vespa. *"You don't want to be caught up in this."*

"Caitlyn—" Alex protests.

"Do it!" I send in a screaming thought, their faces blurring in front of me.

A trooper jabs my chest with a black metal stick and my body shrieks in pain. The shock stiffens my limbs, tears at my nerves—it's a pain greater than anything I've ever felt. It stops, and for a moment, there's relief. But then the trooper tasers me again.

"No! You leave my baby alone!" Mom cries.

I fall to my knees, my body jerking uncontrollably as the jolt grips me, but I will not cry out. I know Daniel endured this many times over the years—Daniel and all the other Government Paras.

"You bullies!" a voice shouts. "Go pick on someone your own size!" It's a familiar voice—the motel owner. If the pain wasn't so bad, I'd laugh. Just imagine—a Parahater defending me.

A torrent of blood gushes from my nose and black spots fill my vision. I'm on my side now, convulsing on the asphalt. I don't know how I got here, but a trooper begins to kick at me. I raise my arms to shield my head. My lip splits open but I can barely feel the pain; the electroshock from the Taser takes all of my focus.

I can hear my mom screaming at them to stop, can feel Alex getting ready to fight, even against such ridiculous odds, all those guns. Rachel is screaming at reporters to make sure they get all of this on tape, but I know their efforts will only make things worse. *"Please—don't fight them,"* I send. *"Just be safe."*

Then I shut myself off from them. When another Government Para arrives, I won't have him targeting my mom and friends because of me. And I don't want them to know my pain, even though they can see it.

I lapse in and out of consciousness and still the troopers shock me. They're furious at what happened to their fellow troopers and they're scared of me and of every other Para. The fear fuels their hate, making them enjoy my pain every time they shock me—they can't get enough of it. I wonder if they'd rather kill me than make me a Para-slave after all.

I get to my knees and try to stagger to my feet.

The crowd is screaming, surging forward and throwing things—but not at me.

"Leave her alone!"

"Trooper brutality!"

"Free Teen Para!"

Their cries fade in and out through the roaring in my ears. I'm sure I must be hallucinating—people can't actually be standing up for me—but when I look up, I see Mrs. Vespa, Netta, Emily, and the motel owner all in front of the crowd, which is being held back by a line of troopers in riot gear. People I don't even know hold makeshift signs and shout for my release.

Swaying, I blink sweat and tears out of my eyes, awed by the sight.

Hope flutters and fills my chest, makes me want to smile even as another jolt tears through my body, tightening every muscle into screeching agony.

I smell burning skin and know it's my own. But I can endure it if it means that people will see that we're not the enemy.

"The crowd's out of control," a trooper says. "Let's get her out of here."

They grab my arms and drag me toward the van.

Mom runs beside me, trying to go with me, but a trooper shoves her aside like a ragdoll.

"I'll find you, baby!" she shouts. "I love you." But we both know that once you're a Para-slave, you're in the system for good—if they don't kill you.

The troopers shove me roughly into the van and slam the door, metal clanging on metal, their guns still pointed at me. I hear a lock turn and a trooper motions me to a hard metal bench, then cuffs me to it.

The engine starts, but we don't move. My body is still spasming in pain and I'm afraid, but I feel hope, too, stronger than I have in years—hope and an almost manic elation. We did it! We got through to people. Even if I'm never free again, the world will be a better place. And the Authority hasn't won.

The roar outside gets louder and turns into a chant—"Free Teen Para! Free Teen Para!"

I lean forward, hardly able to believe what I'm hearing, but I know it's real. And I know it's for me. Tears slide down my cheeks.

The van starts rocking from side to side and I feel heavy pounding along its walls. "Free Teen Para! Free Teen Para!"

The guard beside me swears and I peer through the metal grate separating me from the cab. Through the windshield I can see hundreds of people blocking the van, pressing in around it, waving their fists and chanting.

A sob bursts from my throat. I never really thought we'd get here. I'd fought for it, I'd hoped for it with every molecule in my body, but I didn't really believe that people would let go of their hatred, fear, and prejudice long enough to see us as equals. But here we are, with Normals calling for my release. I wish Dad could see this. I hope Daniel does.

"Free Teen Para!" someone shouts, and a brick hits the trooper van's windshield, cracking it.

"Just run them over!" the guard beside me shouts to the driver.

"Are you crazy? They're filming this, you know—at least a dozen separate news stations."

I let my breath out in a trembling rush. I can't stop the tears.

"Alex?"

"Caitlyn! We're calling for your release," Alex sends, his mind-voice choked. *"We might just pull this off."*

"I told you to go somewhere safe!"

"You didn't really think I was going to listen to you, did you? Besides, I didn't start it. It was some woman in the crowd. And then the rest picked it up pretty fast. They're not used to seeing people brutalized in front of them, Para or not. Not like what those troopers did to you." Alex shudders. *"I think it shook the crowd into action."*

"Yeah!" Rachel says, butting in. *"It made a difference, having it happen right in front of them, seeing you're just as human and vulnerable as the rest of us. It didn't hurt that your mom ran after you and freaked out like that."*

I grow cold. *"My mom! Is she—"*

"She's okay. A trooper started beating on her with his baton, but the crowd stopped him. Most everybody's on your side."

This is the change that for years I've desperately hoped for. And I'm actually a part of it! No matter what else happens, I'll never be sorry for this day.

I lean back as the chanting voices calling for my release go on and on.

The van doors screech open and a man in a black suit and polished black shoes enters, staring down at me. Not a trooper or Government Para—someone much higher up.

The trooper guarding me stands and salutes. The man motions the trooper out of the van with his chin and the trooper scurries out, shutting the doors behind him.

I swallow.

The man stands there, staring down his nose at me, assessing me with his flat, cold eyes. I try not to look away.

"You're a calculating little Para, aren't you?" he finally says.

"What?" I blink at him.

"Setting up that blog, amassing such a huge following,

turning troopers against each other, giving that touching speech before your capture, allowing the troopers to beat you up—"

I stare at him, my mouth dry and my heart pounding.

He goes on: "Riots—worse than the ones ten years ago. Looting, trooper stations burned to the ground, protests, news stories, exposés, people on strike. And even though their own kind was killed, they're still demanding your release. I never thought I'd see the day we'd go backward like this," he says, looking at me bitterly.

I feel like I'm in a dream. But the shrieking pain of my burns and the deep muscle ache from the Taser tells me I'm not.

Then the man uncuffs me.

I stand, wobbling and weak. Hot, fiery needles of pain shoot through my legs. I take in a shallow breath, trying to ignore the ache in my ribs.

"Not so fast," the man spits.

I sink back to the cold metal bench, my legs unable to hold me.

The man opens the van door and motions a medic in. "See to her wounds—all of them," the man raps out. "I'm not going to have people complaining that we used more force on her than we did."

The medic climbs into the van, shutting the door behind him. He bends over me, his shoulders slightly stooped with an unseen weight, his brown hair thinning in a patch on top of his head. His hands are gentle as he checks me over, an apologetic look on his face.

The medic clucks his tongue. "Those are some serious third-degree burns you have there."

"I didn't ask you to tell her what her condition is," the man snaps. "I asked you to patch her up. Now do it."

The medic nods tightly and lays his hands on me, closing his eyes. Bright light glows from his fingers as his hands heat up. I startle, but then I see the metal tracker in his tongue and understand he's a Para-slave, too.

I feel my skin begin to knit itself, the wounds closing over and the pain becoming manageable.

The medic shudders and removes his hands, sweat dripping from his forehead. "You'll be okay now," he says quietly.

"Thank you," I whisper.

His eyes meet mine briefly before he digs into his bag. He pulls out a tube of burn cream and some bandages, applying them deftly.

"A day or two of bed rest and she'll be just fine," he says.

I rub my face, relieved. I feel like I've been dropped from a five-story balcony—repeatedly. But I'm going to be okay. More than okay.

"Very good. You can go," the man says. The medic scurries away even faster than the troopers.

The man stands there, arms crossed, looking at me the way a scientist might look at a rat. I gaze back defiantly.

The man laughs. "You're so like your brother."

He knows Daniel? Knows we're related?

The man pulls a thin bracelet-like metal cuff out of his

pocket and snaps it around my wrist. It locks with a click, the metal sealing so tight I can hardly see the joint. "We may have to let you go, but we sure as hell aren't going to stop watching you," he says. "And when the winds change . . . ."

It's a tracking device! He's put a tracking device on me like I'm a dog. But I hardly care. At least it's not a tracker through my tongue. I'll find a way to get it off.

"I can go?" I ask.

He nods curtly. "We'll be in touch."

He stands back and I open the van doors, then climb out into the bright hot sun. I lift my head, looking around me, and feel the breeze and sunshine caressing my face.

Seeing me, the crowd—even bigger than when I was shoved in the van—roars in approval.

Mom, Alex, Rachel, Mrs. Vespa, and Netta call out to me from the front of the crowd. And behind them, the motel owner stands smiling. Alex's eyes soak me in, and Mom's face is full of love and relief.

I run to them, my body light as air.

A Note from the Author

I drew on many of my own traumatic experiences in writing *Hunted*, just as I did with *Scars*. Like Caitlyn, I know what it's like to have my life threatened, to experience electroshock and other forms of torture, to live under oppression, *and* to break free from oppressors. In my case it was cults; in Caitlyn's, two fairly organized groups of oppressors, one government sanctioned and one not.

I am a ritual abuse survivor; my biological family was part of organized intergenerational cults (meaning that my great-grandparents, my grandparents, and my parents were all part of the interconnected cults). I put a fragment of my experience as a ritual abuse survivor into *Hunted* in the hopes that some of you will recognize the cultlike experience and be more open when survivors talk about ritual abuse. I think fiction helps us hear things we might not otherwise be able to hear.

I also think of *Hunted* as an analogy for oppression that exists in our society—especially homophobia, sexism, and racism, though there is so much more. I hope *Hunted* will inspire you to challenge any form of oppression you may witness.

I hope that reading *Hunted* will show you that healing is possible, and that even when you're facing horrible, soul-killing oppression, you can still find a way to escape it and to surround yourself with a community of people who truly love you, even though it may take time.

I strongly believe in healing, compassion and kindness, and hope you do, too.

Resource Guide for Readers

Remember that you are not alone. No matter what your experience is, there are other people who've been through something similar. I think it can help to know that.

There are many available resources for those of us who've experienced oppression. Many are online, but they also can be found in various communities. I hope you seek out support if you need it; if you don't need the support yourself, I hope you'll consider volunteering or offering support to others who do.

Ritual Abuse Websites

• Ritual Abuse, Ritual Crime, and Healing: *http*://www. ra-info.org/ Information and resources for survivors, therapists, and others. This site has articles, links, and tips on what to do during flashbacks, as well as art and poetry created by survivors.

• Survivorship: *http://www.survivorship.org*. An online community and newsletter for ritual abuse survivors and their allies. This is a longstanding, supportive newsletter and community with lots of good information and resources.

• S.M.A.R.T. (Stop Mind Control and Ritual Abuse Today): *http://ritualabuse.us/* Tons of information on ritual abuse by an organization that works to stop ritual abuse and help survivors through education. The site offers online articles, a bi-monthly newsletter, an email discussion list, and more.

• Persons Against Ritual Abuse Torture: *http://www.ritual-*

abusetorture.org. Lots of information, articles, and resources on ritual abuse and torture. This organization also conducts research on ritual abuse and torture, and engages in activism to stop ritual abuse and torture. Some information on this site may be triggering.

• Sidran Institute: Traumatic Stress Education and Advocacy. *http://www.sidran.org*. Good information on PTSD (post-traumatic stress disorder), abuse, and coping mechanisms.

• Mosaic Minds. *http://www.mosaicminds.org*. An online community for abuse survivors with dissociative identity disorder/multiple personality disorder (DID/MPD). Includes forums, articles, suggestions on keeping safe, and other resources.

Cheryl Rainfield, articles on ritual abuse and programming/mind control: *http://www.cherylrainfield.com/cheryl-Page_Articles.html#ritual*

Books on Ritual Abuse
• *Safe Passage to Healing: A Guide for Survivors of Ritual Abuse* by Chrystine Oksana. Detailed, helpful, and validating book on ritual abuse.

• *Ritual Abuse: What It Is, Why It Happens, and How to Help* by Margaret Smith. Detailed, extensive, and solid information on ritual abuse and programming.

• *The Courage to Heal* by Ellen Bass and Laura Davis. While not specific to ritual abuse (it focuses on incest and sexual abuse), the newer versions have a good section on ritual abuse. The entire book is incredibly encouraging, informative, and healing.

Multiple Personality Gift: A Workbook for You and Your Inside Family. Excellent workbook with some great suggestions, reminders, and information on multiplicity

More Information on Ritual Abuse:
• "Report of the Ritual Abuse Task Force, Los Angeles County Commission for Women" *http://ritualabuse.us/ritualabuse/articles/report-of-the-ritual-abuse-task-force-los-angeles-county-commission-for-women/* One of the best, most comprehensive definitions of ritual abuse. Goes into detail of various forms of abuse, torture, and mind control that many cults use. Much of the information in this article can be triggering.

• CKLN (radio station) *http://www.multistalkervictims.org/raven1/mcf/radio/can-prog.htm*. A series on ritual abuse and mind control.

• Anti Oppression: Making a Positive Difference, Teaching Tolerance: *http://www.tolerance.org*. A wonderful, thoughtful site to find thought-provoking news, conversation, and support for those who care about diversity, equal opportunity, and respect for differences in schools. It covers so much—gender, bullying, race, queer issues, and so much more. Highly recommended!

Change: *http://www.change.org*. Wonderful site to help make a difference NOW about real issues, through signing the petitions and encouraging others to. This site has had petitions against things such as "corrective rape" (rape of lesbians to try to make them straight), making companies apologize for things they've done wrong such as making fun of homeless people, and many forms of discrimination. Check out their "victories" link to get inspired.

• Southern Poverty Law Center: *http://www.splcenter.org*. Fighting hate, teaching tolerance, and seeking justice. A fantastic resource with lots of positive fighting back against current-news oppression, such as various forms of homophobia, racism, sexism, sizism, and more.

• Partners Against Hate: *http://www.partnersagainsthate. org*. A good site with resources on how to stop the hate, teach love and compassion, and discourage hate crimes.

StopViolence.com: *http://stopviolence.com/* A site with tons of links to other sites and reports on the many forms of violence. A great resource.

• Ms. blog: *http://www.msmagazine.com/blog/*. A powerful blog from the pioneering feminists that help raise awareness about sexuality, homophobia, racism, gender, and more in current issues.

• Adios Barbie: http://www.adiosbarbie.com. A fantastic site on body image, class, race, age, ability, sexual orientation, size and gender, with articles, campaigns, and events.

LGBTQ Lesbian, Gay, Bi, Trans, & Queer
http://www.matthewshepard.org/ Matthew Shepard Foundation: Created to honor Matthew who was murdered in an anti-gay hate crime, the foundation works to "Replace Hate

with Understanding, Compassion & Acceptance" through educational, outreach, and advocacy programs, and by telling Matthew's story.

• It Gets Better Project: *http://www.itgetsbetter.org/* A fantastic project made up of tons of YouTube videos by queer people and our supporters who tell LGBTQ youth that it does get better. The project was started by author Dan Savage and his partner Terry, who created a YouTube video to inspire hope for queer youth facing bullying and harassment, following the suicides of several queer students who had been bullied in school. Believe us all—it *does* get better. See the video "It Gets Better" on YouTube: *http://www.youtube.com/watch?v=v_XIpkisWxo*

• Trevor Project: *http://www.thetrevorproject.org/* The Trevor Project works to end suicide among LGBTQ youth through a nationwide, 24/7 crisis intervention lifeline, and digital community and advocacy/educational programs that create a safe, supportive, and positive environment for everyone.

Racism

• Youth Helping To End Racism*http://anti-racismonline. org/* A resource for youth aged 10–21, where you can take a pledge to end racism, read some examples of racism, read about some things you can do to help, and more.

Aware-LA. Alliance of White Anti-Racists Everywhere – Los Angeles: *http://www.awarela.org/* An organization with a great blog that helps to educate and fight against racism and many forms of oppression.

ColorLines—News For Action: *http://www.colorlines.com/*
A daily news site that reports and analyzes racial justice issues.

• Anti-Racist Action (ARA): *http://antiracistaction.org/* An
international network of people from all walks of life who
are dedicated to fighting fascism and eliminating racism,
sexism, homophobia, and other forms of discrimination and
hierarchy from their communities. ARA exposes fascists
and racists in their communities and workplace; shuts down
their meetings, conferences, rallies, and speeches; educates
on what fascism is; supports victims of oppression; defends
clinics from pro-lifers; and acts in solidarity with others
who struggle against oppression.

Sexism
• The Ambivalent Sexism Inventory: *http://www.lawrence.*
edu/fast/glickp/asi.html (Take a quiz—you need to print it
out—to find out if you're sexist, and how much.)

• Killing Us Softly 4: Advertising's Image of Women:
http://www.youtube.com/watch?v=PTlmho_RovY. This video is incredibly powerful, and it will make you think and
see the deep sexism and harmful images to women in advertising. It's important to be able to analyze things for
yourself and not just accept images or ads as truth. Highly
recommended.

• Killing Us Softly 3: *http://www.youtube.com/watch?v=_*
FpyGwP3yzE. Same as above, but with a different segment.

• You can also download and read for free the Study Guide
for Killing Us Softly 4: *http://www.mediaed.org/assets/*

products/241/studyguide_241.pdf The guide has a lot of useful facts that may surprise you about advertising and the way they sexualize and diminish girls and women, the way they focus on and encourage extreme thinness and eating disorders, and more.

Positive Messages for Girls & Youth
• About Face: *http://www.about-face.org/* "About Face promotes positive self-esteem in girls and women of all ages, sizes, races, and backgrounds through a spirited approach to media education, outreach, and activism." A great site that helps girls and women combat negative images of women in the media, and helps them get involved.

• Gurl.com: *http://www.gurl.com/* This site has tons of thought-provoking information, incorporated in their section on labels and in their newsletter, boards where girls can talk, polls, and more. Great graphics, and a nicely laid-out site.

• TeenVoices Online: *http://www.teenvoices.com/* "Because you're more than just a pretty face." A great blog for teen girls that offers thought-provoking information and articles; critiques of ads that distort images of girls (as well as ones that are more positive); book and music reviews; and more.

Shameless Magazine: *http://www.shamelessmag.com/* An independent magazine for smart, strong, sassy young women and trans youth. It's a fresh alternative to typical teen magazines, packed with articles about arts, culture, and current events.

New Moon: *http://www.newmoon.com/* An online community and magazine where girls create and share poetry, artwork, videos, and more; chat together; and learn. All in a fully moderated, educational environment designed to build self-esteem and positive body image. Subscription required.

Acknowledgments

My deep and heartfelt thanks to:

Jean, whose unconditional love, incredible support and encouragement, and faith in me steadied and nurtured me, and helped me find the things I needed to keep writing, dreaming, and being. You have created for me the first real home I have ever known, and the safest, most loving place I can be. You see and love all of me. I love you dearly; you are my family;

Evelyn Fazio, my wonderful editor and now a treasured friend, who not only allowed me to keep my own voice and vision, but helped me enhance it, drawing on what was already there and making it more visible, and who offers me such incredible support and encouragement, understanding not only the writer in me but also the survivor;

Andrea Somberg, my amazing agent, who gave *Hunted* multiple readings and fantastic, detailed, thoughtful feedback which I highly value and which helped spur me on to create the best book I could, and who also gave me encouragement;

Julie Schoerke, my lovely book publicist, who believed in me even before *Scars* was published, and who has offered me not only incredible book publicity and savvy awareness and thinking, but also warm friendship and kindness;

Critique group members over the years for reading various incarnations of *Hunted*, especially Anna Kerz, Carolyn Beck, Anne Carter, Kristyn Dunnion, Erin Thomas, Karen Krossing, Karen Rankin, and most especially Lena Coakley, Erin Thomas, and Nancy Prasad for both reading incarnations of *Hunted* and for writerly support and encouragement. Thanks also to Ellen Hopkins, Libba Bray, Gail Giles, Nancy Werlin, Kathlene Jeffrie Johnson, Annette Curtis Clause, Lois Duncan, Wendy Orr, Peter Carver, Barbara Greenwood, Kathy Stinson, and many others for believing in me as a writer;

The many readers of *Scars* who wrote me to tell me how much they loved *Scars* and how it helped them; your wonderful letters are nourishment for my soul;

The many incredible book bloggers who reviewed *Scars* so glowingly and let me know how much they liked it, and who helped me get the word out about *Scars*. I am grateful to you all!

The wonderful, incredible YA book and writer community on Twitter, including Maureen Johnson and everyone who was a part of #YASaves, who supported and encouraged me when *Scars* was challenged, both in a library and in the *WSJ*; your support made a huge difference for me, helping to turn something that could have been negative into something very positive. Thank you!

Jo Beggs, my dearest and oldest friend, who always makes me feel loved, and knows both the darkest places I have been and the happiest;

Gail Fisher-Taylor, who provided the first real safety and love I ever had, and believed in my memories and in me as a person, and encouraged my healing. You gave me so much!

To my friends, Hilary Cameron and Andrea Medovarski for always believing in me as a writer.

Special thanks to the Ontario Arts Council which awarded me a grant to work on this project, and greatly helped provide the time and ease to work on it without much stress around money. You provide an incredible, much needed service to many Canadian writers. Thank you!